Passion's Song

"You may go to the devil, sir!" Isobel drained her glass. If his lordship wanted her to undress in front of him, then he might as well have his wish.

She strode over to where a dressing gown was draped over a chair and began working the buttons of her frock coat. She let it fall to the floor and in another moment she shrugged out of her waistcoat. At the last minute, she found that she could not undress in front of him, so she took the dressing gown and walked past him into his bedchamber.

He jumped up from his chair and, following, pushed her down on the bed. He growled, "If you don't cover yourself, Miss St. James, I won't answer to the consequences."

She felt a thrill go through her. She meant to protest at what happened next, but his warm hands were stroking her bare legs, moving up to capture her aching breasts; and when he gently pulled the silk gown away from her, she shivered as cool air whispered over her nakedness . . .

PASSION'S SONG

CAROLYN JEWEL

ST. MARTIN'S PRESS/NEW YORK

PASSION'S SONG

Copyright © 1988 by Carolyn Jewel.

ISBN: 0-312-91302-8   Can. ISBN: 0-312-91303-6

Printed in the United States of America

First St. Martin's Press mass market edition / November 1988

10 9 8 7 6 5 4 3 2 1

PROLOGUE

I

30 April 1775
London, England

It was damnably hot in the room, and it was so full of dancing, drunken men and women that Alexander, standing rather stiffly by himself, fairly itched to loosen his cravat. Instead, he unfastened two of the buttons of his coat. He brushed a stray lock of sandy hair from his forehead and longed for the moment when he and his bride might discreetly retire. His present discomfort seemed to him a small price to pay for a lifetime with the woman he adored. His green eyes softened when they fell on the young woman he had married some few hours ago. Lady Sarah was finally his wife. She was dancing with Alexander's father, and she looked radiantly happy as she floated around the crowded dance floor as if there was no one else there. Her white-blond hair was beginning to loosen about her faintly flushed cheeks in a way that made Alexander appreciate his wife's delicate beauty all the more.

Their courtship had been brief, but he thought the six weeks preceding her acceptance of him had been an eternity. He was in love as he had never been before.

And Lady Sarah had let it be known that she was as desperately, passionately, and fashionably in love with him as he was with her. Marriage had been the furthest thing from Alexander's mind when his father had first suggested the match just over a year ago, which was–not coincidentally– some months after Lady Sarah's betrothed, the duke of Worling, was killed in a senseless accident during a sojourn in Paris. As Lord Hartforde had patiently pointed out to his son, Lady Sarah brought a sizeable dowry, she was, it was commonly agreed, the greatest beauty in many a London season and, of course, the match was socially brilliant. Lady Sarah was the only child of the duke of Mallentrye, and Alexander, one hardly need point out, stood heir to his father's considerable estates. It was only because of a sense of filial responsibility that Alexander had started courting Lady Sarah. Much to his surprise, he had soon found himself hopelessly in love.

Alexander's attention was diverted from the dancers, and from his wife in particular, when his father-in-law pushed his way through the press of guests to stand at his side. The duke of Mallentrye was by no means a short man, yet he found himself looking up after his son-in-law straightened from a graceful bow.

"So, there you are!" The duke addressed Alexander more loudly than was strictly necessary from the level of noise in the room. "I trust you and my daughter shall visit me often." The duke thumped him heartily on the back.

"No doubt we shall, Your Grace," Alexander said, taking a cautious step backwards to discourage another demonstration of enthusiasm. He managed a pleasant enough smile and supposed he ought to be grateful the staunch Tory had condescended to bestow his only daughter on an avowed Whig. He already had the utmost respect for the duke, and he was doing his best to like him to the same degree.

"I insist on it, young man! I expect you to continue to spoil her, just as I have."

Alexander began to suspect the duke's unusual exhilaration was due more to an excess of Nantes brandy than to his joy at the marriage of his daughter.

The duke would surely have continued his harangue if he had not been interrupted by Lord Hartforde bringing Lady Sarah over to them. "Thinking of abducting my Sarah, Hartforde?" the duke called out to Alexander's father as the two approached.

"Lord Hartforde dances so divinely, Father, that I am just now recovering my breath." Lady Sarah, still clinging to Lord Hartforde's arm, glanced up at her late dance partner with shining eyes.

After Lord Hartforde greeted the duke, Alexander turned to his wife. "Perhaps, Lady Sarah, we might soon retire," he murmured, reaching to take her hand.

"Oh, no!" she cried. "Laurence, that is, Lord Hartforde"—She blushed at her indiscretion—"has promised he will gavotte with me!" She did not look at her husband.

"I shall never be the one to disappoint you." Alexander spoke lightly, but his eyebrows drew together. "However, afterwards, I am afraid I shall insist." He lifted her hand to his lips and found himself looking into eyes that were a glacial blue.

Later that evening, Alexander was confronted with that same icy gaze as he listened to his wife tell him she could not return his slightest affection. "I love another, my lord," she said plaintively. The expression of sadness on her delicate features lasted the entire length of time it took her to avert her head and seem fascinated by the curtains over the eastward windows.

"If you do not love me, why, then, did you consent to be my wife?" Alexander paced in front of her chair. He found it impossible to be still, and it was only by the greatest exertion of control that he kept his voice steady. Never once had it occurred to him that Sarah did not return his love. He was confounded that he had been such a blockhead as not to see it.

"Because it was what my father wanted!" She raised unhappy eyes to her husband, curling and uncurling her slim fingers as she watched him pace.

He felt a peculiar tension in the region of his chest when she averted her face from him. "Sarah—" He stopped pacing and went down on one knee before her. Grasping one of her hands, he began to speak in an earnest tone. "The Hardwicke act was passed some 25 years ago to prevent just such marriages as this. You need not have been forced to marry against your will. I shall procure an annulment tomorrow if you are so discontent that there is not the slightest chance of your happiness." He kissed her hand and prayed she would refuse his offer of annulment. His head was bent so he did not see her eyes open wide in horror.

"No, my lord!" At her exclamation, he again kissed the tiny hand he held. "But you must understand." She continued in a softer voice. "I was to be the wife of a duke. . . ." She pressed his hand ever so slightly.

"Perhaps, one day, you will come to love me, as I do you." He lifted his head to look into her clear blue eyes. "After all, Sarah, it is I who am alive."

"Oh." The sound was a low whisper. She looked away and caught her lower lip with small white teeth. "You are cruel to remind me of my loss, my lord."

"And you are cruel to have consented to marry me if you do not love me!" he cried. He laid his head in her lap, and she smoothed his brow with two slim fingers.

"But, I have married you," she said. Lady Sarah was delighted that her pronouncement had achieved such wild success. He was absolutely prostrated with love for her! The possibility of having to marry a man twice her age had been enough to make her privately agree with her father that the some-day-to-be 11th marquess was a most suitable husband. Marchioness was perhaps not so good as duchess, but it would certainly do. The family was wealthy enough, and Alexander was at least a little handsome. Getting Alexander to fall in love with her had not been half as hard as she had believed it might be, and when she perceived the number of other young ladies who were disappointed at the news of their engagement, it had turned out to be twice the success. Her grief at the loss of her young duke was played to just the right pitch; he had fallen, just like all the others.

Lady Sarah touched his golden hair and fervently hoped her husband would age as gracefully as his father. Lord Hartforde was an exceptionally handsome man.

30 April 1775
Boston, Massachusetts

II

Isobel Frederica Rowland was a charming girl who had, one week ago, turned six years old. She was standing next to the fortepiano while she listened to her mother play a popular new song with a great deal of emotion but, alas, not quite the same degree of skill. When Mrs. Rowland finished playing, she rested her hands on the keys and turned to look at her daughter. Her blue eyes sparkled, as they often did when they rested on her only child.

There was no doubt the two were mother and daughter. Both had light blond hair and pale rose-tinted complexions, but where Mrs. Rowland's blue eyes were cerulean, Isobel had her father's expressive

deep blue eyes. In temperament the two were as alike
as night and day. Mrs. Rowland was by nature a light-
hearted woman, and even though she'd had her share
of misfortune during her five and twenty years, she
never quite lost the sunny disposition that, in spite of
everything, had made her husband fall in love with
her. Isobel was like her father. She was prone to
moodiness and had so serious an aspect one might
never have suspected her of being capable of laughter.
Although she was only six years old, she most em-
phatically had a mind of her own.

Mr. Rowland doted on Isobel, and when the girl
was four he had begun to teach her to read, despite his
wife's most vehement entreaties not to. Mrs. Rowland
did not care much for books, or for learning, either,
and she was fond of telling her husband no good
would come of trying to teach a girl so much. To Mrs.
Rowland's horror her daughter became a voracious
reader. Had she not been convinced Isobel could never
grasp it, she would have been aghast when her husband began to teach her Latin and Greek. He was constantly filling her head with, it seemed to her, anything
and everything without regard to what it was proper
for a girl to know.

Not content to sit in a distant chair when her mother
was playing the fortepiano, Isobel always stood close
by the instrument and stared at the keys so intently
that Mrs. Rowland was tempted to believe she meant
to memorize every note she heard. "So, my little Isobel," Mrs. Rowland said in her clipped British tones.
"Do you want to learn to play?" There was no mistaking Isobel's joy at her mother's long-awaited question.
Mrs. Rowland reached down to swing her onto the
bench. "Oof! You are getting too big to lift!" she
gasped. "Shall I show you how to play?"

"I already know how to play, Mother," Isobel said.

"Oh?" There was only the barest smile at the corners of her mouth. "Then you must play for me." Just as she was about to chide Isobel gently for her boast, the girl put her hands to the keys and began to play, with uncanny accuracy, the tune she had just heard her mother play for the first time.

Chapter 1

London—1781

I

Lady Sarah grimaced when her maid pulled a little too sharply on her hair. "Mary! Have a care!" She rebuked the diminutive woman who was painstakingly attempting an elaborate coiffure.

"Forgive me, my lady." She looked properly chastised and Sarah decided to leave it be this time, though she resolved the woman would have to be let go if she tugged on her hair like that again. "His Lordship will be pleased at you tonight, Lady Sarah." Mary stepped back to check the tortured style milady had insisted on.

"Think you so, Mary?" she said absently as the woman patiently went back to work on the stubborn locks.

It did not occur to Sarah to care what her husband might think of her appearance. She never called him by his given name, nor did she encourage the little shows of affection he insisted on making to her, even in public. She found his attentions to her acutely embarrassing. It was not that she did not want her husband to be in love with her, on the contrary, she depended on the fact. She only wished that he were not so obvious about the depth of his feeling for her.

Sarah was so sure Alexander doted on her that when she made the astounding discovery that he had taken a mistress, her first reaction was to be angry that he could even think of going to another woman's arms when he was so desperately in love with her. Her second reaction was to think that he must have noticed her attraction to his father after all, and the woman was just an attempt to return tit for tat. She discarded the theory on the grounds that her husband believed her incapable of infidelity and, in any event, she had had no real luck with the marquess. Sarah was puzzled, and a trifle put out, when, although Alexander continued to come to her with regularity, in all other aspects of their marriage, he began to affect a distant politeness. She complained bitterly to her father of her husband's indifference, with the eventual effect that relations between son-in-law and father-in-law were severely tested as the duke became convinced Alexander was deliberately cruel to Lady Sarah.

Alexander's demeanor warmed after Sarah began to make the effort to be more charming to him. It was a great relief to her, for one of her greatest fears was that he might become so jealous that he would forbid her to go out or, even worse, send her to Hartfordeshire where she would surely die of boredom. As long as he continued to come to her bed, she was certain of his love and their marriage.

She waited while Mary put the final touches to her toilette and then went downstairs to supper with her husband.

II

"Will you go out tonight, Lady Sarah?" Alexander asked when she came into the salon where his sister, Julia, and Lord Hartforde were waiting.

She nodded to the dark-haired girl, but Julia's greeting in return was cold. The animosity of a fourteen-year-old was of no concern to Sarah, and she merely shrugged her shoulders at the child's rudeness. "Yes," she answered, turning her head to glance at Alexander when she took Lord Hartforde's arm to go into supper. She was smiling because Lord Hartforde appeared to notice she had taken especial care with her dress. It was a new Paris gown that set off her coloring to distinct advantage.

Alexander took his sister's arm and followed his wife in to table.

As usual when they were all present, the atmosphere was strained, and Lady Sarah filled the frequent silences with chatter, though she directed it mainly at Lord Hartforde. A dessert of pudding and fruit was being cleared before there was another lull in the conversation.

"And where are you going tonight, Lady Sarah?" Julia's question filled in the quiet.

"To the opera." She watched the two men at the table.

"And with whom do you go?" Julia persisted.

"Well, since you are so interested, my dear, I am to go with Lady Braithewaite and one or two others." If she had been looking at her husband she would have seen he understood quite well that she was to meet her lover. Because of her profound deafness, Lady Braithewaite was a popular companion for women bent on adventure. They were interrupted by a servant announcing her carriage was ready. "I take my leave of you then." She stood up and was almost to the door when Alexander's query stopped her.

"Lady Sarah?"

"Yes?" She turned back.

"I would have a word with you tomorrow."

"Until tomorrow, my lord," she said gaily as she went out.

"How do you stand her, Alexander?" Julia threw down her napkin and frowned at her brother.

"Julia, such childish behavior ill becomes you."

III

"How can you accuse me of such a thing?" Sarah fumed as Alexander stretched out his long legs and settled himself more comfortably in his favorite chair.

"Do you deny you and Wolperton have shared a bed?" He sighed at her outraged expression. "Sarah, you misunderstand me. I am not asking you to end your *affaire de coeur,* I only desire you to be more discreet. 'Tis obvious you don't care to spare my feelings, but, I might remind you, I am well within my rights to insist that you not flaunt your liaisons quite so publicly."

Sarah was shocked to discover that she had been mistaken in thinking his silence on the subject of her lovers was due to his ignorance of them. It came as an even greater shock to discover that he knew and did not care in the least. This reaction was incomprehensible—he was in love with her! Every man she took a care to humor loved her, and she had eventually humored her husband. "Do you hate me so much?" she asked in a small voice, hoping to throw him off guard by a change in tactics.

"Hate you? No, I don't believe I hate you."

"Then you do care!" she cried.

Alexander lifted his eyebrows in two perfectly matched arches. "Don't misunderstand me further. I care for you just as my father cares for you, or Lord Fistersham, or any of the lovers you have not bothered to hide from me. Which, as you may gather, means

not a great deal. It seems they tired of you rather
sooner than I did. It should be a comfort to you to
know that I have decided to give up our bed. Neither
one of us has particularly enjoyed that aspect of our
marriage."

"But what about an heir?" She blurted out the question because she had never ever imagined he would
stop trying for an heir. Although she would be the last
to admit it, she had come to look forward to his caresses. He was a most skillful lover, she had learned as
much by comparison. She felt herself flushing from the
sudden fear that he might decide to divorce her. The
humiliation would be too much for her to stand. She
was well aware that if he should actually take such an
extreme course, society would no longer turn a blind
eye to her behavior.

"If not having to lie with you means the title reverts
to some other branch of the family"—he shrugged—
"'tis a small price to pay."

On 25 July, Lord Hartforde died and Alexander
Spencer Grey became the 11th marquess of Hartforde.

Chapter 2

Boston—1781

Isobel hurried home, a few flaxen curls falling out of the heavy braid hanging down her back, humming to herself as she walked briskly down the street. She held a brown paper-wrapped package in her arms and every third step or so she gave an exuberant skip and threw the book up in the air, slapping it safely between her hands when it fell to the level of her chest. At this juncture in her life, Isobel had but three passions. The first was her music and the second was ancient Greece. She could never read enough about Socrates, Plato, or Alcibiades, and her father would have been scandalized to learn she had managed to read nearly all of Sappho. Her third passion was her music teacher, Mr. Standifer. With the steadfast conviction of her twelve years, she fancied herself deeply and enduringly in love with Mr. Standifer. To her unmitigated joy, the object of her affection had been at the bookstore. He had made her an elegant bow and kissed her hand just as though she were grown up, which she naturally considered herself to be. She refused to acknowledge Mr. Stand-

ifer's wife as an obstacle to her (as yet) unrequited
love, and in any event, her very existence made her
love for Mr. Standifer all the more tragic. So, she had
dallied at the bookseller's instead of going straight
home, as she had promised her nursemaid, Miss
Forbes, she would. She knew Miss Forbes would be
angry with her for having been gone so long, but she
accounted the golden moments she was able to spend
with Mr. Standifer as well worth whatever punish-
ment her governess might see fit to mete out.

When at last she reached the gates of the neat clap-
board house, she was only a little out of breath. She
paused long enough to let her panting abate before
continuing up the flower-bordered path to the door.
Ever since her mother's death two years ago, her father
had insisted on planting bluebells because, he said,
even though they were English flowers, they reminded
him of Catherine. Isobel thought they were depress-
ing. Every time she saw bluebells she thought of
death. The war with England, her father's lengthy absences, and her mother's death had all somehow become associated with the flower. Her hand was on the
latch when she suddenly stopped. She was still standing, looking at the flowers, when Miss Forbes herself
opened the door.

"Where have you been?" Miss Forbes pulled her inside and pushed the door so hard it shut with a bang.
Her normally bright eyes were reddened with tears and
she let go of Isobel to dab at her eyes with the hem of
her lace apron.

"Father?" Isobel felt her stomach tighten with sickening apprehension.

"Your father has taken a turn for the worse." Miss
Forbes took her hand and gave her a pitying look. She
had let Isobel go to the bookseller's because she did not
want the girl to worry when she summoned the physic

for the third time in as many days. Never had she
dreamed Mr. Rowland was so close to death.

Jonathon Rowland had made his fortune from the
English trade in the American colonies, and by the
1770s he was the owner of one of the largest fleet of
ships in the Massachusetts Bay Colony. At the outset
of the revolution, there were those who wondered exactly where his sympathies lay; after all, his wife was
British, and the war threatened his very livelihood.
Rowland, however, ended such speculations when he
threw his substantial resources behind the revolution-
aries. In the process, he made a second fortune reliev-
ing British ships of supplies being transported to
occupied New York. He knew the Hudson tributaries
better than almost any man alive, and time after time
the British found themselves cursing the luck of the
American pirate. It wasn't until the death of his wife
that Rowland's luck changed. Shortly afterward he was
seriously wounded during an escape so narrow that
half his crew swore they would never set foot on another Rowland ship, not even if General Washington
himself ordered it. Sent back to Boston to recuperate,
his health slowly worsened, and not even the devoted
attentions of his daughter could improve his condition.

It was at night when Isobel could hear him coughing
that she could not keep back the fear he would die.
"'Tis only a cough," she would tell herself fiercely.
But the racking sounds sometimes continued for
hours. She could not close her eyes until it stopped,
and as soon as it did, she would creep down the hall to
her father's room to push open the door and peer into
the dark until she could make out the shallow rise and
fall of the blankets drawn over the slender form in the
bed.

*   *   *

"Is he dead?" The book slipped from her hands and hit the floor with a thud.

Miss Forbes held Isobel's arm to prevent her from going into the room from which they could faintly hear the soft muttering of prayer. "You mustn't go in there." She pulled Isobel into her arms. "My poor little girl. First your mother, and now . . ." Her voice lowered to a whisper as she stroked her hair.

"Is he dead?" As soon as the Reverend William Grafton came out of the room, she knew that he was, but she desperately wanted to hear, by some miracle, he was alive. After all, she thought, had he not recovered from other attacks of his illness? Why should this time be any different?

"My child . . ." Reverend Grafton briefly pressed a soft hand to Isobel's bare arm, and she could not suppress a shudder at the dampness of his touch. "God has called your father to his side. He suffers no more." He noticed her relief when he took his hand away, and his plump lips tightened while he pressed the palms of his hands together. "God's will is done," he said, looking a little unsettled at her stare. "Here." He thrust something into her hand. "Your father requested that I give you this." His chin tripled as he bent his head to watch her take the silver pendant.

It was galling to let the man see her cry, but she knew she ought to show some emotion. If she did not, he might refuse to pray for her father's soul. She summoned the tears he seemed to want from her. "Why did God let him die?" she moaned, looking up from her hand and clenching her fist around the necklace.

"God's will is done," Reverend Grafton repeated. His grim expression relaxed, but still Isobel shuddered when his moist hands touched her arms again. "You are an orphan now, my child. Perhaps"—he glanced up at Miss Forbes—"she will be thrust upon the mercy of the Church?"

"I can take care of her!" Miss Forbes answered him so quickly that Isobel looked over at her in surprise.

"You will pray for him?" Isobel wiped at the tears trickling down her cheeks and was relieved to see him nodding, his chin briefly appearing out of folds of fat.

"What did he give you?" Miss Forbes asked when Reverend Grafton was gone. She bent down to see what Isobel was clutching in her hand.

She opened her palm. "Mother's locket." She held it up, and the silver oval her father had cherished as a memento of his wife glinted in the light as it spun on its chain.

"Here, I'll put it on you." Miss Forbes took the chain and fastened it around Isobel's neck. "You will always remember your parents and how much they loved you every time you look at this."

"I'll never take it off."

Chapter 3

British-Occupied New York

I

Isobel stood in the drawing room and glowered while the man the court had named as her guardian until she was twenty-one introduced himself. Carter Samuels hadn't even bothered to come to Boston after receiving the news of his cousin's death. As a vehement Tory, Samuels had no interest in living in Boston. He had sent his attorney to handle the sale of the house and most of its contents. The attorney had curtly informed Isobel that the proceeds of the sale were to be held in trust for her by Mr. Samuels and that as soon as she felt able she was to travel to New York, where, he was pleased to tell her, she was welcome to live with her relative until her majority, at which time her inheritance would be released to her. To her great relief, it was agreed that Miss Forbes should go with her to New York.

"So, you are little Isobel Rowland?" Samuels held out a thin hand. "I am Mr. Carter Samuels, your poor father's cousin." He shook his head to show how sad he was at the death of a relative he believed to be a

traitor to his country and whose demise had brought
him into control of a fortune of nearly one hundred
twenty thousand American dollars. He bent over in a
small bow, and Isobel could not help thinking that his
horsehair peruke probably covered a balding pate.
When, with a flourish, he drew out an enameled snuffbox and shoved a prodigious amount of the tobacco up
his nostrils, she despised him for his pretension. She
smiled politely when he dabbed at his nose with a
slightly yellowed kerchief after a series of artificially
loud sneezes. "I am Mr. Samuels," he repeated
breathily. "And this is my wife, Mrs. Samuels." He
put a hand on his wife's shoulder.

"Good afternoon, Mrs. Samuels." Isobel took a
deep breath because she instantly disliked the mousy-
haired woman.

Mrs. Samuels nodded when Isobel finished a dutiful
curtsy. "You and my little Emily will be good friends,
I am sure!" Mrs. Samuels put an arm around a plump
girl of about nine or ten whose hair was exactly the
same mousy brown as her mother's. "Say 'good afternoon' to your cousin Isobel, Emily." The girl obeyed
her mother in a surprisingly loud voice. As soon as
Mrs. Samuels looked away, Emily glared at Isobel and
screwed up her face.

"Good afternoon, Emily." Isobel tried her best to
sound pleased to meet her.

"You must call her 'Miss Emily,'" Mrs. Samuels re-
monstrated. Isobel's disdain for fat Miss Emily increased tenfold. Ever after, she never thought of Emily
without somehow including the adjective "fat" in the
thought.

"And this"—Mr. Samuels indicated a sullen boy of
about sixteen or seventeen—"this is your cousin, Mr.
Philip Carter Samuels." Mr. Samuels's sharp chin
lifted a little after the pronunciation of each name.

"Good afternoon, Mr. Philip." Isobel curtsied again.

"Cousin." He bent his head briefly in her direction.

His arrogant nod inexplicably endeared him to her, and she favored him with her most winning smile. His eyes reminded her of her father's eyes; they were precisely the same deep shade of brown.

"Well, little Isobel, you must be very tired after such a long journey." Mr. Samuels did not sound as if he cared that it might be true. "A servant will show you to your room. And to yours as well . . . Miss Forbes, is it not?"

A maid came in a few minutes later, and as soon as Isobel had again curtsied to the family, Isobel and Miss Forbes followed her to a small room at the very far end of the second floor. She stood for a few minutes, staring after Miss Forbes, who had hugged her tightly before leaving her alone. Isobel threw herself into a chair by the bed and held her head in her hands, trying, but failing, to keep back the tears. The future was not going to be pleasant, that much she knew. That Samuels was in charge of her father's estate, and of her, until she turned twenty-one filled her with despair. It would be years (practically forever! she cried to herself) until she would be able to go back to Boston. Tears of frustration burned her eyes as she was suddenly hit by how alone she was now. There was only Miss Forbes to remind her of happier times.

II

The day after Isobel arrived in New York, Mrs. Samuels went through Isobel's closet and pulled out all but six or seven dresses, saying as she did so that her dresses would fit Miss Emily so much better it was a shame for them to go to waste. Isobel was so aghast she could do nothing but stare. "Your father may have spoiled you, young lady," Mrs. Samuels said, "but you'll get no special treatment here!"

As for Mr. Samuels, he proved to be a strangely penurious man. He kept but two horses, yet three carriages, and there was no doubt that the house was understaffed. Isobel counted herself lucky that Miss Forbes was kept on as governess for the two girls. Mr. Samuels complained bitterly about the expense of keeping the house warm during the winter, and he rationed out the coal in so niggardly a fashion he had difficulty keeping the servants through the season. It was obvious, though, that he had an excellent tailor; he followed the fashions without regard to cost. Then there was Philip; he was the breath of life to his parents, they rarely denied him anything. Mrs. Samuels spoiled fat Emily as though she were a princess of the blood and not merely a chubby, plain, and whining little brat. *For heaven's sake,* Isobel thought with disgust, *she is only ten, and Mrs. Samuels acts as though she is likely to attract the attention of any of a score of suitors!* Worse than fat Emily, worse even than Mr. Samuels and his faded wife, was being required to be polite to the British soldiers who were their frequent guests. It was intolerable, she raged to herself. Why, any one of them could be the man who had wounded her father! She yearned to be twenty-one, old enough to leave New York and go back to Boston.

It was in the middle of the spring of 1782 that, with a look obviously not meant to be interpreted as the glee it was, Mrs. Samuels told Isobel that Mr. Samuels wished to speak with her. "He's waiting for you in the study," she said with a sly grin.

Isobel stood before Mr. Samuels, hands clasped behind her back. He was sitting in his favorite chair, and as he turned to face her he placed his feet on an ottoman and hooked his fingers in the pockets of his satin waistcoat because he fancied it made him appear kindly. His peruke was so heavily powdered that his

shoulders were covered with a fine layer of flour. He
cleared his throat. "I have a great deal to discuss with
you, my dear. I have just come from the lawyers'.
There appears to be some difficulty about your birth
certificate, a trifle, I assure you, that will no doubt
soon be cleared up to our mutual satisfaction. It seems
to have been misplaced. There is no record of your
birth that my lawyers can locate. Do you, by chance,
happen to know where you were born?" A smile
pulled at his lips.

"I was born in Boston, of course, Mr. Samuels."
She did not understand why it mattered and she shifted
impatiently.

"How interesting. Are you certain of that? I see I
shall have to send Mr. Michaels to Boston again so this
little unpleasantness may be cleared up. There is no
need to worry about this at all, my dear little one. You
may rely on me to see that your interests are repre-
sented." He paused. "You understand that without
your birth certificate there is some difficulty about
your father's will?" When she nodded, he said, "Well,
my dear child, well, we must also talk about your music lessons." He smiled, and it made his hollow cheeks
wrinkle at the edges of his lips. She nodded again. "In
times like these . . . well . . . the lessons are quite expensive. This talk of a British withdrawal . . . but"—
he gave a deep sigh—"but your father inexplicably set
out that the lessons are to continue as long as you want
them." He had been of a mind to put a stop to the
lessons on his own until it occurred to him the girl was
likely to make a fuss. He decided it would be unwise
to chance having anyone take an interest in his ward.
Though he held out little hope she would agree to
stop, in light of the cost he felt it was more than worth
the attempt. "The lawyers assure me," he continued,
"that such conditions in a will . . . er . . . until other
matters are cleared up, it is wisest—that is, there is no

difficulty about the lessons. But, it is so very hard to meet expenses. The war, you know, has taken its toll on everyone." He kept a regretful expression as he let his voice trail off.

"You can't make me quit." She spoke quietly, but in a voice leaving no room for argument.

"Make you quit? Make you quit? Why, the very idea!" He managed to look as though he had been wounded to the quick. He put a hand to his wig and then, in an unconscious mannerism, stroked his meager thigh.

"You want to keep my father's money," she accused levelly, her gaze on him steady because she knew it bothered him when she looked at him calmly.

"How could you think such a thing? My dear child, I have only your best interests at heart!" Here he sighed again and, as if it pained him greatly, said, "Very well, then, we will have to let one of the servants go. The extra work will be very hard on Mrs. Samuels; she's a frail woman. I expect you will have to help her out."

"Yes, Mr. Samuels."

"Run along now. Go to your room. And tell Miss Forbes I wish to see her." Isobel paused at the door at these last words. When she turned to look at him, the expression on her face said the hateful words in her heart.

"Insufferable little brat," he snorted when she was gone. He brushed futilely at the white dust on his favorite velvet breeches. He never did get around to telling the lawyers Isobel claimed to have been born in Boston.

Isobel sat on Miss Forbes's bed, eyes fixed on the wall where a print titled "Royal Sport" was still hanging. It had not yet been packed away. Miss Forbes had caught Isobel staring at it once and had told her that although it seemed an odd thing for a woman to have on her wall, it was the only thing of value she possessed. Miss Forbes's father had brought it with him to the colonies in 1760 and it was the only thing, besides his debts, that she had inherited from him. It occurred to Isobel that every man in the drawing had a look of greed on his face. She wondered if the artist could have known Carter Samuels.

Miss Forbes's trunk was in the middle of the floor. It was open and Isobel could see that there were already neatly folded clothes in it. Two weeks ago, Miss Forbes's leaving had seemed a long way off. Now, instead of counting the days they had left together, Isobel was counting the hours. She closed her eyes and tried to imagine what it would be like when the room was empty and the walls were bare.

Miss Forbes came in, and looked a little surprised to see Isobel sitting on her bed. "What are you doing in here, all alone?"

Isobel quickly pressed the tips of her fingers over her eyes. "I don't want you to go!" she cried when she thought she could speak, in spite of the catch in her throat.

"I also wish I wasn't going, Isobel." She sat down on the bed and put her arms around the girl. "But, there's nothing to be done about it." She took out her handkerchief and with it dabbed at Isobel's face. "I shall miss you and your fortepiano." They sat together for several minutes that Isobel wished with all her heart she could keep from passing. "You mustn't cry about me, Isobel," said Miss Forbes.

III

After Miss Forbes was let go, Isobel took on more and more of the housekeeping duties until she was practically running the household. There was virtually nothing for Mrs. Samuels to do except complain that

Isobel did not know the meaning of the word "economy." Isobel oversaw the servants, planned the meals, and generally succeeded in adhering to the pitifully small budget provided by Mr. Samuels. She got up at half past five, worked until the afternoon, went to Mr. Archer's for her music lessons or practiced the forte-piano, had dinner, and went to sleep. The weeks passed with comforting dullness. She stayed away from Mr. Samuels and fat Miss Emily and occasionally endured one of Mrs. Samuels's tirades. Sometimes a servant would quit and she would look about for another one.

The only change in the routine of Isobel's days occurred when she was fifteen, and soon it became more or less a part of the monotony. At first she was convinced the bleeding meant she was dying, and when she finally confided her fears to the only person whom she might call a friend, she began to cry when the cook laughed at her.

"Die? You aren't going to die!" Mrs. Morris wiped her eyes and put a hand on Isobel's shoulder and then handed her kerchief to her. "Did no one ever tell you? It means you're a woman now, little darling!"

That night, Isobel examined her face in the mirror to see if she did, indeed, look like a woman. She thought she looked the same as always: very much like her mother and not at all like her father. Neither did she feel different. If this meant she was a woman, she thought it nothing more or less than an inconvenience. Isobel's whole life was so centered around her music that she was the only one who did not notice her figure was no longer girlish. She merely altered her clothing and thought to herself she might yet grow as tall as her father. Still, if anyone had bothered to ask her if she was happy, she would have said she was. She had all her body needed: food, a place to sleep, three dresses, a pair of leather shoes to keep out the mud and snow,

and a woolen cloak that was warm during the fall and
spring and very nearly warm enough during the
winter. And she had all her soul required: her music.

It was some time before Mr. Archer commented on
the gradual change in her—the ugly dresses and the
plain boots that looked as if they might split at the
sides at the least pressure—and soon he became concerned by her increasing thinness and pallor. His eventual questions about the Samuelses and her obviously
worsening appearance were invariably met with stubborn silence, and he stopped questioning her. It was
enough that his most able pupil—for all she was only a
girl—was improving every day. He relieved his conscience by telling himself Miss Rowland had the constitution of a great artist, and if she was thin, it was no
wonder what with all her nervous energy. Anyway,
his bill was always promptly paid.

Isobel began staying at Mr. Archer's later and later,
not just for the extra practice, but because by doing so
she missed the dreadful dinners with the Samuelses.
The food that could be bought on the sum Mr. Samuels saw fit to allow was not typically the best to be
had, and in spite of Mrs. Morris's culinary skill, it
tasted like it. And by staying away, she was almost
entirely able to avoid the British soldiers who were frequent guests. Mrs. Morris would generally set something aside for Isobel to eat when she got back from
her lessons. They would talk companionably while she
ate, though this usually meant she listened to Mrs.
Morris tell her why she should leave the Samuelses.
Although Mrs. Morris was some twenty years older
than Isobel, she, like no other, understood Isobel's
misery when she talked about the Samuelses.

Mrs. Morris repeatedly said she would help Isobel
find good paying work as a lady's maid or, with her
ability to read and write, as a governess. "Why stay
here and let Samuels have your work for free? If you

got a position, in a year or two you might save enough to go to England to find your mother's family!" What she did not say was how unlikely she thought it was that Isobel would see even a penny of her father's money.

"But I could never leave America!" she said.

"Why not?" Mrs. Morris persisted.

"When I'm twenty-one I'm going back to Boston to study music with Mr. Standifer."

"But right now you're no better than a slave for Mr. Samuels," was Mrs. Morris's invariable response. "And anyway," she continued once, "why couldn't you study music in England? There's nothing for you in Boston; you said yourself the house was sold."

"Boston is my home, Mrs. Morris!" One day she would be a very wealthy young lady, and when that time came, there was nothing that could stop her from doing whatever she wanted.

On the afternoons when she did not go to Mr. Archer's, and when she had spare time after practicing, she sometimes sought out Philip. Mr. Samuels had engaged a tutor for him, his son's education apparently being one of the few things about which he did not think to economize. Isobel usually found him in the library drawing swirls on the paper he was supposed to be using to copy Latin declensions. She was always careful to make some small noise to alert him that she was coming in so he could turn the sheets over. She would ask him about his studies, and though he answered her only because otherwise she wouldn't go away, Philip discovered it made him feel important to have her hanging on his every word. It had the added benefit of making him remember his lessons, something he attributed to a natural intelligence, since it never occurred to him that his recitations to his cousin might be helping him remember the information.

It amused Philip to have Isobel dote on him. She sometimes saved him desserts and sneaked them to his room after dinner. She never asked him to share, which was a fortunate thing, because he never thought to do so, and if she had, he would have laughed at her for the presumption. Occasionally, he rewarded her devotion by allowing her to borrow one of his books. It was thus that Philip discovered Isobel's proficiency at mathematics. He had given her a text on algebra because it was sure to confound her and lead to his explaining the impossibility of the female mind grasping the complexities of mathematics, a moment to which he looked forward. The day she returned the book, he decided it would be amusing to make her try to solve a problem before starting his speech. As it turned out, she solved it, as well as all the other problems he gave her. Initially, he was put out, but it occurred to him there was a silver lining to this cloud. He took to having her do his exercises for him, and she regarded him with all the adoration of a little sister.

IV

Isobel was all of seventeen when she realized she was in love with Philip Samuels. Philip had much to recommend him; he was young, and he was handsome, with thickly lashed brown eyes that sometimes looked soulful. His hair was saved from being mousy because of its reddish tint. He was taller than Isobel by only a few inches, but he was powerfully built. Most important, he was the only person besides Mrs. Morris who ever listened to her.

At Mr. Samuels's insistence, Philip had enrolled in law school. Consequently, he was often out, but when he was home he would talk with her as he had in times past and, now and again, he would lend her a book. Isobel attributed his shortness with her to the stress of his law studies. His frequent demands for money from his father were due, she knew, to his desire to better himself. Philip was discerning enough to perceive a man was judged first by his appearance. She looked forward to his homecomings with all the impatience of a girl deeply in love.

It was as little a thing as failing to firmly shut the door to her tiny room one night when she was in her bath that changed everything. The warmth of the water made her drowsy, and as she scrubbed herself she indulged in her favorite fantasy that there was a maid standing ready to wash her back if she so much as lifted a finger in her direction. Squeezing her eyes shut to keep out the harsh foam, she poured water over her head until the last of the soap was gone. She stepped out of the bath, leaning over to let the water from her wet hair fall into the tub, and groped for her comb on the table. Drops of water hit the bare wooden floor as she worked the tangles out of her hair. She was combing out a stubborn snarl when she felt an almost imperceptible swirl of air pulling at the dampness of her skin. It was an odd sensation that moved over her arms and back in waves of prickly tension. She told herself she was imagining things and refused to give in to the temptation to look behind her. Finally, though, she pulled her hair away from her face and twisted around to look.

"Good evening, Isobel."

"Philip!" She snatched up the towel draped over the chair. Her mortification was so acute that she spoke only when he made no move to leave her to her embarrassment. "What do you want?"

"I came to get Euclid."

The book he had let her borrow more than a month ago was on her table, and as she reached over to hand it to him, she held the towel tightly around her. She didn't at all like the look on his face as he took the book from her shaking hand. "If you were a gentleman, Mr. Philip, you would have knocked!" she said, hardly able to believe she could utter the criticism.

"If you were a lady," he said slowly, "your door would have been shut." He tapped the book against his open palm and looked at her for a long moment before turning to leave, closing the door firmly behind him.

Philip walked back to his room with a strange excitement boiling in him. As he'd said, he had come to get his book. The sound of water sloshing in the tub told him his cousin must be in her bath, and he suddenly found himself curious to see what she looked like without those hideous clothes she wore. She had just stepped out of the tub when he pushed open the door. He saw water glistening on her pale skin and darkening the wooden floor under dainty feet and long elegant legs. He was instantly hard when she bent at the waist to grope for a comb. He'd damned near taken her right then, but he knew what a prim little thing she was. A little finesse would be necessary with her. She might be skinny, but she was surprisingly well shaped. "Surprisingly well shaped," he mused as he dressed to go out. He felt a tingle of arousal in his belly at the thought of those long legs wrapped around him, hips moving in unison with his. He had got only a glimpse of her breasts, but they had looked to be generous. His cousin worshipped him, he knew, and he did not think for even a minute it would be difficult to get her to turn that adoration into something more physically rewarding.

V

Isobel might have convinced herself the humiliating episode was forgotten, except Philip now stared at her in an unsettling manner. Or at least she thought he did. She did not know if his gaze disturbed her because of what had happened or whether he really did look at her differently. She told herself her carelessness had brought this on her. He was right; a lady would have made sure the door was firmly shut. It was unfair to blame Philip because he had unwittingly embarrassed her; it was not his fault she left the door ajar. She dismissed the persistent thought that he had been standing in the doorway for some time, and convinced herself that it was she who was really to blame.

One day, when Isobel was in the study settling the household accounts, Philip entered the room so quietly his greeting startled her.

"Ah, here you are!"

It was a moment before her heart stopped its wild pounding. "Good afternoon, Mr. Philip. Is there something you need?" She dismissed the uncomfortable feeling that whatever he was thinking was not at all proper, still unable to believe a base thought could enter his mind.

"I've brought you a book." This was evidently true; there was a book tucked under his arm.

"You have?" He sounded amiable enough and she relaxed at this obvious sign of his high regard for her. "What is it?" She took the heavy volume he held out to her. It was a leather-bound edition of Aristotle. "Philip, it's beautiful! It must have cost you a fortune."

"I thought you might like to have it."

"Oh, yes!"

"You're very pretty when you smile, Isobel." He rested his hand on her shoulder. Though she did not want to spoil this return to normal relations, she shook off his hand. "I'll be extremely interested to hear your thoughts on it." He glanced at the clock hanging on the wall above the desk where she sat. "Well, I'd better be going!"

*   *   *

When Isobel got back from Mr. Archer's later
that evening, she went directly to her room and sat
down at her desk, her head nearly bursting with music. She immediately pulled out her pen and ink and
began to lose herself in the exhilaration of seeing her
music captured on paper. Mr. Archer did not know
she had started composing on her own, and she intended to surprise him with a piece for fortepiano,
flute, and continuo. She spent all of her free time on
the fortepiano at home so he would not suspect her
surprise.

It was ten o'clock before she put down her pen and
shook her hand. The copy of Aristotle lay on the desk,
and, knowing she would be unable to sleep right
away, she tossed it onto the bed. When she was settled
under the covers with the candle moved to the bed
table, she held the book to her nose, closing her eyes
and breathing in the smell of the leather. When she
opened it she was surprised to see a folded sheet of
paper fall from the pages. She immediately recognized
Philip's cramped writing.

The short letter read:

> My sweet Isobel,
>
> I know I take the chance of offending you by this
> desperate letter, but I beg of you, read through to the
> end and you will see I have no choice but to take such
> a risk. I am sick with love for you. I cannot think, I
> cannot eat, I cannot attend to my studies, I offend my
> friends with my despondency. I have been unable to
> think of anything but you since—but, I expect you
> know to what I cannot refer. I begin to fear I am in
> grave danger from this fever threatening to consume
> me with a greater violence for every day that passes
> without a salve for the ravage it causes me. If you have

any feeling for me at all, you will consent to meet me so I may tell you how I have been suffering for love of you.

   Tomorrow evening, number 16 Acton Street. I will wait all day and all night for you.

Isobel read the letter twice over before she could begin to think calmly. He loved her! She read the letter for a fourth time before thinking that if he was so terribly in love with her, he ought never have written such a letter asking her to compromise herself. It bothered her enough that the next day she showed it to Mrs. Morris.

"Don't you dare think of going!" she gasped. "If he loves you, he will declare himself like a gentleman. You're a lady, and he must treat you like one!"

"But, if he loves me, he will not compromise me!" Isobel took back the letter.

Mrs. Morris shook her head. Master Philip was a young man obsessed with bedding every wench in sight, though she could not bring herself to tell Isobel so. "Listen to me," she said, "a gentleman does not ask a lady to meet him alone. You know this. That letter is nothing but an insult. Do you not know in your heart that it would be wrong to meet him?"

"But he says he loves me!"

"No, Isobel, he does not say he loves you. Read it again. He says he hopes you will disgrace yourself. Will you damn yourself to hell for such a man? Will you do what you know is wrong? There is no greater sin than that, Isobel."

"Mrs. Morris, if you can read this letter and tell me Philip does not love me, I will not go."

"He will love you all the more if you prove to him you will not do what you know to be a sin."

*   *   *

For some time afterward, Philip came home only to ask his father for money. On the few occasions when Isobel saw him he refused to do anything but scowl at her. She had adored him for so long she could not believe he could be angry with her for refusing to compromise herself.

One day, when Philip was again home to ask his father for a few more dollars, she passed him in the hall, and to her surprise he caught her arm and made her stop.

"Good afternoon, cousin Isobel."

She gave him a strained smile. "Philip." When he did not let go of her arm, she tried to shake loose. "What do you want? Your mother will not be very pleased if she finds you are keeping me from my work." Her warning had no effect, for he continued to grip her arm.

"Why didn't you come?"

"Philip, if you truly loved me, you would never have insulted me by asking me to meet you!" She met his gaze unblinkingly.

He pulled her close to him until she was pressed up against his chest. "Isobel, you are a cruel and cold woman."

There was a hungry look in his eyes that frightened her, but she was unable to look away. His face was so close to hers she could feel his breath on her cheek. "Let me go!" She tried to twist away, but he only held her tighter.

"Isobel, I do love you." He stared into her eyes and then let them close as he lowered his head to her mouth. His lips were hard on hers, and when she felt him trying to thrust his tongue into her mouth, she kicked out at him as hard as she could. To her great relief he suddenly released her. "You'll regret that, you little bitch!" he snarled, bending over to rub his bruised shin.

"You are a gentleman, Philip Samuels, but you seem to have forgotten it!" she cried, resisting the urge to wipe her mouth.

He straightened up and sneered, "If you want to get on in the world, cousin, stop your airs and remember your station. There're easier ways for a woman to make a living. Even one like you!" He stepped back. "You won't be so proud when Father boots you out of here. You won't think yourself too good for me then!" He brushed against her as he went down the stairs.

She leaned against the wall after he was gone and pressed the back of her hand to her mouth. She finally understood that Philip Samuels meant her no good.

VI

Philip had not been home for several weeks when Isobel found herself enjoying a rare evening of solitude after Mr. Samuels took Mrs. Samuels and fat Miss Emily to supper and a new Italian opera. When she came home from Mr. Archer's she discovered Mrs. Morris was also out, probably taking advantage of the empty house to visit her brother, and so Isobel ate a very lonely supper. She was in her room, brushing out her hair, when she decided she would read for an hour or so before going to bed. She pulled on a cotton wrapper, then went downstairs to the library. In this quiet room, surrounded by books, she could pretend she was in Boston, that her father was still alive and was going to come into the room to talk with her as of old, or that her mother would come in to say she was going to play the fortepiano. She opened her book and was soon so utterly absorbed in the death of Socrates that she did not hear the door open.

"Good evening, cousin." Philip leaned one shoulder against the doorway and crossed his arms over his chest, eyes fixed somewhere below her shoulders.

"What are you doing here?" Isobel snapped the book closed and stood up, startled because she had not heard him come in.

"I live here," he said. He stepped inside and closed the door behind him.

She wasn't sure, but she thought his voice sounded just the tiniest bit slurred. "It's quite late, Philip, and I must be going." She started toward the door, but the look on his face stopped her. His lips were pressed together in a thin smile. "You leave me alone!" She tried to fight her panic when he took a step toward her.

He shook his head and let his eyes drop to where her wrapper failed to hide the swell of her breasts. "Do you know, my dear little Isobel, there's no one here but us?"

"Mrs. Morris is here!" Her eyes darted to the door, judging whether she could get past him.

"I've given Mrs. Morris the night off."

"What do you want, Philip? It's very late."

"Do you remember my letter? I meant every word I said, and I still mean it." He reached out to touch her hair.

He was close enough that she could smell liquor on his breath. "You're drunk!"

"Ah, but not too drunk to appreciate how pretty you are," he spoke softly, and before she knew what he was doing, he took another step toward her.

"Philip!" she said, backing away from his uncomfortable closeness.

"I've been thinking about you, Isobel," he said in a low voice, "almost every night." She put her hand out to stop him from coming any closer. "You know I love you. Let me prove it to you." When she saw he meant to try to kiss her, she pushed him away.

"I don't want—"

"Why not? You know, Isobel, you're the one who made me think you were in love with me." He scowled angrily and stepped toward her again. "You followed me all over! And now you're surprised I'm attracted to you? I'm a man, after all, I'm only human."

"Philip!"

"Come here," he snarled, suddenly grabbing her arm.

Her reaction was instinctive. She jerked her arm from his grasp and pushed him away as hard as she could. He stumbled backward and then fell, hitting his head against the side of a small table.

Chapter 4

"Philip! Are you all right?" Isobel bent over him, relieved to hear a drunken moan.

"Good God! What's happened here?" Samuels was standing in the doorway, his wife behind him, clutching his arm.

"My son!" Mrs. Samuels exclaimed when she saw Philip. She pushed past her husband to kneel at his side. "My son, my son," she said in a choked voice. "You've killed him!" Mrs. Samuels twisted to look at Isobel.

"I have not!" Isobel protested.

Another groan from Philip made Mrs. Samuels return her attention to him. "Hush! Don't talk right now. Thank God we came back before she could do you even greater harm!" Mrs. Samuels turned to her husband. "She might have killed him, Mr. Samuels! I told you that girl would be nothing but trouble."

"I did not! He was trying to—"

"Think twice before you accuse my son of something you can't prove," Samuels cut in. "I think, young lady, you had better go to your room and stay there until I call you."

"Yes, sir."

Some quarter of an hour later, Samuels rapped sternly on Isobel's door. "Please give me the key to this door," he said.

"But—"

"The key." When she turned it over to him, he stood stiffly with his hand gripping the side of the door. "Philip assures me," he said, "that your attack on him was unprovoked. I suggest you spend some time thinking about the consequences of falsehood."

"It's Philip who ought to be punished, not I!" she cried as the door shut in her face.

"Philip," she heard him say as he turned the key in the lock, "is at least a member of this family."

A week later, Philip found Isobel in the study. She jumped when he put his hand on her shoulder.

"Unless you intend to apologize, I have nothing to say to you, Mr. Philip Carter Samuels," she said stiffly.

"So, you still think you're too good for me, do you?"

"If you ever touch me again, I swear I'll tell your father!"

"Really?" He sneered. "And when I deny it, who do you think he'll believe—his only son, or some distant relation? If you are related at all, that is."

"I would die before I let you touch me, Philip!"

"I promise you, I'll make you the sorriest woman in New York." He whirled around and left, slamming the door after him.

Isobel stared at the papers scattered on the desk and tried to fight her rising panic. It was becoming all too clear they meant to rob her of her inheritance, and there was no one in New York she could turn to for help.

The next day she told Mrs. Morris of her fears. "I've got to find someone to help me!" She slapped the tabletop angrily.

Mrs. Morris patted Isobel's hand. "My nephew is a law clerk for Mr. Horace Bartless. Maybe he'll help you."

"Do you think he would?"

"Well, it never hurts to ask."

Isobel's reply was interrupted by someone's knocking loudly at the door. When she realized no one was going to answer it, she stood up. "I'll be right back, Mrs. Morris," she said over her shoulder.

Chapter 5

I

Mr. Edward Fairfax St. James had no great love for America. He'd been shot at by the damned colonists during the war and he had the uncomfortable feeling that they'd still like to shoot an Englishman. He wanted nothing more than to put an end to this wild-goose chase his brother had sent him on and go home to good solid English soil. He was of the opinion that his niece was dead. If she was still alive, Catherine Rowland, who had once cherished the hope his brother would one day recognize their daughter, would never have stopped sending the letters. The war had interrupted his brother's search for the girl, and though Edward was convinced the twice-yearly communications had stopped because the girl was dead, Robert had been adamant that he go to the colonies and confirm it. If she were alive, she was to be brought to England. Edward would never have gone but for the fact his brother had given him a goodly sum of money and the promise of a lucrative post in the government on his return. Since he had recently resigned his commission in the army, and had nothing much better to do, he had gone. He had already spent the better part of a month trying to discover what had happened to the American Catherine Rowland had married. He'd spent even more time trying to locate their daughter. It was several weeks before he discovered she'd moved from Boston to New York. By then, he was more than ready to go home. It was so like those deuced colonists to make things difficult, Edward told himself. He knocked at the door of the house where he had been told Catherine Rowland's only child now resided. He glanced around while he waited for someone to answer the door. The dingy building was not large, but it looked as if it might once have been rather pretty. Now, it was in need of some whitewash and, he thought as he looked out over the side lawns, a good gardener. An appallingly pale girl opened the door. Judging by her appearance, the owner did not treat his servants too well. She was as drab as the house. Her skirt and blouse were clean but faded to a uniform gray, having seen better days long ago. Her hair was covered by a dark kerchief, though a few strands of light-colored hair had escaped to curl around her wan face.

"Yes, sir?" Her voice was soft.

Edward thought it was odd that he should notice her eyelashes made a dusty curve on her cheeks. Something about her made him whip the hat off his head as he spoke. "Would you be so kind as to tell me if I have found the relatives of Mr. Jonathon Rowland?"

"His cousin, Mr. Carter Samuels, lives here."

"Mr. Carter Samuels," he repeated, looking at her more closely and deciding if she weren't so thin she might, almost, be considered handsome. She had high cheekbones and a slender nose, and the hand that held the edge of the door had long fingers. Because she was standing in the shadows, he couldn't see the color of her eyes.

"Mr. Samuels isn't in. Perhaps you might leave your card?"

"Perhaps, miss, you may be of service," he said, handing her his card with a little flourish. "Is there, by any chance, a young girl by name of Isobel, seventeen or so, living here?"

"Yes, Mr. St. James, there is," she said.

He masked his surprise at her being able to read. "I should be extremely grateful if I could speak with her." He sighed with relief. He could taste good English roast beef even now. All he had to do was collect the girl and head for home.

"Why?"

"I'm afraid that's confidential." He was nonplussed at the question, as if it were any business of hers! He was of a mind to chastise her for her impertinence, but instead, he forced a smile and said, "If you would tell her I am here, I would be in your debt."

"If she knew why you wanted to speak with her, I'm sure she would consent to see you."

It was a shame she was relegated to a life of petty labor. Poverty ruined women at a regrettably young age. She was no older than sixteen or seventeen, and he was certain that inside of ten years her looks would be entirely spoiled. He took out a coin and pressed it into her hand. "Perhaps I might convince you to tell her I am here?"

"I don't want your money." She held out the coin until he took it back.

"As you wish." He shrugged and pocketed it, restraining himself from telling her she looked as though she could ill afford to refuse any coin. "I am staying at the DeWitt Hotel. If you would be so kind, please tell your mistress where she might find me and that I wish to speak with her on a matter of the utmost importance." He was about to go when his eye was caught by a flash of light off something around the girl's neck as she took a step toward him. He tried to hide his excitement as he reached out to examine it. "What an unusual locket! May I see it?" She quickly covered the locket with slim fingers. "I only want to look at it," Edward protested. She was silent while he examined the motto engraved on its reverse side. "Where did you get this?" It was no wonder she hadn't wanted him to look at it; the little thief had stolen it!

She tucked the locket back into her shirt before answering him in an offended tone. "It was given to me by my father. Now, if you do not mind, my cousin will be upset if you take up any more of my time, so unless you have a message for him . . . ?"

"Your cousin?"

"Yes."

"You are a servant here?" He could keep the incredulity from neither his voice nor his face.

"Mr. Samuels is kind enough to allow me to earn my keep," she answered stiffly, looking him full in the face. He saw then the unmistakable deep blue of her eyes.

"You are Isobel?" She nodded. "Then, I have the pleasure of telling you that I am your Uncle Edward." He bowed and, when he straightened up, continued: "I am gratified to have found you at last."

She was looking at him with a stare unnervingly like the one his brother had used on him just before ordering him to America. "I don't find your little joke at all amusing," she said, anger flashing in her eyes. "Philip put you up to this, didn't he? You will tell him, if you please, that it did not work." She would have shut the door in his face if he had not quickly put his foot in the way.

"I assure you this is no joke! My brother—that is,

your father—has spent the last several years and a great deal of money trying to locate you. He expects me to return to London with you."

"My father is dead."

"His lordship would be surprised to hear that."

"His lordship? Oh, really!" Her voice was dripping with sarcasm. "Do you think me so stupid as to believe such nonsense? Next you will be telling me King George has decided to ask for my hand!"

"I can prove I tell the truth!" Edward exclaimed. The last thing he had expected was to be disbelieved. Provided he even found his niece, he had envisioned informing her of her good fortune and taking the grateful girl back to England. No arguments, no reluctance, and certainly no suspicions about his veracity.

"How?" she asked skeptically.

"Do you recognize this?" He took a miniature out of his pocket and held it out to her.

"No," she said bluntly, barely glancing at the painting of a small blond child before thrusting it back at him. He refused to take it.

"Turn it over."

Isobel read the inscription on the back:

Your daughter, Isobel St. James on the occasion of her 3rd anniversary, 23rd April 1772.

She looked at him. "So?"

"Your mother sent this to your father."

"If she sent it to my father, how did you get it?" She handed the miniature back to him.

"Jonathon Rowland was not your father." He pocketed the painting with a long sigh of frustration.

"Perhaps you have the wrong Isobel?" She had offered the suggestion to be helpful and she looked taken aback at his sharp reply.

"No! And that necklace proves it." He jabbed a finger at her chest. "It was a gift from my brother to your mother."

"And just who is it you say is your brother?" She crossed her arms over her chest as though challenging him.

"Your father is Robert St. James, third earl of Chessingham. Your mother sent him news of you every year on your birthday and at Christmas. Her letters stopped coming several years ago."

"My mother died when I was ten. Why didn't he try to find me then?"

"I think that's a subject you'd best discuss with your father." Edward began to have hope he might be back in England before too long.

"Am I to understand I am to meet him sometime?" She spoke slowly, trying desperately to absorb what this stranger was telling her.

"Your father has instructed me to find you and bring you back to England."

"But I don't want—" She was going to say she did not want to go to England, but stopped herself. What was there for her in New York if what he was saying was true? "Miss Isobel St. James." She said the words as though savoring their sound. She looked at him and asked, "Is he very rich?"

Though Edward was surprised by her question, he did not show it. "He's a wealthy man, yes." If finding out his brother was rich would get her to go with him, he was willing to tell her he was Croesus.

"Perhaps you had best speak to Mr. Samuels." She opened the door and let him in. "If you don't mind waiting, I think he would be very interested in hearing your story."

II

Edward took Isobel's arm as they boarded the English packet bound for Bristol, concerned that she

would be frightened to be on a ship for the first time.
As it turned out, he needn't have worried, for, as she
told him, she'd been sailing with Rowland more than
once. During the weeks it took to cross the Atlantic,
she did not suffer a moment of seasickness, not even
when the weather turned foul. She spent hours standing on the deck looking out over the water as though
she expected the shores of England to magically appear.

Isobel spent the nearly ten weeks it took to cross the
Atlantic in a state of constant turmoil. Though she
often longed to go back to Boston, and sometimes
wished she had refused to go with Mr. St. James, she
had to admit that if she were to go back, there would
be nothing there for her. She felt lost, as adrift as the
ship she was on. When she thought about England she
found it impossible to put aside her loyalty to the
country she had grown up in. Just the sound of the
word "England" brought up a feeling of dread and a
vague sense that she was sailing toward the enemy. Yet
England was to be her home. The irony was that even
if she had refused to go, her music would likely have
taken her there sooner or later.

She listened carefully when Mr. St. James talked
about his brother, hoping she might hear some clue
about herself in his words and she alternated between
dreading their arrival in England and being impatient
to have the waiting over.

Though she was fully prepared to dislike London on
principle, Isobel fell in love with it as soon as her carriage entered the city gates. It was utterly and completely different from New York, and as the carriage
rolled along the crowded streets she pulled down the
glass to peer out the window. The air was filled with
the shouts of street merchants hawking their wares,
and their cries assaulted her ears. For his part, Edward

kept up a constant stream of conversation, pointing out sights of interest and taking care to inform her of their connection with men of importance. The carriage bounced over the cobbles past a man standing on a box, head and shoulders above the small group gathered around him, one arm raised skyward extolling the properties of his miracle potion, guaranteed to cure anything and everything from boils to the gout, the pox, and fevers of the brain. "Will it cure me of me wife?" shouted one skeptic.

"How do you stand the jouncing?" she complained after she was nearly thrown off the seat when they abruptly turned a corner.

Edward did not seem to be the least affected by the joint-destroying ride and he assured her it was a skill she could learn. "This coach isn't really suited to the city streets," he told her, "but I'm afraid it will have to do until we get to Redruth."

She had to wonder if they would arrive at all. The streets were clogged with carriages of all sizes, all being driven as if each one were the only vehicle on the road. Drivers cursed one another with an inventiveness that, when she could decipher the accent, made Isobel blush and Edward look sheepish. Still, she could see it was better to be in a carriage than to be on foot. Crossing the street was obviously a perilous undertaking. It wasn't until they reached some better-appointed streets that she saw barricades set up for the protection of any poor souls unlucky enough not to make it all the way on the first attempt. Edward jokingly told her the more timid had been known to wait for weeks before deciding it was safe to cross.

The carriage turned one last corner onto Albemarle Street. "Albemarle Street is named after Christopher Monck," he began, "the second duke of Albemarle, who bought Clarendon House for twenty-five thousands of pounds, then leveled it to the ground and built

Albemarle Street on the site of the old mansion. The
Duke of Albemarle Publick House is hard by on Dover
Street." He nodded his head in that direction.

"Do you go there often?" The carriage pulled to a
stop and Edward escaped having to answer when the
door was pulled open by a servant wearing the earl of
Chessingham's blue-and-gold livery. "This is where
your brother lives?" She blinked in disbelief when the
footman handed her down. Edward bobbed his head in
assent as he stepped down beside her. Redruth was a
forbidding blackish-gray building three stories high,
with two curving staircases that met at the second
story before carved wooden doors. Another liveried
servant pulled the doors open just as they arrived, and
when they stepped over the threshold they were met
by a doleful-looking butler who took Edward's overcoat and hat and waited patiently for Isobel to give him
her cloak. At Edward's prodding, she handed it to him
and felt very shabby indeed when she saw the butler's
clothes were of far better quality than her own. As
soon as she handed over the threadbare garment, the
butler passed their things to another servant, who disappeared with them to Lord only knew where.

Edward looked at her self-conscious stance and
wished he'd had the sense to buy her some decent
clothes before they left New York. He ought to have
known—he had berated himself several times—that
she had so few dresses and such a woefully inadequate
cloak. Ten weeks on the open sea did not seem to have
bothered her in the least. He'd often seen her standing
on the deck, that pitiful excuse for a cloak pulled
closely about her, staring out over the water as if the
seas were calm and it was not bitterly cold.

She had not complained even once during the long
post-chaise trip to London. It was impossible for her
not to have been uncomfortable; in spite of its being
late in May, the weather was unseasonably cool. After

spending the night at Bristol, where Edward sent word
to his brother that they expected to arrive in three or
four days, they began the overland trip to London.
The roads had not been in good condition; they were
muddy and the going had been unpleasant, to say the
least. Still, she had not uttered one word of complaint
until they hit the cobbles of London.

"His lordship is expecting you." The butler sounded
as though the phrase was one he was used to repeating.
He motioned for them to follow him. Isobel kept her
eyes on the floor and listened to the soft tapping of her
boots on the black-and-green squares of marble until
they turned a corner and stopped in front of a door
halfway down another hall. She glanced up at the gilt
molding arching up into the ceiling, while the butler
pulled open the paneled doors and took two short steps
into the room. "Miss St. James and Mr. St. James,
milord," he announced. She followed Edward inside.

The room was large and rectangular, with a marble-
topped desk that took up nearly all of one end. The
walls were covered with dark wainscoting, and, had it
not been for a large window overlooking the gardens,
the room would have been quite dim. Nearly all the
available space on the walls above the wainscoting was
taken up by portraits, all the way up to the ceiling, and
it gave the room a cramped feeling to have so many
faces staring down from the walls. An intricately pat-
terned blue-and-white rug covered nearly the whole of
the wood floor she had seen at the edge of the carpet.
Her feet sank into the wool and she wished fervently
that it could hide her scuffed boots. She looked up
from her feet and was surprised to see no one. She was
about to turn to Edward and ask him where her father
was when she was startled to hear a deep voice say,
"Do come in." Someone stood up from a sofa that was
turned to face the fireplace. "So, I have finally found
you."

The earl, only slightly taller than average, was a solidly built man whose eyes were exactly the same dark blue as Isobel's. It was at the eyes that the resemblance between them began and ended. He looked about forty, but she later found out he was nearer fifty. His nose was aquiline, and his eyes were nearly overshadowed by heavy eyebrows. His forehead was high and his chin long. His lips were plump but they stretched tightly over his teeth when his mouth was closed. His skin was lightly marked from the effects of the smallpox that had taken his wife and son. He had the beginnings of a paunch, yet he stood so straight he seemed slender. His graying black hair was curled at the sides and tied at the back of his neck with a black ribbon. His neck was covered around with a snow-white cravat tied into an elegant knot at the front. The ends of the cravat were tucked into a soberly decorated waistcoat sporting a heavy gold watch chain across the stomach. One foot was very neatly bandaged and it rested lightly on the floor. His shoe was black, and recently polished, with a gleaming gold buckle; his stockings, too, were black, and they were tucked nicely into the bottoms of his breeches. He wore a large gold ring on the little finger of his right hand, and on his left hand two large yellow diamonds.

Robert St. James, third earl of Chessingham, leaned on an ivory-handled cane of a highly polished black wood as he walked toward the girl who stood quietly at his brother's side. Except for the unmistakable color of her eyes, he would never have guessed she was his daughter. She was far too thin, poorly dressed, plain, and worst of all, she looked like some bloody serving girl, though he doubted it was her fault, seeing as how she had been brought up in the wilds of America. He stopped in front of her and reached out to move her chin to get a look at her profile. He hoped it would not be an impossible task to make her into a proper Englishwoman. She did not seem to be ill at ease in his presence, and he took her poise to be a sign that she might be made into something. With any luck, Catherine would have given her some breeding. "You may call me 'Father,'" he said when he let go of her chin. "Where did Edward find you?" He turned to his brother.

"She was in New York. Both Catherine and her husband are dead. She was living with the man's cousin," Edward answered.

"Was he unable to clothe her properly? She looks like a deuced chambermaid!" The earl swept a disdainful eye in Isobel's direction and addressed his brother, who only looked uncomfortable and did not answer.

"How old are you now, child?" He jabbed the silver-tipped end of his cane at her.

"She is just seventeen," Edward answered again.

"Does she not speak English?" he asked coldly, raising one heavy eyebrow to underscore his sarcasm.

"Of course I do, Father." Isobel's voice was soft. "I'm afraid Mr. St. James"—she looked at Edward— "found me in reduced circumstances."

He turned to his brother. "I trust there was no trouble with the cousin?"

"Indeed, he did not seem loath to see her go."

The earl shifted uncomfortably on his feet. "Come, child, sit with me. My foot begins to bother me." Isobel sat on the chair he indicated when he sat down again on the sofa. She picked up a cushion and put it underneath his outstretched leg. "Thank you, my girl." He looked down to where his foot pressed into the silk of the pillow.

"Does it hurt much?" she asked.

"Damnably." He winced as he settled his foot on the pillow.

"What happened?" She tucked her booted feet out of

sight under the chair when she saw the pained glance
he gave them.

"Gout."

"Why did you bring me here?"

Edward had to smile when he saw her using the
same forthright glance his brother had used so effectively on him.

"You get right to the point, don't you?" Lord
Chessingham gave her a sharp look. "I think perhaps
you need to learn some English manners." He thought
such American boldness was entirely unfeminine and
that to be plain on top of it would be nothing short of
disaster.

"I am sorry, Father, if I have offended you," she
said contritely, shrugging her shoulders in a curiously
elegant movement that made the earl raise his eyebrows. "But, less than a month ago I thought myself
an orphan, and now I find I am really the daughter of
an English aristocrat." She was impatient from wondering what her future was to be, but still she was surprised to hear how bluntly she spoke.

"Your mother was a beautiful woman," he said,
"and I should have married her had her station been
only a little higher. The second earl did not think the
difference could be overcome. He had already arranged
a marriage. But I did not bring you here to discuss my
past." He rapped his cane on the floor. "May I see the
locket?"

"The locket?" It took a moment for her to understand what he meant. "Of course." She reached to unfasten it and hand it to him.

"This was the only thing I gave Catherine that she
did not return." While he held the locket in his palm,
there was an instant when Isobel could believe he had
once been a young man. The moment ended when he

looked up and handed the necklace back to her. "You look a great deal like her."

"You could have married her anyway!" she blurted out.

"It was my duty to obey my father's wishes, and my father did not wish for me to marry your mother."

"Then you must not have loved her very much." The words were accusing and bitter.

"I loved her enough to bring you here!" His face was stony and there was a tense moment of silence. "My wife and children are dead," he said at last, staring intently at the carved handle of his stick. Their eyes met when he finally lifted his head. "I intend for you to marry and provide me with a grandson."

"Won't you have a difficult time marrying off your bastard daughter?" She rankled at his imperious tone. How could her mother have loved such a cold-hearted man?

"Since I intend to acknowledge you as my daughter there will be no shortage of young bucks clamoring for your hand. Damme, there won't, I own! You might be plain, but wealth has a way of blinding men to such shortcomings. Edward, ring for me!" Only after his brother had complied did he turn back to Isobel. When a servant appeared not three minutes later, he gave terse instructions. "See that Miss St. James's things are taken to her room. And send for a dressmaker immediately. My daughter is in urgent need of a new wardrobe." He looked at Isobel. "I am engaged tonight, but we shall speak further at a later time. Mrs. Godwaite"—he nodded at the woman who was standing deferentially at the door—"shall see to it you obtain clothes appropriate to your new station. You are to follow her advice exactly."

"Of course, Father."

"Tonight, you will do me the goodness of having a tray sent up to your room, as I shan't be dining with you." He looked steadily at her. "You have suddenly become a woman with prospects. I hope you are up to the challenge." He nodded his head in dismissal.

Isobel followed Mrs. Godwaite down the hall and into a sitting room, where the woman told her in a tight little voice to please wait and left her to her own devices. She amused herself by walking slowly around the room but quickly pounced on a newspaper she found lying on a small end table. She was more than halfway through an account of the bills before the House of Commons when she began to wonder if perhaps she might have been forgotten. She had just stood up to find someone who might tell her what was expected of her when the door opened. Mrs. Godwaite came in, followed by another woman who turned out to be the sempstress, and one of the housemaids.

"Miss St. James will be needing a complete wardrobe," Mrs. Godwaite said sternly to the woman, who nodded and put down her basket. "See to it at least three or four gowns are delivered immediately." Isobel watched Mrs. Godwaite while the sempstress pulled out a dress of a horrid brown color and waited patiently while the maid helped her into it. "Have undergarments sent as soon as possible," Mrs. Godwaite added when Isobel stood clad only in her shift. Mrs. Godwaite was a dark-haired woman who looked as though she thought Isobel might sprout the devil's horns at any moment. Her tiny brown eyes were nearly buried in her puffy face, and Isobel was afraid if she were to smile they would disappear completely. Mrs. Godwaite stood impassively while Isobel was prodded and poked and generally made to feel put out. Not one word more was spoken during the entire ordeal, and she was grateful when at last the sempstress packed away her things and Mrs. Godwaite silently showed her to her room.

Her room really consisted of three rooms, a bed-

chamber and a smaller anteroom, and there was also a
small lavatory. The walls of both rooms were hung
with a golden-yellow silk, and the hangings of the
huge four-poster bed were of a matching silk taffeta.
The chairs were all of the same style of Chippendale.
In the anteroom there was a pair of large oval mirrors
in carved gilt-wood, more of the dark chairs, and a
dressing table of a pretty, light-colored wood. There
were gilt chandeliers in both rooms, and there were
lamps and candlesticks scattered throughout. From the
windows in the bedchamber she had a view of the interior gardens, and from the opposite side of her quarters
she could see part of Albemarle Street, a portion of the
gates, and a bit of the drive.

   She was glad to be left alone, for, in addition to
Mrs. Godwaite's being the last person she might
choose to spend her time with, she was exhausted
from the days of travel. Her joints, not yet recovered
from being bounced from one end of London to the
other, were aching, and she longed to lie down and
sleep, something she would have done were it not that
her mind was so full of her new surroundings she was
convinced sleep would be impossible.

   She stood looking out the window and wondered if
it was her father's arranged marriage that had made
him such a bitter man. She turned away from the window. Or, had wealth made it easy to abandon her
mother?

Chapter 6

I

Isobel stayed only one week at Albemarle Street. The London season was over on June 4, the King's birthday, and, like most persons of quality, the earl spent the summer in the country. They left London together, but when they reached a small estate of his near the village of Mawbury, he stayed only the night before continuing on to Bath, where he hoped to obtain relief from his gout. He left Isobel there with only the servants, her new abigail, Bridget, and a governess, Miss Agatha Steadly, for company. Her father had also engaged a tutor for her, but after Miss Steadly informed the earl via the post to Bath that his daughter knew quite enough for a young lady, the lessons were stopped. Dresses continued to arrive from London, and her days generally consisted of tedious mornings of additional fittings and dull afternoons of listening to Miss Steadly tell her everything it was essential for a young lady of position to know. Miss Steadly started every day with the pronouncement that, as the acknowledged daughter of a peer, she was exceedingly marriageable and could be expected to make an excellent match. However, she would add in her sternest tones, the slightest defect in her deportment would surely prevent her from making a truly exceptional marriage.

Isobel spent a good deal of time, after Miss Steadly was finished with her, reading newspapers and pamphlets, and soon found herself becoming interested in the English system of government. How was it, she often asked herself, that it had failed so miserably in America? She never got the opportunity to discuss what she read, or much else of interest, for that matter, since Miss Steadly refused to entertain the notion of a young lady's knowing anything about Parliament until after she was married. Her riding lessons provided some diversion, but it was so terribly hot that the only comfortable time for riding was early morning or late evening, and she reserved her evenings for the fortepiano. It seemed a luxury to be able to play for as many hours as she wished, and it was several weeks before she stopped feeling guilty for the hours she spent at the instrument.

Her stay at Mawbury wrought a gradual change in her appearance. For the first time in a long while she was getting enough to eat, and it was food of infinitely better quality than she had eaten in New York. She could sleep all morning if it suited her, but it was some time before she stayed in bed past eight o'clock. She began to gain a little weight and, though she was still pale, she lost the ghastly pallor that had made her look so unhealthy. And her clothes! Never had she had so many dresses (she gave a sigh of relief to see not a single one of that hideous brown color), and she had enough underthings to last a lifetime. There was a pair of slippers for each gown and dozens upon dozens of silk stockings. There were garters, hats, and gloves and she was already collecting rich muffs, scarves, wraps, and even a beautiful black fur cape that she would be able to wear in winter. She shouldn't have been surprised to learn she was expected to change her clothes several times a day: one dress for morning, one for afternoon, a blue habit for riding, a dress for walking in the park, and yet another gown for the evening. Sometimes it seemed to her that she did nothing but change her clothes.

Isobel passed the summer in tolerable comfort, and if she was sometimes a little lonely, all she had to do was think of New York and even Miss Steadly seemed good company. If she had not been anxious to find the music teacher Mr. Archer had recommended to her, she would have been happy to stay at Mawbury indefinitely.

In mid-September, the earl finally requested she come to London. She could not help feeling hurt when she found he had been in London for nearly two weeks before sending for her. When she arrived at Redruth she was informed by an unsmiling Mrs. Godwaite that his lordship had left word he was out for the day but expected to return in time to dine with her at half past four. At a quarter past four, he sent word that he would be joining her for tea at six, as he was engaged for dinner. He arrived at half past six and, after a perfunctory apology for having kept her waiting, received a shock when he actually took the trouble to look at her. She was still pale, but her skin had taken on a translucence that made her complexion seem delicate instead of sickly. Her nose, which had seemed a trifle too long in her thin face, now seemed perfectly suited to her high cheekbones. Most of all, she radiated good health, her golden hair was shiny, and, though she remained slim, she had lost the angular, half-starved look that had so concerned her Uncle Edward.

II

Isobel and her father had dinner together almost
every day, but though there were often several people
waiting for him, he never invited callers to stay. He
would, however, repeat their stories to her so she
could almost feel she had met them herself. Isobel
looked forward to their dinners because it was the only
time she might expect to have an intelligent conversation. Her father was invariably engaged for supper and
Isobel generally spent the evening meal alone. The earl
enjoyed their afternoons together for many reasons,
not the least of which was the increasing evidence that
his daughter might actually be considered a beauty.
More than once, however, he took her to task for her
blunt way of speaking.

"Ladies," he warned her, "should not be so accomplished as you seem to be. It is well established that
intellectual pursuits have proven to be too much of a
strain on the fragile constitution of the fair sex, leading
to ill health and, in dire cases, insanity."

"Oh, Father! That's nonsense!"

"Nevertheless, one would be hard pressed to find a
husband who would appreciate such accomplishments.
As the late Lord Chesterfield has said"—he raised a finger to make his point—"'Women, then, are only children of a larger growth.' You would do well not to
forget it." He shook his fork at her to emphasize the
seriousness of his words.

"But, Father, if I really were only a child, would
you need to remind me to act like one?" She looked at
him as though puzzled.

"Your impertinence is not appreciated," he snorted.

"Well, then, I think it unlikely I shall marry," she
said, looking down to cut into her roast beef in order
to hide her smile.

"Who would have such an impudent little snip as you, I can't imagine!"

"I promise you, Father, when at last I am presented to society, no one will ever suspect I've a brain in my head!" She waved her fork in the air.

"I do believe you're too clever for your own good." He was unable to suppress a smile, and he actually grinned when she began to laugh.

"Father, I know I am not all you might have desired in a daughter, but I can scarce be anything other than myself. You will have to be satisfied with me as I am."

"Friday se'nnight there will be guests for supper. You may attend," he said gruffly.

"And who is invited?" She failed to hide her excitement at the prospect of meeting some of his circle.

"Lord Burke, Lord Hartforde, his sister Lady Julia, Edward and his wife; and Mr. Mansfield Swaffing has prevailed upon me to have Mrs. Vincent. Mrs. Vincent is the widow of Mr. Humphrey Vincent."

"I shall be a model of femininity, I promise." She put a hand to her heart as she spoke. Mr. Swaffing, she knew, was a member of Parliament for one of the boroughs under her father's control. About Lord Burke she knew little except that his father had been the earl's closest friend. The marquess of Hartforde, however, was a man about whom she knew a great deal. His name was mentioned frequently in the political papers her father read. She knew he had held some post or other in the government until the death of his father, when he took his seat in the House of Lords and had proceeded to make his name known. She had found and read several pamphlets containing the texts of some of his speeches, and she was anxious to meet the man who could compose such inspiring words. Lord Hartforde was a man of impassioned beliefs who could temper his fiery rhetoric with good sense if it was necessary. She distinctly remembered reading somewhere

that there were some who speculated Lord Hartforde
might well be the next Prime Minister.

III

Isobel had to smile when Mr. Swaffing arrived on
the heels of Mrs. Vincent. Angelica Vincent could not
possibly be a day over twenty-two, which was about
twenty years fewer than her escort could claim. She
was a beautiful woman with dark hair and dark eyes,
that, Isobel thought at first seemed introspective but,
much later, realized was the result of her complete dis-
interest in any person not attired in breeches. She wore
an exceedingly low-cut gown of watered green silk
sprigged with darker green. From the jewels fairly
dripping off her, Isobel surmised the woman's late
husband had left her quite well off. Mr. Swaffing was
a roundish little man whose claim to good looks lay
chiefly in the abundance of his dark hair and his having
found an excellent tailor. His effusive greeting to Isobel was cut short by the arrival of Lord Burke.

"'Tis an honor to make your acquaintance, Miss St.
James." Lord Burke bent over her hand. "I am your
servant."

When he spoke, he gave the impression he was a
sober man for all that the ruffles of his shirtlace and
cravat bordered, by British standards, on the excessive.
Though not a small man, he was by no means cor-
pulent, and his auburn hair was artfully curled at the
nape of his neck. He was almost handsome, with light
brown eyes and a ready smile. He greeted Edward and
Mr. Swaffing, then kissed Mrs. St. James's hand before bending over Mrs. Vincent's hand. Edward's wife
was a gracious and still pretty woman who, it was
clear, was very fond of her husband. Isobel sat next to
Mrs. St. James, sipping from the small glass of wine
the earl had permitted her, quite happy to let Mrs.

Vincent monopolize the conversation until Lord Hartforde and his sister were announced. The earl rose and
took her arm as Lady Julia came in.

"This enchanting young woman is the Lady Julia
Grey," the earl said as Lady Julia reached out to take
Isobel's hands in hers.

"My brother," Lady Julia said to Lord Chessingham, "is fussing over his horses and will be here
just as soon as he can bear to tear himself away."

"Lady Julia, my daughter, Miss Isobel St. James."

"Your daughter!" Lady Julia looked at the earl in
surprise, her pale green eyes questioning before ex-
tending a hand to him. Her voice was warm as she
spoke. "Miss St. James, it is a pleasure to meet you.
You must tell me why Lord Chessingham is trying to
keep you such a secret when all of London is talking
about you! Shame on you, sir, for not introducing her
to us sooner." She shook her raven head at him.

"I have only just found her." The earl placed a hand
on Isobel's elbow. "My daughter has been in London a
very short time."

"Good evening, Lady Julia," Isobel said, already liking her. Lady Julia was about her own age, certainly
no older than nineteen or twenty. Her smooth complexion was set off by glossy black hair, and her light
eyes were open and friendly. She was not tall and her
fine features and slender figure gave an impression of
fragility. Isobel thought she seemed terribly young to
be the marquess's sister. She had expected a much
older woman. She was soon so busy answering Lady
Julia's questions (How did she like London? Had she
seen many wild Indians when she lived in America?)
that she did not notice the tall gentleman who came
into the room and greeted her father.

Julia turned her head and said, "I see my brother is
being his usual graceless self."

"On the contrary," Lord Hartforde responded with

a smile, "I merely choose to let my sister exhaust herself first. I find it is quite useless to speak until she has finished." Isobel was surprised to see Lord Hartforde was much younger than she had supposed, and even from this distance she could see his eyes were not the piercing gray she had imagined.

"My Lord Hartforde, may I present to you my daughter, Miss Isobel St. James," the earl said. "The most noble Alexander, Marquess of Hartforde."

Lord Hartforde stepped forward and took her hand. "I am at your service."

She inclined her head toward him, and when he straightened she found herself looking up into brilliant green eyes. Where Julia was dark, her brother was fair; his thick sandy hair was streaked with darker blond and his skin was faintly golden from the sun. His nose was straight and his lips were curved in a smile that did not reach the moss green of his eyes. No one feature was responsible for his extraordinary looks; it was rather the combination of them all that made him so handsome. What was remarkable was that it was quite plain he was utterly unaware of his beauty. Perhaps because he was so fair, he never had to give it much thought. He had such an air of quiet confidence that Isobel was convinced even if he had been a homely man it would have made no difference in the effect he had on her. He was not at all what she had expected. From what she had read about him, she had been fully prepared for a paunchy older man about her father's age with a dignified but stuffy demeanor who, perhaps, walked with a slight limp from the gout.

"Lord Hartforde," she murmured, feeling as though she might drown in those eyes. She forced herself to look away when she suddenly realized that, as he continued to look at her, there was a flicker of amusement in his gaze. She did not want to seem foolish or unsophisticated to anyone and, for some reason, especially to this man. She was quite, quite certain that Lord Hartforde had more than his share of women who made fools of themselves over him.

He turned away from her to speak to her father. He was wearing a suit of dark blue with gilt buttons, and the snug fit of his breeches showed the legs of a man who kept himself active. Isobel was glad that, like any man of fashion, he did not wear a wig; instead, his own tawny hair was pulled back from his forehead and tied at the nape of his neck with a blue ribbon. His cravat was simple; he forbore the frothy lace so popular among certain men of society, though the lace at his cuffs was not so plain as to miss being fashionable. She sat back down to talk to Lady Julia, but she could not take her eyes off him. Though she tried to resist, her gaze constantly moved to him. He was talking with Lord Burke and Mr. Swaffing, and she felt herself color when he saw her looking at him. After that, she succeeded in keeping her attention focused elsewhere until supper was announced.

Lord Burke lost no opportunity in taking Lady Julia's arm. When Edward took his wife's arm, and Mr. Swaffing Mrs. Vincent's arm, Isobel had no choice but to take the arm Lord Hartforde offered her. She stared at the buckles of his shoes as they walked; they were fairly sparkling with diamonds. Isobel sat on her father's left, with Lord Hartforde across from her. She hardly noticed where anyone else sat.

"And, of course, you are planning to give a ball for Miss St. James sometime soon . . . ?" Julia smiled over at Isobel before giving the earl a stern look.

"I had thought at the new year," he replied.

"Wonderful! Everyone will be back from the country, bored to tears and anxious to start the new season!" Julia clapped her hands. "Isobel, I shall give you the name of my dressmaker." She fixed the earl with a grim stare. "She will need a gown, my lord! And this one must be exceptional!"

The conversation turned to horses, and Lord Burke was, he declared, shocked to discover Isobel had not been at Ascot. Lady Julia proved knowledgeable on the subject and soon engaged Lord Burke and Mr. Swaffing in a heated debate over a horse Lord Burke claimed to be worth its weight in gold. He professed to be stunned, therefore, when the earl announced he owned the fastest filly in the empire, bar none. "You do not know what you say!" he cried.

Mr. Swaffing was strangely quiet.

"A thousand pounds says my Gazetta outruns your nag, Burke!"

"Done!"

Mrs. Vincent, during all this, did her utmost to be charming to Lord Hartforde, who, it seemed to Isobel, was spending a great deal of time leaning her way. Lord Hartforde smiled when Mrs. Vincent avowed she simply did not see the sense in racing, though she would allow a race could be an exciting thing to see.

Lord Hartforde thought Mrs. Vincent was an extremely pretty woman, and he glanced around the table to confirm his estimation that she was the handsomest woman present. He would go so far as to admit the earl's daughter was practically lovely, and, though she was rather too slender for his taste, he did not fail to note her figure was not in the least displeasing. He considered Chessingham to be a good friend and an important ally in the House, but he had absolutely no doubt that he was hoping for a match between them, and no matter how advantageous such a union might be, he had no desire to be married again. Once had been quite enough for him, and he could not help but believe his wife's death had been a blessing in disguise. They had all too soon discovered they detested each other. He was in no particular hurry to be-

get an heir while there was still so much time left in
which to accomplish the deed.

The conversation turned to the opening of Parliament the next week, and Lord Hartforde was impressed to find Miss St. James knew something about
English politics. He laughed when she turned to him
after demanding to know Lord Burke's political lean-
ings and bluntly asked, "Of course, you are a Whig,
are you not, my lord?"

"Naturally, Miss St. James," he responded. "And
yourself?"

"As you know, all women are disfranchised so I can
be neither Whig nor Tory," she said tartly.

"But if you were?" he insisted.

"A Whig. And I should work tirelessly to see that all
English people, men and women, have the right to
vote!"

"Your daughter certainly sounds like one of those
dashed colonists, Chessingham!" He turned away from
a pair of flashing eyes.

Not long afterwards, the earl asked Lady Julia for
any suggestions she might offer to ensure the success
of the ball he meant to give for Isobel. Lord Hartforde
tried to hide his amusement when he saw the look
Miss St. James gave her father for changing the subject. The topic next was society, and, though he had
turned his attention to the delightfully ignorant Mrs.
Vincent, from the corner of his eye he watched Miss
St. James lean back in her chair and push her un-
touched veal around her plate with the tip of her knife.
She listened to Lord Burke with an air of utter fascina-
tion, while she absently poked holes into the chop until
she had almost shredded it. She looked down at her
plate, evidently surprised at what she had done, then
looked guiltily at her father. There was such a touching mix of apprehension and affection in the look that
Lord Hartforde thought to himself, *Why, she is quite*

fond of him! And for some ridiculous reason, when she smiled at her father he felt a familiar tightening in his belly. He was staring at her so intently, wondering what made him react that way, that when Mrs. St. James asked him a question, he had to ask her to repeat herself.

By the end of the evening, when the men had joined the women in the drawing room, Isobel and Lady Julia had agreed to meet the next day for a ride in Hyde Park, Mrs. Vincent having begged off by virtue of a prior engagement.

"May I have your permission, Father?" Isobel looked at him, wondering if he would refuse her again. To her relief, he nodded his agreement. "At last!" she cried. "I have a lovely riding habit I thought was going to be out of fashion before Father allowed me out of the house! I am given to understand the design is French," she told Julia. "All I know is that it is exceedingly uncomfortable and it matches my eyes!"

Lord Hartforde smiled at her sally, but he politely refused his sister's entreaty to join them, though Lord Burke readily agreed. He knew his sister too well not to think she wasn't already scheming to throw Miss St. James in his way. Julia had taken a liking to the girl, and he knew she would be matchmaking in no time. It was a shame he had no intention of marrying again, because Miss St. James was a very fascinating and beautiful young lady.

Chapter 7

I

Julia liked Isobel from the moment she saw her standing at Lord Chessingham's side looking a little nervous but determined to put a brave face on it. The close friendship that sprang up between them was aided by Lord Hartforde's London house being just down the street at number 10 Albemarle Street. There was a strength about Isobel that fascinated Julia. She had always thought Lord Chessingham a hard man, yet he seemed softened by his daughter, and Julia thought anyone who could accomplish such a thing was worth befriending. She had not been disappointed. She was pleased to find she and Isobel thought alike on many subjects and that their tastes in all things were remarkably similar.

The earl encouraged their friendship. He knew very well how important it was for someone with Lady Julia's connections to be seen with his daughter. He hoped curiosity about Isobel would be brought to a pitch by the time he formally introduced her to society. And, if the truth be known, he hoped Lord Hart-

forde might, by reason of their being previously
introduced, feel he had a better claim to her than anyone else. That Isobel should marry Hartforde was Lord
Chessingham's fondest wish. It was much to the earl's
delight, therefore, that he began receiving numerous
inquiries about whether his daughter was "out" or not.
Until then, it was not proper for a gentleman to speak
with her. Only Hartforde and Burke had that privilege.

Julia expected to be surrounded by men when she
and Isobel went abroad, whether it was to a concert,
an at-home, riding in Hyde Park, or walking at Kensington Gardens, but Isobel, she knew, was ill at ease.
Her friend's awkwardness, however slight, was a
source of great concern to her. She was very anxious
for Isobel to make an impression in society. She was
beautiful enough and her manner natural enough that
her lack of polish could be overlooked, but Julia was
determined Isobel should acquire it, for she had decided that Isobel should marry her brother. She knew
precisely the kind of woman who might entice him
into an offer of marriage, and Isobel possessed all those
qualities but one. Julia meant for her brother to fall
hard and she devoted herself to seeing that Isobel
quickly acquired the sophistication provided only by
associating with people of fashion.

Julia's campaign to make Isobel into a woman of ir-
resistible charm proceeded well. She quickly mastered
the art of the noncommittal response, and it was entirely due to her own kindness that she listened to less
than scintillating conversationalists with an air of avid
interest that early gained her the reputation of being a
fascinating young woman. Julia soon decided it was
time to make the pilgrimage to Chelsea so Isobel
might see, and be seen at, the gardens of Ranelagh.

Lord Burke was easily persuaded to escort them,
and, as he plunked down the admission price of half a

crown for each of them, he proclaimed it a small price
to pay for the privilege of accompanying the two most
beautiful women in London. Isobel was quite taken
with the gardens, and while they walked along the ca-
nal, both Julia and Lord Burke were pleased to hear her
praise. The three wandered through one of the pagodas
until Julia suggested they have coffee and rest for a few
moments. They had arrived early, and while they
walked, more and more people began filling the gardens. Couples strolled arm in arm down the paths,
groups formed and reformed, and unattached men and
women looked out for someone to whom they might
become attached, however briefly. Isobel had been
rather enjoying herself during the afternoon. It was beginning to dawn on her that she was attractive to men,
and the interested looks sent her way as she walked
with Lord Burke and Julia did much to increase her
confidence. From time to time they were joined by ac-
quaintances of Julia's or Lord Burke's. Julia assured her
there would be no great harm done if she found herself
participating in conversation. Two or three times she
even ventured to express an opinion, and once, to de-
fend it heatedly.

The crowd became quite thick as they made their
way toward the coffeehouse, and by the time they
reached the bridge Isobel was distinctly uncomfortable.
A boisterous party of some fifteen or twenty couples
was just coming off the bridge, oblivious that they
were blocking the way for people headed in any direction but their own. Several of the party were shouting,
and the men who weren't were waving their hand-
kerchiefs as they listened to a handsome blond woman
sing the last refrain of a song so off color one wondered at its being sung in public, let alone in mixed
company. When the group continued down the path
toward them, Lord Burke briefly let go of Isobel's arm
to chastise a fellow who had jostled Julia, and that was

enough for Isobel to be separated from them. Though she tried to keep sight of them, after she had shaken off a too familiar hand and disentangled herself from the group, it was some minutes before she had regained the bridge. She could see Lord Burke and Julia nowhere. She walked for a while in the direction where she thought the coffee house might be, but it was soon evident she had not gone the right way. When she realized that she had got completely turned around, she looked about, trying to suppress her growing panic. She had no idea how to get to the coffeehouse, nor even how to get back to the entrance, and she had so hopelessly lost her sense of direction she had no clue as to which way she had first come. She shut her mouth firmly but felt unwanted tears when she briefly closed her eyes.

"Forgive me if I am forward," someone said, "but might I be of assistance?" Isobel turned to see a handsomely dressed gentleman standing to one side of her. "Mr. Rupert Selwynn, at your service." He bowed, smiled kindly, and smoothed his moustache.

Mr. Rupert Henry Selwynn was a gentleman of some five and thirty years with reddish-blond hair and a moustache of a slightly darker hue, which he was in the habit of stroking. He was of average height, about five feet and seven or eight inches, and he held himself in a soldierly posture so as to appear taller than he actually was. He kept six horses, had two very fine carriages, and a German valet who barely spoke a syllable of English but who had absolutely mastered the art of arranging his employer's hair. Mr. Selwynn knew appearances were everything, and, therefore, he adeptly hid a black heart and the soul of a libertine under a veneer of gallantry. He spent six hundred pounds a year on clothing alone. He had a house in the vicinity of Tottenham Court Road, and there was a steady parade of chambermaids through its elegant doors. He was a halfhearted Whig who secretly agreed with the Tories that something ought to be done about the disgraceful increase in the numbers of vagabonds and beggars, chiefly in the shape of more workhouses where they would learn the value of a day's honest work. He hedged his bets and had memberships in both Whig and Tory clubs. Mr. Selwynn, Sr., was a tobbaconist who, when he died at the age of eighty-five, left his only son a fortune of one hundred ninety-five thousand pounds, 6s, 8d, by which Mr. Selwynn, Jr., was almost able to sever himself completely from the stigma of his connection with trade. Rupert Selwynn had never worked a day in his life. He had three children, for none of whom he spent a farthing to support, their mothers being, respectively, a chambermaid, a parson's daughter who had made an ill-advised trip to London to visit her best friend, and the sister of an impoverished Grub Street hack. He was unmarried and likely to remain that way. He went often to Ranelagh, and when he saw Isobel he was immediately struck by two things: she was devilishly pretty, and she looked as though she was about to burst into tears.

"Oh, please, sir, I am lost!" She knew she ought on no account speak to a stranger, but, when faced with the prospect of staying lost, she decided propriety might this once be disregarded.

"Permit me to escort you from this den of iniquity." He held out an arm for her to take. "And whom have I the pleasure of rescuing from such a terrible distress?" He stuffed his handkerchief into his pocket.

"Please, sir, I am with a party, and I must rejoin them before they miss me! They were going to have coffee." She took his arm.

"You are an angel of incomparable beauty, Miss . . . ?" When she did not fill in his pause with her name, he continued in a languishing tone: "I must know who you are, my dear little beauty!" He was certain she was the daughter of some merchant who had brought his child to London in order to find her a husband. That she was so willing to trust him spoke volumes for her innocence. It also suggested she had not been brought up as strictly as she might have been. Indulgent fathers had been the ruin of more than one young lady visiting London for the first time. He covered her hand with his and began strolling in the direction of one of the more remote corners of the gardens.

Isobel did not recognize where they were until they passed the edge of a flowered border she did remember. "At last!" she cried when she recalled that, should they cut through, they would be very near the entrance. "Oh, but that way is to the gates!" She stopped when he continued straight ahead.

"Indeed, it is not, miss."

"No, sir, you are mistaken," she insisted when he tried to urge her on. She began to have a sense of how reckless she had been to trust a stranger.

"I assure you, 'tis you, angel though you are, who are mistaken," he said smoothly.

He walked on and she had no choice but to walk with him. With every step they took she was more and more certain he was leading her away from the entrance, especially since she did not see any buildings that looked as if they might be the coffeehouse. She pulled to a sudden halt when, to her great relief, she saw Mrs. Vincent walking out of one of the Chinese-style buildings.

"I see my party now!" She jerked her arm free and called out to Mrs. Vincent. She waved frantically when she saw the woman look around.

"Miss St. James, what a pleasure," she said when Isobel reached her side.

"Is Mr. Swaffing here?" she asked, so relieved to see someone she knew that she failed to note her "rescuer" had followed her and was standing next to her, listening with great interest to every word.

"Miss St. James!"

"Lord Hartforde," purred Mrs. Vincent, smiling and half turning to look behind her.

"Lord Hartforde!" Isobel jerked her head up as he reached Mrs. Vincent's side.

"My Lord Hartforde," said Mr. Selwynn, while he straightened up from a deferential bow, "Miss St. James was lost and she prevailed upon me to escort her to safety." Isobel was horrified to hear Mr. Selwynn giving him the impression that she had accosted a complete stranger, and she turned to stare at him. "I trust, my lord, I am leaving her in capable hands." He bowed and would have kissed Isobel's hand had she not snatched it away. He bowed again and, smoothing his moustache, left Isobel staring after him.

"I presume, Miss St. James, you are no longer lost?" Lord Hartforde queried.

"I was with Lady Julia and Lord Burke and we were separated, and I did not know where I was nor how to reach anywhere I knew! And he addressed me, my lord!"

"And where are my sister and Burke now?" A large diamond flashed on his finger as he brushed a speck of dust from his immaculate cuff.

"We were going to have coffee when we were separated." Isobel was so close to tears that her voice trembled.

"We were just going that way." He indicated the group that had exited the building after Mrs. Vincent. Mr. Swaffing was not among them.

"I just want to go home!" She was positively mortified to feel her cheeks burning and tears welling up again.

"Please, Miss St. James, consider my carriage at

your disposal." He made a neat little bow before turning to Mrs. Vincent. "Mrs. Vincent . . . Angelica," he
murmured. "If you would be so kind as to allow me to
escort Miss St. James to my carriage, I shall rejoin our
party in a thrice."

"Of course, my lord," said Mrs. Vincent, looking at
Isobel a little smugly and, evidently, feeling she was in
a position to be magnanimous.

Lord Hartforde took Isobel's arm and, as soon as
they were out of earshot, cleared his throat. "Miss St.
James," he said sternly, "I feel it my duty to tell you a
young lady never, upon any account whatsoever, ap-
proaches a stranger. I understand you are new to England, and no doubt things are done differently in
America, but 'tis little excuse for acting so unwisely."

"I did no such thing!" She looked away as soon as
she met the brilliant green of his eyes, unsettled at the
strange sensation it caused in her. She found it helpful
to concentrate on his sword, gently hitting the skirt of
her gown.

"Then you know Mr. Selwynn?" He glanced down
at her.

"Of course not!" she denied hotly, trying not to take
offense at what she thought was a patronizing tone.

"Then, forgive me, if you will, Miss St. James, you
must have approached a stranger. Q.E.D."

His voice was so full of condescension that for a moment she entirely forgot to be cowed by him. "Forgive
me, Lord Hartforde, but he approached me. I did not
approach a stranger. *Quod erat demonstrandum.*"

"*Verbum sat sapienti est,* Miss St. James."

"'Yet do I hold that mortal foolish who strives
against the stress of necessity.'" She was angry enough
at him for scolding her for something she had considered only in desperation that she forgot how upset
she had been at Mr. Selwynn for implying what had
not been the case.

"Good heavens! A woman who quotes the classics!"
He was laughing, and Isobel frowned at him. "Pray
tell, Miss St. James, when had you occasion to read
Euripides?"

"When I was eleven," she said shortly.

There was an incredulous pause. "Indeed?" he said.
There was another pause, during which Isobel glared
at him, and after which he said, smiling, though his
voice was serious, "Should a woman as learned as
yourself deign to take my humble advice, you would
do well to avoid Mr. Selwynn in the future."

By then they had reached his carriage and he handed
her up when the footman jumped to attention and
opened the door. She heard him giving the coachman
instructions after the door was shut but didn't know he
stood looking after the carriage long after it was out of
sight.

II

Later, Julia was effusively apologetic for Lord
Burke's clumsiness in losing hold of her at Ranelagh
and she repeated her brother's advice to avoid Mr. Selwynn.

The next day, promptly at ten in the morning—the
earliest one might call without rudeness—one of the
servants brought her a card with the name "Mr.
Rupert Henry Selwynn" embossed in ornate letters beneath the silhouette of a carriage and four. "He sends
his best regards for your health and begs you to see
him, miss," the servant said when Isobel took the card
from the tray.

"Show Mr. Selwynn to the west drawing room,"
Isobel said. "And tell him I will join him momen-
tarily." She finished her coffee, then went to see Mr.
Rupert Henry Selwynn.

"Miss St. James! It is indeed a pleasure and an honor

to see you." He took the hand she extended to him and bent over it. As he did so, he thought he had never held a hand so pretty. The sapphires she wore could be worth no less than a thousand pounds.

Isobel took her hand back. "Have you come to apologize, Mr. Selwynn?"

"Miss St. James, I can only think you refer to your misapprehension that I was not leading you to the coffeehouse." He looked stricken at the thought. "I assure you, I was not leading you astray! May I be struck down as I speak if I am capable of such a base act!" Fortunately, Mr. Selwynn was not a religious man, or he could not have kept his composure so well.

"Yet, I know you were not taking me to the entrance, Mr. Selwynn. I had at least remembered that much!" She remained standing.

"You are quite mistaken, Miss St. James." He stroked his upper lip. "I was merely taking you by a route which you, apparently, did not recognize. I would never—never!—do such a thing as you accuse me of." He went down on one knee before her and grasped her hand. "Miss St. James, I beg of you, I beseech you! I shall throw myself in front of the first carriage to pass your door if you persist in thinking me capable of such a base and dishonorable act!" He stood up when she gently took her hand away.

"Yet, you allowed Lord Hartforde to think I approached you, a stranger."

"I?" He put a hand to his breast. "I only recall helping to safety a beautiful woman who was in distress. If my Lord Hartforde received the impression that you approached me, why, 'tis false!"

"But so he thinks."

"Then I shall go to him directly I leave here and explain his error!"

"I think you had best do so, Mr. Selwynn." She rose and rang for a servant to show Mr. Selwynn out.

"I shall go on the instant, Miss St. James." He took her hand and bowed over it. "Will the lovely Miss St. James have pity on my poor soul and permit me the honor of calling on her again?"

"Perhaps, Mr. Selwynn." At least Lord Hartforde would no longer think her morals loose. Mr. Selwynn seemed so sincere she did not at all doubt he would keep his promise.

"Then, I am your slave, Miss St. James." And he followed the servant out of the room.

Rupert Selwynn paused on the steps of number 5 Albemarle, feeling extremely pleased that Miss St. James had so easily forgiven him. She was twice the beauty he had remembered. A few well-placed questions since their first encounter had gleaned him the information that she was the natural daughter of the earl of Chessingham, an intimate friend of the Lady Julia Grey, and in a fair way of becoming an heiress. *Here,* he told himself, *is a woman who could almost make me look fondly upon the tortures of matrimony.* The very thought of her expected fortune combined with his was nearly enough to make him consider the deed. When he first saw her at Ranelagh, he did not have the slightest suspicion she was so well connected, or he would never have attempted to make off with her. It had been quite a shock to discover she knew Lord Hartforde. There was a man he chose not to cross again. He smoothed his moustache. Then, pulling on his kid gloves, he softly whistled a tune as he skipped down the steps. He signaled his driver to follow him and walked off in the direction of Charing Cross Road.

Shortly after Mr. Selwynn disappeared around the corner, Lord Burke arrived to beg Isobel's forgiveness for his stupidity in losing hold of her for even a second, and he looked so abjectly ashamed that she really did forgive him and they parted on the best of terms.

Chapter 8

I

Not long after the outing at Ranelagh, Lady Julia arrived at Redruth determined to entice Isobel into going out once more; this time she had arranged a large party from which she could not possibly be separated. Julia was shown to the music room, where she found Isobel so intent on the fortepiano that she did not hear the servant's announcement. Julia signaled the footman to go and stood in the doorway to listen with rapt attention. She had never heard anything so sad in her life. The notes cried out to her, slowing, softening, yet never losing a clarity that made her wonder how anyone could have stood such sorrow except to express it exactly so.

"Who was that?" she asked when Isobel sat tapping one finger on the sheets of music in front of her. She jumped at the sound of Julia's voice and hastily placed a songbook over the sheaf of papers before turning to smile at her. Julia sat down next to her. "It was very sad. And beautiful."

"'Twas nothing." She shrugged and played a trill,

her fingers moving rapidly over the keys. "Just something I made up. I'm afraid I'm out of practice. I played badly." She gave a disappointed smile.

"It was you? I mean," she said, when Isobel raised her eyebrows, "was it you who wrote it?"

"The very same." Julia was silent and Isobel gave a little half smile. "I had lessons in America."

"Surely you have lessons here?" She leaned one arm on the fortepiano and alternately tapped two keys with the fingers of the other.

"The man I want to study with won't take on a woman student. He said I played very nicely and he was sure my husband would be proud to have such an accomplished wife. It was so unfair!"

"Oh, pshaw!" Julia laughed and played a scale. "Women have music lessons all the time. I had lessons myself. As you can hear, they were quite a success."

"You don't understand." Isobel shook her head. "I don't want to play just the fortepiano; anyone can do that. I write music, and not only for fortepiano, but for the orchestra . . . symphonies! I want to hear my music performed someday. It *will* be performed! It's worse here than it was in America. An Englishwoman with any ambition beyond having children might as well be dead!" She banged her hands down on the keys in frustration.

"But, Isobel—"

"At least let me fail after I have tried my best. To fail because I am not permitted to try is a crime against my soul. I refuse to believe I am inferior! You heard me play, Julia. Did you think the music inferior? No, you thought it must have been written by a man. Not even Mr. Walters could call it inferior. He simply refused to believe I had written it."

"So, find another teacher."

"But who? I don't know of anyone else."

"John Faircourt," Julia said.

"I doubt he'd take me on as a serious student."

John Faircourt had no small reputation as a composer, and he was said to be highly discriminating about whom he chose to study with him.

"I think I might have some influence with him," Julia said. "My father was his patron, you know."

"If I was a man, Mr. Walters would not have hesitated to work with me."

"I'm sure Mr. Faircourt will have no such hesitation. Do promise me you'll go to him. I'll even write you a letter of introduction."

When Isobel and Bridget arrived at John Faircourt's house, Isobel's mouth was dry and she swallowed nervously before knocking. What would she do if he refused to accept her? He was, after all, one of London's most well known musicians. "Is Mr. Faircourt at home?" she asked the servant who opened the door.

"Who shall I say is calling?"

"Miss Isobel St. James. I've a letter of introduction." She presented Julia's letter.

She did not have to wait long before the servant came back to usher her into Mr. Faircourt's drawing room. He rose when she came in and, smiling warmly, bent over her hand.

"So, you desire to continue your music lessons with me, do you, Miss St. James?" He held Julia's letter in his other hand. He was about fifty years of age and was not a particularly tall man. His prodigious stomach was proof he enjoyed his roast beef and pudding to the utmost. He wore gray breeches, none too loose at that, and a gold-embroidered waistcoat of the same color. His shirt was a fine silk, and frothy point lace fairly dripped from his cuffs and cravat. His receding hair was worn long and was excessively pomaded and curled, Isobel thought.

"Yes, Mr. Faircourt, I do."

"Tell me, Miss St. James, have you a favorite musician?" He refolded Julia's letter and slipped it into his pocket. "Is there someone you wish to style yourself after?"

Isobel could not help suspecting that he was humoring her and it rankled her. "I wish to style myself after no one but myself, Mr. Faircourt. But, if I may say so, I think there is a great deal for me to learn from you." Faircourt chuckled at that. "I want to be a composer," she rushed on, "not merely a fortepiano player. I may never be as great as Wolfgang Mozart, but I feel I have something."

"So, you think Herr Mozart is great, do you?"

"I believe he is a genius, Mr. Faircourt," she said fervently.

"I do not share your enthusiasm for the Austrians." He looked down his nose at her and raised his eyebrows. "However, I suppose my students are entitled to an opinion or two of their own."

"Would you care to hear me play?"

"Oh, I don't think that will be necessary, Miss St. James. Lady Julia's recommendation is quite enough for me."

"But, what if I have no talent?"

"If the Lady Julia says you have talent, then it is so!" Isobel must have looked surprised, because he coughed and said, "Well, perhaps you might play something, if only to prove your patroness right." He indicated the fortepiano with one hand.

She sat down, hands poised over the keys, looking at him expectantly.

"Anything you like, Miss St. James," he said with a little shrug of his shoulders. She chose Mozart's C-minor sonata for fortepiano, and when she finished, he cleared his throat. "I think that is adequate. I should, of course, be most pleased to have you as a pupil."

"Thank you, Mr. Faircourt, I am honored, indeed!"
Isobel smiled triumphantly.

"Though Lady Julia intimated in her letter you may
not be able to devote all your energies to music, I
should be happy to help you when you may come."

"Yes, I'm afraid my father heartily disapproves of
my musical inclination," Isobel said.

"How very unfortunate."

"Is now too soon to start?"

II

Although their sessions were shorter than Isobel
would have liked, Faircourt agreed he could work with
her at least twice a week without risking unpleasant
gossip. She was delighted when the two-hour practices
soon stretched to three hours and then gradually to
four. It was not long before she was encouraged
enough at her progress to play one of her own compositions for Faircourt.

Isobel winced at the expression on his face. "Well,
what did you think?" she asked timidly. He was silent
for so long that she finally said, "Was it so terrible?"

"Quite the contrary. Miss St. James, you are tal-
ented, of that there can be no doubt. In addition to
talent, you possess something few others have: the
ability to work hard. Believe me, 'tis a rare combination, and under different circumstances your success
would not be in doubt." He looked at her intently,
lifting his eyebrows in an expression of uncertainty.
"Wednesday fortnight I am engaged to play at Lord
Huntingdon's. I should like to have you perform,
among other works, the piece you just played for me.
But"—he held up his hand to stop her interruption—
"Miss St. James, how badly do you want to be a musician?" Faircourt clasped his hands behind his back and
began pacing.

"It's all I've ever wanted."

"Do you want it badly enough to do something a little . . . er . . . unusual?"

"What exactly do you mean?"

"I mean that you should play at Lord Huntingdon's in the guise of a man."

"You can't mean it!" She laughed.

"Miss St. James, which do you want to be—a musician, or a woman musician? If you performed as a man, they would hear only your music." He paused. "I admit the idea is a shocking one," he said, when he saw Isobel was staring at him.

"I think the idea is a splendid one."

Isobel was surprised at how easily Julia was convinced to help her. "You Americans are so daring," she said. "But think of the scandal if you are discovered!"

"If you help me, I won't be discovered, Julia. I need to change my clothes here at Hartforde House. If my father or Mrs. Godwaite ever found out, it would be the end of everything. You've simply got to help me!"

"You're not going to be talked out of this, are you?"

"No."

"I suppose it's my fault for sending you to Mr. Faircourt." She sighed.

"Then you'll help me?"

They spent two entire afternoons during the week before her performance sequestered in Julia's room altering the suit she was to wear.

They chose the finest clothes from those Julia had procured from her brother's valet by telling him she needed clothing to donate to the poor. Most of them were more than acceptable for a young gentleman; many of the shirts were a fine white lawn, a little worn about the cuffs, but with tolerably lacy cravats. There

were also three waistcoats, two frock coats, three pairs
of breeches, and Isobel had succeeded in obtaining a
pair of soft leather boots and a pair of buckled shoes
that fit her well enough.

It was the things that had belonged to Lord Hartforde that they were frantically altering. There was a
hardly-worn silk shirt, a frothy cravat, and a pair of
gray breeches along with a matching waist coat sporting gold-embroidered pockets. But the glory of her
suit was to be the frock coat. It was green satin lined in
a darker green with gold buttons in the shape of a
lion's head, and, most impressive of all, the entire coat
was embroidered with gold thread. Worn but once, it
was marred only by a small stain at the bottom of the
hem that was cut away in making it small enough to fit
Isobel's considerably smaller frame.

The day before the performance, Julia watched as
Isobel pulled on a pair of hose and secured them to
garters before pulling on the breeches, fastened at the
bottom with a row of silver buttons and tied with a
bow just below the knee. She examined her reflection
in the mirror.

"It's hopeless, Julia!"

Julia pursed her lips thoughtfully while shaking her
head. "Put on the waistcoat. Maybe you won't show
so much." But the waistcoat made little difference; the
curves of Isobel's bosom were still obvious.

"I just knew it was too good to be true." She threw
a small pillow across the room before plopping down
on the bed.

"What if you keep your coat fastened all the time?"

"That won't work—I'll have to take it off sometime." She stared morosely at the spot where the pillow had landed. "But, of course!" She jumped up and
started to loosen her shirt, smiling gleefully as she
pulled it over her head.

"What is it?"

"If I cannot flatten myself, then I must do the opposite." She grabbed another pillow and held it to her stomach so the top of it was level with the bottom of her breasts. "Give me a sash or something." She held out a hand. She took the stocking Julia handed her and tied it securely around herself. This time when she had her clothes buttoned—shirt, waistcoat and frock coat—the effect was to make her look slightly plump. After she had secured a black wig on her head, she no longer recognized herself. "Well?" She held her hands out to Julia for her approval after she had pulled on the boots.

"How pleasant to meet you, Mr. Boxham!" Julia curtsied prettily, calling her by the name Isobel had chosen—Boxham, after her mother's maiden name, and Ian Frederick, after her initials.

Isobel took up a handkerchief and waved it about in a foppish manner. "Oh, Lady Julia," she minced, "'pon honor, you're a devilishly pretty woman! Has anyone ever told you that?" They dissolved into giggles when she rested all her weight on one leg and made a show of brushing at the lace of her cuffs. "A bloody shame if you're engaged, I vow!"

III

The concert at Lord Huntingdon's was a nerve-wracking affair, for though Isobel was entirely ignored before she played, afterward she became the darling of the guests. She was amazed to find no one seemed even the least bit suspicious. There were several inquiries about where to send invitations for future playing engagements, which she answered by responding that at the moment she was entirely in the hands of Mr. Faircourt.

In the carriage on the way home, she leaned back in the seat and closed her eyes. "Thank God that's over!"

she said. "I thought I was going to faint from nerves! Can you believe not one person guessed?" She opened her eyes to look at Faircourt.

"You were a huge success, Miss St. James, as I knew you would be."

"Is everything all right?" she asked, concerned at the odd tone of his voice.

"Perfectly."

"I'm exhausted."

"You had better get used to it, for you have a future in this."

"Then, I have everything I could possibly want."

"No one must suspect you, Miss St. James. We must be more careful than ever, now society's eye is fixed on Master Ian Boxham." Faircourt leaned forward and tapped her knee with his knuckles. "Isobel St. James must take care to develop habits that will provide explanations for her absences from society, once you are formally introduced, that is."

"Whatever you say, Mr. Faircourt. We are, both of us, entirely in your hands."

Chapter 9

I

Isobel and her father spent Christmas at Marblestone Park, in South Oxon, the seat of the Chessingham earldom. She spent a great many hours at the forte-piano, much to the pleasure of her father, though it concerned him that she spent so long at the instrument. The countryside was lovely and, until the house was overrun by guests, going on long morning rides with her father and afternoon walks by herself were her chief recreations while they remained there.

Once, during one of her walks, she came upon what looked to be an ancient Roman ruin, and that night she anxiously awaited her father's explanation. Was it a pagan temple? The residence of some provincial Caesar? She was deflated to learn the ruins were nothing more than the landscaper's conception of the picture-esque. The ruined building was hardly much older than herself. She laughed outright when her father told her the copse of trees in the rear gardens had been de-liberately planted with dead trees for the same reason. The earl agreed it was ridiculous, but, he told her, at the time it was all the fashion and, feeling like a fool, he had let the man haul in dead trees and one or two boulders to complete the scene. "Luckily I stopped short of letting him have a go at the hedges," he remarked. "If I had, the place would be uninhabitable!"

Shortly after Christmas, a shooting party descended on Marblestone Park at the invitation of the earl, but although some of the gentlemen had brought their wives, until she was officially "out," the earl did not permit her to talk with any of the guests. Consequently, she was forced to have most of her meals in her room. Also, consequently, there was rampant speculation about and admiration of Lord Chessingham's terribly handsome daughter. On the inevitable occasions when she came upon one of the guests, she could do no more than nod her head politely and either leave the room or continue on her way if they had happened to pass in the halls. Until she was introduced, it would be exceedingly improper to do any more, and at any rate, her experience with Mr. Selwynn had made her a great deal more cautious.

One of the earl's guests was James Stanton Fredericks, Viscount Strathemoore, who, at twenty-four, was a charming and amiable young man, well liked among men of fashion for his impeccable taste, his ready wit, and the ease with which he lost at hazard. He was of above-average height, not yet portly, with black hair and startling blue eyes that made him a favorite among women. He was a Whig who, before his father's death, had stood as Member of Parliament for one of the boroughs. He had but once shown his face at the Commons. He took snuff, donated generous sums to the poor, patronized two painters and one writer, and attended church on an irregular basis, and after dozing through the sermon sincerely told himself he would go more often but never did. His father had left him a large fortune, a country house in Middlesex to which he repaired during Christmas, Easter, and summertime, and a medium-sized estate in the county of Devon that gave him about eighty thousand pounds a year. He was only able to spend about half of the income from the Devon estate because the men he left to oversee the place were robbing him of the other half. The family seat was some one hundred miles or so southwest of Bath, and he fully meant to visit the place again sometime soon. Even at the rate the viscount was spending his fortune, it would be some time before he would need to consider acquiring less prodigal habits. Currently, he was considering marriage, it being high time he got himself an heir. The trouble lay in deciding whom to marry. There were any number of deucedly pretty women to whom he was quite attracted, but there were slightly fewer who were rich enough. He had come to Marblestone Park for the sport and because he had heard the earl's cook was incomparable. When he saw Lord Chessingham's daughter, he saw the woman he meant to marry.

Young Lord Strathemoore rose early one day and set out with the rest of the guests for a morning of shooting. Two dead pheasants later he turned back, claiming an injury to his foot. It so happened he had been able to discover that Miss St. James took the morning air in the rear gardens, and his trek back to Marblestone was a circuitous one by way of the back of the house. He was elated to discover the object of his interest sitting not twenty feet away from a copse of trees into which he promptly stepped. He stood there for some minutes while he decided which of a variety of strategies occurring to him was mostly likely to succeed in attaining his object. He was just throwing down the pheasants when somehow his gun got tangled up in the twigs of a dead tree, and in jerking it free it went off, but, to his great relief, not in the direction of Miss St. James. He yelped in surprise and had just enough time to throw himself to the ground when he heard her cry out.

II

Isobel was startled when she heard the report of a gun and, immediately afterward, a shout. She jumped up from her seat. "Oh, my!" she exclaimed. "Who's there?" She heard groaning from the trees. "Are you hurt?" she called out, making her way toward the agonized moans. She pushed past the branches. "Oh, dear God!" she cried when she saw a young man lying prostrate on the ground. She ran to his side and bent down on her knees. "Are you shot?" She took one of his hands in hers. "Don't move. I'll get one of the servants!" She was about to get up, but his hand tightening on hers prevented it.

"No, I'm not shot," he said through a grimace of pain. "But I've given my ankle a nasty turn." He struggled to sit up and held a hand to one booted foot, gingerly attempting to move it. "Give me but a minute. I'm sure 'twill come round." He looked up at her through thick eyelashes.

"What were you doing here?" She eyed the dead birds with distaste. "I'm quite certain there are no grouse so close to the house."

"Pheasants. Miss . . . ?" He looked at her hopefully.

"Perhaps you ought to take off your boot. There's bound to be some swelling." She reached out to his foot but snatched back her hand when he shouted in pain.

"I would not be so indelicate as to expose my unshod foot to your beauteous eye . . . Miss St. James, is it not?" He saw her frown and quickly continued: "Would you be so kind as to help me up? If I could just get to the house, I could have my man take care of me." He leaned heavily on her, swaying when he was upright.

"What about your things?" She glanced down at his gun and the two dead birds.

"I'll send my man for them later," he said as they began to make their way out of the copse.

"So, you have not yet told me why you were lurking in the trees."

"I am ashamed to admit it, miss, but I was lost! I was heading back to the house and thought to take a shorter route and somehow I got myself rather turned round."

"I should say you did. Are you all right?" she cried out when he shouted in agony after he tried stepping down on his foot. "Oh, dear, I do hope it isn't broken. You seem in such pain!" Her voice was all concern now. "You'd best use me as a crutch." She placed his arm around her shoulders.

"That would be most unseemly, Miss St. James!" He sounded embarrassed.

"Well, I can't carry you," she said in frustration. "Can you wait till I get one of the servants to help you?"

His arm curled around her shoulder. "No," he said with a groan, taking a hopping step forward. They were almost to the house before one of the servants came running out to them.

"Oh, my lord! Have you broken your leg?" The chambermaid held her hands to her face when she saw the leg he held bent back at the knee.

"Please send my valet down," he ordered, before Isobel could tell the maid to take her place.

"Yes, milord." She curtsied, then ran back inside. Isobel helped him to a seat in the entrance hall while they waited for his valet to appear.

"How can I thank you, Miss St. James?"

"Thanks are not necessary, sir."

He grasped her hand. "James Stanton Fredericks, Viscount Strathemoore, your most humble servant." He pressed his lips to her hand. He looked forlornly at her when he saw his man hurrying down the stairs. He kissed her hand again. "I am your slave, Miss St. James." He let go of her hand when the servant arrived.

"Good day." She curtsied and walked hurriedly up the stairs.

Lord Strathemoore and his valet hobbled up the stairs to his room. Once inside he shook off the man's helping hands. "I'm quite all right, Lowther." A puzzled Lowther watched Lord Strathemoore stride to the door and look out into the hall. "I left my gun and two birds in the trees in the back," he said when he shut the door. "Wait a few minutes and then go get them. Should anyone ask, tell them I am not as badly hurt as you feared."

"Yes, my lord."

III

"Rum luck, Strathemoore, your turning your ankle like that," Lord Campston said over cards later that evening. "The cover was excellent!"

"It's luck, I'll own, Campston."

"'Pon honor, you sound glad of it!" Lord Fistersham said, laying down his cards and scooping up the pot.

Once sure Chessingham was out of hearing, Viscount Strathemoore made his announcement. "My friends, I have met Miss St. James!"

"The devil, you did!"

"You don't say!"

"She is an angel!" Strathemoore said.

Chapter 10

I

Isobel was glad to return to London. The countryside was beautiful, but she had had enough of fake ruins, deliberately planted dead trees, and wild undergrowth left to choke out prettier bushes. She considered it utter nonsense. The city was a welcome relief after the solitude her father had imposed on her by adamantly refusing to introduce her to his guests. Avoiding Lord Strathemoore had been a trying enough endeavor, but she was looking forward to the time when she would be properly introduced to the man. She thought him rather good-looking.

As soon as she arrived in London, she and Julia were caught up in plans for Isobel's ball. Lord Chessingham approved whatever Julia recommended, and Isobel was more than happy to let her plan the affair. She hadn't the faintest idea how to go about such a thing. Her time was taken up with dancing lessons, fittings, and the fortepiano. In the week before the ball, Julia spent hours telling Isobel what to expect of every one of her guests. She even attended one of Isobel's dancing

lessons and pronounced her as graceful as any woman
could hope to be.

When at last the day of the ball arrived, she was
calm while Bridget painstakingly pulled her hair into
an upsweep and adorned it with a ribbon of the same
sky-blue satin as her gown. It was a color she had always disliked, but Julia had insisted she looked divine
in it, and Isobel reluctantly deferred to her judgment
on the matter. The underskirt was a darker blue silk
revealed all around at the points where small dark blue
bows held up the overskirt. She had been adamant that
the rows of bows at the elbow-length sleeves be removed in favor of just one at each cuff. She was calm
while the buttons of her dress were being fastened. By
the time the maid had fastened the gold buckles of her
dark blue satin slippers, she felt like someone's pattern
doll and she was thoroughly disgusted with the entire
process. Up until she took her father's arm and stood
with him at the door to greet the guests, she was calm.
But as people began to arrive and she saw the looks of
curiosity on their faces, she began to wish she could
just go upstairs and wait until the ordeal was over.

As her father escorted her into the ballroom to dance
the first minuet with her, she felt her mouth go dry.
When it was over she whispered to him to take her to
the punch bowl so she might wet her parched throat. It
would also give her something to do. She was not at
all convinced anyone would ask her to dance, and she
was surprised when she was instantly surrounded by
men begging for the honor. She supposed they were
obliged to out of courtesy. Soon, however, all the glib
phrases Miss Steadly had taught her became indispens-
able as she was spun around the floor and handed
through the intricate dance patterns. Did these ele-
gantly dressed men really think her stupid enough to
believe the nonsensical drivel they were spouting at
her? Could she do anything but look away as though

suddenly shy when some ridiculous fop told her she was a divine creature, that her eyes reminded him of a stormy sea, or that she was more graceful than any swan? It would have been funny if they had not so sincerely expected her to believe them. She was grateful it was considered polite to look away at such times; at least then she could hide her scorn for some of the more outrageous comments.

Isobel took a deep breath as Lord Hartforde expertly handed her through another minuet. She was looking fixedly past him and so missed the raised eyebrows and appreciative look downward as he took in the sudden swell of her breasts against her neckline. Until she saw the décolletage of the gowns other women wore, she had thought her own to be terribly daring. She had been watching him surreptitiously all evening, hoping he would dance with her. Just when she had given up, he had bowed gracefully and asked her. She had been half inclined to tell him she was engaged, but when she looked into those green eyes she was mesmerized. She was so intrigued by the man that she had actually gone to the trouble of obtaining copies of all his speeches. She had learned that, in spite of his comment that she sounded like a "dashed colonist," Lord Hartforde had been a vehement supporter of the colonists in the American war, having upon the opening of Parliament in October of '81 made his first impassioned speech against continuing a war that, in addition to being immoral, he argued was incapable of being won. The news of the fall of Yorktown on 19 October, received just a few weeks after his speech, had been an incalculable embarrassment to George III and his prediction of disaster had not endeared him to his Sovereign. Isobel sighed again. Her studied indifference to him was becoming difficult to continue. His hand, whenever it rested lightly on her back, seemed to burn through the fabric of her gown. He was a wonderfully graceful dancer; the other men she had danced with were oafs by comparison. And he was so unconcernedly handsome!

"Is something amiss, Miss St. James?" he asked, dismayed that she seemed distracted.

"I'm afraid I'll make a fool of myself and step on your toes." She looked directly at him for the first time and blushed when she realized what a ninny she sounded like.

"But you dance divinely." He laughed at this example of what he took to be coquettishness, and when next he held her hand, he grasped it a little closer. He decided he liked the sound of her American accent after all. She was quite striking when she smiled, he thought, and, truly, she filled the modest neckline of her gown in a most fascinating manner. It was no wonder every man in the place was panting for a chance to dance with her. Rich and beautiful—what man could resist that combination?

"To tell you the truth, my lord, I feel like somebody's prize horse at an auction," she said, surprised that, after an evening of guarding her tongue, she could say what she really thought. But, then, how could she let him think she hadn't a thought in her head but the fear of stepping on his toes? "My father can't wait to marry me off so I may produce him an heir. I'll wager he spends his evenings working up bloodlines." She was hurt when he threw back his head and laughed. "You wouldn't think it so amusing if you were in my place!"

"But I am in your place, or, rather, one like it. Being widowed, I find people constantly throwing their daughters my way in the hopes she shall be the next marchioness of Hartforde."

"I see," she said stiffly. "What a trial it must be for you." She was not so dense that she could not appreciate the relevance of his comment to herself. She gave him her most dazzling smile when the dance ended, and as he led her off the floor, she turned to him and said softly so no one but he would hear, "Rest assured, sir, I shall resist being thrown."

Someone quickly claimed the next dance and Isobel soon lost sight of Lord Hartforde. She was absolutely mortified that such a great man thought she was the sort of woman concerned only with snatching a marquess. She sighed to herself as she recalled she had not exactly been a brilliant conversationalist. He was justified if he thought her dull.

"I have been waiting an eternity for this dance," her new partner said earnestly, bowing as he offered her his hand. "James Stanton Fredericks, Lord Strathemoore, at your service," he reintroduced himself to her. "Your beauty has dazzled me so, I have done nothing but pine until now." His blue eyes twinkled as he swept her onto the floor.

"My lord, you'll turn my head with talk like that!"

"Then I shall continue. You may depend on it!"

"Rascal!" She caught a glimpse of Lord Hartforde talking to Mrs. Vincent, who was wearing a dangerously low-cut gown. If he thought for even a minute she was the least bit interested in being the next marchioness of Hartforde, he was seriously mistaken, she decided, when she saw Mrs. Vincent place her hand on his arm. "I see your ankle has fully recovered, my lord," she said, flashing a smile at Strathemoore.

"You were cruel to leave me at Marblestone as you did, Miss St. James. I was so desperate for an introduction, I own, I was willing to risk my life to get it!"

"Come, now, my lord, would you have me believe you would be so reckless?"

"Any man who would do such a thing would have to be desperately in love, do you not agree, Miss St. James?"

"He would be a fool at best, sir. But an endearing one," she added, when he looked crestfallen.

Lord Strathemoore brightened, then continued a stream of easy conversation until the dance ended and she was snatched up by her next partner. He watched her thoughtfully as she danced, admiring the bright upswept curls, and he wondered what she would look like with her hair loosened. He thought to himself that she was a damned fine woman. And it certainly didn't hurt that she was an heiress.

II

At last Isobel could stand it no longer. Her feet were tired and sore from being stepped on, and she could feel her carefully coiffed hair coming loose. She wanted nothing more than to rest a moment where she would be undisturbed by a gaggle of men who cared more for her prospects than they did for her. As soon as the next dance started, she excused herself and sought refuge in the hallway.

She went about halfway up the stairs before sitting down and resting her chin in her hands to listen to the strains of music floating up from the ballroom. It felt good to sit down. Her thoughts drifted again to Lord Hartforde and she sighed when she thought of his obvious disdain for her. "You absolutely must not make a fool of yourself over him!" she admonished herself. Besides, what reason had she to think such a man would have even the slightest interest in her? His comment to her about the number of women who wished to be the next marchioness of Hartforde was a point well taken. He had every right to warn her he was not interested. Men like Lord Hartforde did not concern themselves with anybody's bastard daughter, and she would do well to remember it. She was startled out of her reverie by the sound of voices from down the hall and she leaned into the shadows of the rails to avoid being seen. A dark-haired woman was walking slowly along the hallway doing nothing to fend off the hands of a tall gentleman whose face Isobel could not see on account of his being absorbed in a contemplation of the front of the woman's dress. She recognized the brunette as Mrs. Vincent, and as soon as the light glinted off the man's golden hair she recognized Lord Hartforde.

"Why not, my lord?" Mrs. Vincent was saying in a cajoling tone.

"Perhaps you have convinced me, after all." Lord Hartforde raised his head from his study of Mrs. Vincent's bosom and looked at the library door, a short way down the hall.

Why, he's nothing but a common womanizer! she thought as she watched him pull Mrs. Vincent to him.

"Alexander . . . my lord." She stopped walking and sank down on a small bench. He sat next to her and began kissing her. Isobel was unable to look away, amazed to see Mrs. Vincent actually seemed to be enjoying it. "Alexander . . ." she moaned as her arms went around his shoulders.

He lifted his head. "Yes, Angelica?"

"Not here, my lord," she said breathlessly, pushing away his hand and adjusting the front of her gown before standing up. "Come with me." Her face was flushed with some emotion Isobel could not identify.

He followed her down the hall and, reaching in front of her, put a hand to the door. He grasped her shoulder and kissed her full on the lips. He broke their embrace with a look of reluctance, while one hand fumbled behind him to open the door. He whispered her name as he pushed her through. The door closed firmly after them.

Isobel blinked at the spot where they had stood.

"Miss St. James!" Lord Strathemoore took a few

steps up the stairs toward where Isobel still sat. His blue eyes were concerned. "Are you ill?"

"I'm quite all right. I only needed a respite from the crowd." She wondered what it would feel like if Lord Hartforde were to kiss her like that.

"I had hoped to persuade you to dance with me again," he said, encouraged by the peculiar look she was giving him.

"Oh, come, now, surely you don't expect me to believe you have been frantically searching for me all in the hopes of another dance?" She laughed and took the hand he offered her.

"Well, perhaps not frantically." He smiled. "But will you dance with me again?"

"Perhaps we might just have a glass of punch. I find I'm somewhat in need of refreshment. It's rather warm, don't you think?" She took his arm and smiled up at him again.

The viscount thoroughly enjoyed the envious looks sent his way as he escorted Isobel to the table where punch was being served by liveried footmen. Lord Chessingham's daughter had caused quite a stir, and any man with pretensions to fashion was anxious to make her acquaintance. He had been watching her carefully during the evening and his vigilance had been rewarded by the discovery that she was most receptive to the men who were more circumspect in their attentions. When he went to claim his first dance, he had carefully tailored his behavior to that discovery. His jesting imitation of his rivals he now judged to have been a success. He handed Isobel a glass of punch before taking a glass for himself.

Isobel was sitting down when she saw Lord Hartforde coming toward her. "No, Lord Strathemoore," she was saying, "it would be positively wicked to dance with you yet again. Besides, I promised this one to someone else." James was laughing as she put a finger to her lips and wrinkled her brow. "If only I could remember who it was!" He frowned when he saw the light that came into her eyes when she caught sight of Hartforde.

"I believe 'twas I." He bowed and extended his hand to Isobel.

"Why, Lord Hartforde, I thought you had gone!" She took his hand and suppressed a tremble as he placed his hand around her waist and swept her out among the dancers.

"How could I leave when you had promised this dance to me?"

She thought she heard a faintly mocking tone in his voice. "My, your gallantry quite overcomes me," she said dryly. Why, she wondered, did his hand over hers have to be so warm? His lips curved into a smile at her words and Isobel felt herself blushing.

"I do seem to have that effect on you," he remarked, taking in her flush and, mistaking its cause, increasing the pressure of his hand against her back when the opportunity arose. He had thought her beautiful before, but tonight she was disturbingly so.

"I believe you overestimate your appeal, Lord Hartforde," she said curtly. "Not every woman in this room is dying to find herself in your arms."

In spite of his prior experience with her candor, he was taken aback. "Just most of them," he teased.

"You're nothing but an arrogant . . . arrogant . . ." She stuttered with indignation, unable to think of a suitable word to put an end to his mocking.

"Rake?" he supplied. "It makes life so much more pleasant." His eyebrows arched at her outraged expression.

"It is unbecoming of a gentleman, especially one such as yourself, my lord, to think himself the object of every woman's desire," she sniffed primly.

"But am I the object of yours?" He leaned closer and

he suddenly found himself intrigued by the soft pout of her lips and the flush coloring her cheeks. For a brief moment, he let himself imagine what it would be like to kiss those curving lips, and there was a disturbing sensation in his belly.

"What a loathsome thing to say!" She would have pulled away from him if he had not held tightly onto her hand. "I shall cause a scene if you do not let go of me, sir," she said through clenched teeth.

"My dear Miss St. James, I apologize if I have offended you." He knew full well it was an outrageous thing to say to any young woman, and he was at a loss to explain just why it was that he found himself deliberately provoking her.

"You most certainly have offended me!"

"Forgive me, I was not aware you were unused to gallantry." Her eyes looked almost purple, they were so dark. He shook himself, annoyed that he had even noticed such a thing.

"Sir"—Isobel was furious now—"if you had told me I am the loveliest creature on the face of this earth, that would be gallantry. Asking me if you are the object of my desire is rudeness in the extreme! And I shall not tell you even if you were. Which you aren't!" she added.

"I am put firmly in my place." He inclined his head and attempted to look regretful. He let a few moments pass and then smiled wickedly. "Ah, Miss St. James." He sighed. "You are the loveliest creature on the face of this earth."

"And you, sir, are certainly the rudest!" The dance ended and she walked away from him, his laughter ringing in her ears. She looked quickly around and when she saw Julia talking to Lord Burke, she made her way to them. Lord Burke made an elegant bow when she approached and Julia took her hand and squeezed it.

"Why, Isobel! Lord Burke and I were just talking about you!"

"Miss St. James"—Lord Burke nodded—"I was just praising your beauty to Lady Julia."

"You flatter me," she said. She glanced around the room and when she saw Lord Hartforde staring at her she lifted her eyebrows at him in an expression of disdain. She colored when she saw him laughing at her and she steadfastly refused to look his way again.

III

Isobel awoke the next morning and quickly shut her eyes against the faint light penetrating the curtains. She had no immediate inclination to leave her warm bed, so she pulled the covers up to her chin and drifted back to a semi-sleep, remembering every dreamy detail of the previous night: the way men had crowded around her, anxious to dance with her, how they had begged first for the privilege of walking with her to the punch bowl, and then for the honor of handing her a glass. She could see herself dancing. The refrains echoed in her mind as she was gavotted and pavaned and minueted nigh on to exhaustion. It was no wonder she had eventually needed a rest! The scene she had witnessed while sitting on the stairs . . . Lord Hartforde kissing . . . in her dreaming mind it wasn't Angelica he held so closely. The woman in his arms was blond and she was having trouble getting her breath. There was an aching, fluttering feeling that burst into a longing for . . . she didn't know what.

Her eyes opened and she sat up, angrily ringing for Bridget. Even the thought of letting that man kiss her was humiliating! Why, he was nothing but an arrogant rake! His behavior toward her the past evening had bordered on the rude, and if he hoped she was going to make a fool of herself over a common rake, he had

best think again! Further expostulating Lord Hartforde
was interrupted by Bridget's coming in and opening
the curtains.

When she came downstairs at last, her father was
waiting for her. He reached to fill her cup with coffee
when she sat down and then leaned back in his chair,
looking pleased with himself.

"What is it, Father?" she asked, wondering at his
being in such a happy mood.

"Were I to judge only by our drawing room, my
dear, you were quite a success last night."

Isobel put down her delicate china cup. "What do
you mean?"

"We are virtually inundated with flowers and vari-
ous fancy gewgaws!"

"We, Father?" She cocked her head at him.

"Go look for yourself!" He followed her to the
drawing room and stood in the doorway while she
looked through the cards piled on a tray at one end of
the table.

"Small reward for my sore feet!" she commented,
pleased to hear him laugh. She opened a note that ac-
companied a bouquet of tulips. She could barely recall
the earl who had sent them. "But what am I to do
with all this?" She gestured at the flowers covering the
table.

"You will have to acknowledge them. Of course,
you must return jewelry or anything else of value."

"But it will take all day! This is ridiculous." She
picked up a box of chocolates, then let them fall back
on the table with a thump. She reached for the card
with a huge vase of fragrant blood-red roses. They
were from Lord Strathemoore.

"Do you continue to think I shall have trouble finding a husband for you?" He paused. "I have received
no fewer than five offers for you just this morning."

Isobel turned to him. "Will I have any choice in the matter, Father?"

"As long as I approve. As long as I approve," he said slowly.

"Only Hobson's choice, then?" She hid a bitter smile by bending her head to the roses Lord Strathemoore had sent. Had Lord Hartforde sent her roses? she wondered.

Chapter 11

I

One of Lady Julia's passions was going to the Haymarket to see the Italian opera, and after she had persuaded Isobel to accompany her once, they became regular visitors on Tuesday nights. Lord Burke frequently escorted them, and even when he did not, he could always be counted on to arrive before the last act to join them for coffee afterward. When Isobel hinted that he might be in love with Julia, she only laughed and professed not to care more for one man than she did for any other. Still, when he did not accompany them to the theater, Julia seemed distracted until he arrived

One Tuesday night Julia and Isobel were escorted to the Haymarket by Lord Hartforde, who was making a rare appearance at the opera. This was one evening when Isobel could not attend to the singing onstage. All three of them were out of sorts, and trouble had started in the carriage. Julia was put out because Lord Burke was absent. Isobel was trying to pretend Lord Hartforde's presence did not unnerve her in the least. She was sitting quietly with her hands folded in her lap staring out the carriage window, from which she could see absolutely nothing, while she listened to Julia and her brother chatting. Lord Hartforde seemed put out at Isobel's presence. He had greeted her coldly and proceeded to act as though she was not there. She was, therefore, startled when he spoke to her.

"Has our conversation bored you, Miss St. James?" he inquired in a voice of gallingly false concern.

"Certainly not, my lord." She hoped she succeeded in sounding surprised at the thought of being bored by any word chancing to fall from his lips.

"I think, then, you must have been reciting one of the classics to yourself, you are so quiet."

"Gallia est omnis . . ." she intoned, making a wry face at him.

"And have you the idea to conquer Gaul?" he asked. "You've come to the wrong country for that!"

"No, sir, I shall be happy enough with just a small part of London, I think."

Julia laughed and pretended not to notice the glare Isobel sent her brother's way.

They took their seats in the box engaged for the season at a cost of fifty guineas, and Lord Hartforde, sitting some three seats away from Isobel, began stirring restlessly and tapping his fingers on the arm of his chair. Isobel was tempted to tell him to go away if he could not bear to let others enjoy the singing. Instead, she contented herself with a stern frown in his direction. His look in return was one of innocence, but the tapping did not begin again until some quarter of an hour later during an aria she particularly wanted to hear. She finally screwed up enough courage to lean over and briefly cover his hand. He stopped, but thereafter she was unable to think of anything but how warm his hand had felt.

During the first intermission they were joined by Lord Allryn, an anemic young man who seemed delighted to find Julia without Lord Burke in attendance.

He sat next to her and earnestly engaged her in conversation. Just before the end of the intermission, Lord Burke stepped into the box.

"Good evening," he greeted Isobel and Lord Hartforde before turning to Julia, who very coldly said how surprised she was he had been able to tear himself away from his engagement and then turned back to Lord Allryn as though she could not bear to miss anything he might say.

The second act started and for all of five minutes the box was quiet. Then Lord Hartforde started his fidgeting again and Lord Allryn kept up a constant sibilant chatter. Isobel could hardly follow the performance because of all the whispering and finger-tapping going on in the box. Lord Hartforde smiled when she propped her elbows up on the railing and leaned forward in an attempt to follow the music. She would have covered his hand again, but he was tapping—deliberately, she surmised, from the grin he gave her when she glared at him, with the hand farthest from her.

The second act ended and Lord Allryn, clearing his throat, said, "My dears, it occurs to me Easter is almost upon us! I go to Bath at Easter, you know. It is becoming an annual pilgrimage for me." He leaned back in his chair and fingered a button on his coat. "I expect that during the fortnight I shall be there, my health shall be vastly improved. I took physic for a certain complaint of mine." He coughed behind his hand. "I suffer so, you understand, that at last the doctor quite insisted I should go to Bath." Just as he was getting into his stride, he was interrupted by Lord Hartforde, who rose and excused himself to the company. "Hartforde, my good man," Lord Allryn called out before he could leave, "you ought to go to Bath yourself. One's health is such a delicate thing. And if I may be so bold, I might ask you to bring your vastly lovely sister with you, and of course"—he looked at Isobel—"if you can persuade the vastly lovely

Miss St. James to come as well, Bath will be the pleasant-
est spot in all England." Proud of his gallantry, he looked
to see if Julia was impressed.

"I am afraid, Lord Allryn, that my sister makes her
own schedule, and as for Miss St. James, I have no
influence with her at all. If you will excuse me." He
nodded and left the box.

After Alexander was gone, Lord Burke did his best to
divert Julia's attention from Lord Allryn, but his reserve
of manner and good breeding prevented him from having any success. He sighed and, except for a single glance
at Isobel, kept his gaze steadily fixed on Julia. Lord
Allryn, not being completely obtuse, perceived he had
Julia's undivided attention and proceeded to take full
advantage of it by relating to her in particular detail the
diet recommended him by his physic. His fervent recita-
tion of the condition of his stomach was brought to a halt
by Lord Hartforde's return—this time with Mrs. Vincent on his arm. The brief silence ended when Allryn
turned to Mrs. Vincent and began telling her about the
shocking consequences of inattention to diet.

There was no finger-tapping during the last act.

When the final scene was over, Isobel leaned over to
Lord Hartforde and whispered, "Really, sir, you might
have found a more private place for your assignation!"

She felt a warm hand on her bare shoulder and his
breath in her ear. "The idea, I do confess, was not
mine, but if I have succeeded in annoying you, Miss
St. James, my happiness is complete."

When she turned to scowl at him, he was engrossed
in kissing Mrs. Vincent's hand.

At Mrs. Vincent's urging, the whole party went to
take coffee. Though she tried to avoid it, Isobel ended
by sitting between Lord Hartforde and Lord Allryn,
who turned his attention to her once he saw Lord
Burke had usurped Lady Julia. They were soon joined
by Lord Strathemoore, who took the seat closest to

Isobel and struggled unsuccessfully to divert her attention from Allryn. Mrs. Vincent saw how frequently Lord Hartforde's eyes fell on Isobel, and her plump lips turned down in displeasure.

"My lord"—she put a hand on Alexander's arm and gave him a weak smile—"I do not feel at all well. May I impose upon you to drive me home?"

"Of course, madam," he said, almost instantly erasing the wrinkle of annoyance that appeared on his forehead. "If you will excuse me," he said to the company as he rose and extended his hand to Mrs. Vincent. "I trust I am leaving my sister and Miss St. James in good company." He nodded at Julia and, as he bent over Isobel's hand, murmured, "I leave you, then, with some small part of London yet to be conquered."

"I shall be happy only if that part includes yourself!" Isobel retorted, chagrined that he had so easily divined her feelings and did not care to spare them one iota.

II

After the night when Lord Hartforde had so clearly demonstrated his disdain for her, Isobel swore to herself she would give up thinking about him. To that end she decided she would take more interest in other men than she had in the past.

One exceedingly fine morning she let herself be persuaded to go to Hyde Park with Julia. They had just joined the line of carriages when Isobel saw Lord Burke and Lord Strathemoore waving to them. From Burke's expression of relief, Isobel suspected he had been looking for them. She leaned forward and instructed the driver to slow down. When the two men reached them they exchanged idle banter for a few minutes before Lord Burke finally mentioned he had tickets to a masquerade.

"I should be honored if you two ladies would accompany me." He looked at Julia with such sheep's eyes that Isobel had to glance away so he would not see her smile.

"Oh," said Julia, sounding terribly disappointed, "my lord, at another time we should have been delighted, but Miss St. James and myself are engaged for the next fortnight!" Lord Burke's hopeful smile faded. She turned to Isobel. "Lord Allryn's invitation was so kind, do you not agree, Miss St. James?"

"Indeed, Lady Julia, vastly so," answered a startled Isobel.

"And really"—Julia looked back at Lord Burke—"as I said to Allryn, I do not want to wait until Easter for Miss St. James to see Bath."

Lord Burke, who was trying not to look crestfallen, wished them a safe journey and a pleasant visit, then begged their leave to go.

"You don't really mean to go to Bath, do you?" Isobel asked when the two men had left them.

"Of course not!"

"Well, don't you think Lord Burke will notice when we are still in London during the next fortnight?"

"Have you ever been to Sussex?" she answered. "We have an estate near Ashdown Forest, and I find I have a sudden hankering to visit it."

As it happened, Lord Burke proposed to Julia the day before they were to leave for Sussex, but Julia declared that she was not at all certain she ought to accept him. She thought him too somber and not nearly romantic enough for her. She assured Isobel that their trip to Sussex was more necessary than ever in order that she might determine without distraction what she ought to tell Lord Burke. And, anyway, she had no intention of accepting a man the first time he asked.

Chapter 12

I

Ashdown Grey sat impressively at the top of a slight incline about five miles from the closest village. The long approach was lined with chestnut trees up to the iron gates, where the road curved around immaculately kept lawns. Rolling fields of green spread out on three sides, and on the fourth the edges of Ashdown Forest made a smudge on the horizon. The house itself was a huge stone building. The original central portion had been built during the time of Elizabeth, but the rest of the house was intricately ornamented with balusters, pilasters, and other fancy masonwork. There were two brick side wings that had been added under the Hanovers. The effect was not at all displeasing, if somewhat eccentric.

The interior of the house lived up to the promise of its facade. The massive oak doors swung open into a large marble-floored hallway, with gilt arches curving up into high, frescoed ceilings.

"Is there a music room here?" Isobel asked as they followed a footman up the stairs.

Julia laughed and took her hand. "Yes, there is, and as soon as we're settled, I'll show it to you. You're an angel to humor me!" They spent the afternoon exploring the entire house and by the time they had finished a late dinner, they went to bed pleasantly exhausted.

Julia sat on Isobel's bed the next morning and watched Bridget brushing out her bright hair. "Do you mind that I've made you come here?" she asked.

"Not at all." Isobel sat still while Bridget braided and pinned her hair.

"I expect we shall be utterly bored in a day or two. Everyone is in London." She sighed and lay down on the bed. "We could go for a ride this morning, I suppose."

Isobel agreed it would be a pleasant way to pass the morning and consoled herself with the thought that they would be back in London before two days had passed.

After lingering over a light breakfast of coffee and rolls, they went back to their rooms and changed to the obligatory blue riding habits. While they waited outside the stable for the groom to saddle their horses, Julia scratched the ears of a brown-and-white dog that was followed by a chubby brown puppy. It wasn't long before the rest of the litter appeared and Isobel bent down to play with them. A black-and-white puppy bullied its way to her and she picked it up to hold it to her face. "What a little darling you are!" she said when it licked her face. She put it down reluctantly when the groom brought out the horses. He helped Isobel to mount a bay gelding named Boots, and she waited for Julia before trotting out toward the forest.

"Ashdown Grey has been standing since the crusades," Julia told her. "The first marquess acquired the place when he was elevated from earl of Northem for some favor rendered to Henry the Eighth, though I understand the 'favor' was something along the line of a few thousand pounds. For some reason he never lived in it. My grandfather had the place remodeled. He added the south wing and was going to do the other side, too, but then he dismissed the architect and by the time he found another to suit him, he hadn't the inclination anymore. My father added the north wing. He spent much more on the inside than out—and I'm afraid he let the lands go rather dreadfully. Hartforde has made them pay ten times what they paid under my father. He's enclosed thousands more acres and now, I'm told, the lands turn a handsome profit. Sussex," she continued after a pause, "is almost as lovely as Hartfordeshire. Someday you and I must visit there. I expect, though, you will have your fill of them both after you and Hartforde are married."

"Married? To your brother?" She felt she ought to protest the idea, though she didn't quite know why.

"Who else would he marry?"

Angelica Vincent, thought Isobel.

"You are the perfect wife for him."

"But, would he be the perfect husband for me?"

"But, of course!"

"I don't think your brother wants to marry anybody." She remembered very well his warnings to her on the subject. "And, Julia, begging your pardon, I think your brother is an arrogant, self-important—"

"That must be why you like him so much!"

"Is it so obvious?" She felt herself blushing. "I'm afraid he has made it clear he does not like me. The thing is impossible. Surely you have noticed his affections are very much engaged?"

"If you want to think so." At her ball, Hartforde had danced with Isobel twice, something he never did with any woman. He'd looked in Isobel's direction several times throughout the evening, and, if that weren't enough, Julia knew for a fact he hated the opera. And never before had she known him to take an interest in bedeviling one of her friends; yet, whenever he and Isobel were together, the atmosphere was positively thick! She felt quite sure her brother had met his match in Isobel St. James. All that was required was for her to continue her careful management of the situation. Nature would do the rest. "So," she said, "tell me about Lord Strathemoore."

"Lord Strathemoore? There isn't anything to tell, Julia."

"Why haven't you told me he sends you roses every day? Everyone is talking about his terrible extravagance."

"Surely not everyone!"

"Everyone."

"He's awfully nice." That much was true. Lord Strathemoore was very nice to her. He had taken her twice to see a play and had escorted her to the Kensington Gardens one morning when she had wanted to avoid the crush at Hyde Park. "What about you, Julia? Have you made up your mind about Lord Burke?" She decided it would be best to change the subject to one less uncomfortable.

"Oh, I don't know what to think! I am convinced he loves me, and I should not hesitate to accept him, but he is so restrained." She sighed. "I'm positive the man is incapable of passion! But, then, he is so terribly attractive. . . . I wish I knew what to do!" Julia kicked her horse into a gallop and Isobel took off after her, cursing under her breath when she nearly toppled off the animal's back. She denigrated the sidesaddle for being a dangerous contraption designed for the sole purpose of discouraging women from getting any real enjoyment from riding.

II

The next night while they were having supper and Isobel was telling Julia about the progress she was making on her music, the butler announced Lord Hartforde's arrival and his intent to join them at table. Isobel shook her head when Julia gave her a meaningful look.

"Hartforde! What are you doing here?" Julia asked when he joined them.

"Is it so unusual that I visit my own home?" he responded as he sat down at the head of the table, where a place was always kept set for him.

"Well, of course it is always a pleasure to see you, Hartforde. 'Tis only, we did not expect you." Julia filled his glass with wine, trying to suppress a smile. "We were sure you were too busy thwarting the Tories to bother with us."

"I needed to get away from London for a while. Besides, I have something to discuss with you, Julia." He looked at Isobel, as if suddenly noticing her presence. "Good evening, Miss St. James." He frowned because he had been telling himself he would not find her half as pretty as she had seemed in London, and now he saw that he'd been quite wrong. He clearly recalled a particular Tuesday night when she had distracted him so much he had been hard pressed to maintain his aloofness. He certainly did not think he ought to remember so well how soft the skin of her shoulder had felt when he had briefly touched her. He gave a little smile of triumph when a particularly long look succeeded in making her blush.

III

Isobel rose early the next day, and though she took her time getting ready, by the time she had dressed and

finished with a not insubstantial breakfast, Julia was
still asleep. Sleeping late was one habit to which Isobel
could not accustom herself. She rarely stayed in bed
past nine, and she could not understand how her friend
managed to stay abed until well after noon. She sighed
and decided to find the library so she could read until
Julia joined her. She was exceedingly anxious to discover whether they were to return to London that day.

She opened the door to the library and sighed with
happiness when she looked around. The room was
large and books covered the walls from floor to ceiling. The only wall not entirely taken up with shelves
had a fireplace with an ornate marble mantel on which
there sat a large ormulu clock. Confronted with so
many titles, she was at a momentary loss to decide
what to read, but at last she settled on a thick book
called *The London Spy*. She had never heard of its author, but it sounded too promising to pass over.

Such a large room was not to her taste for reading
in; it was tomblike in its musty silence. She preferred
to read in a cozier drawing room or parlor. The library
was in the section of the north wing nearest the center
of the house, and because she remembered seeing a
great many windows when she was in the rear gardens, she decided the back of the old section held the
most promise for a pleasant place to read. In fact, she
opened three doors before finding a room that looked
inviting. This one had one wall taken up by windows
overlooking the gardens. There was even a comfort-
able-looking sofa facing the view. The floor was covered by a red-and-gray Chinese rug that instantly
reminded her of the carpet in her father's study in
Boston. She had loved to walk barefoot over it while
he sat reading or writing out his correspondence.

The fireplace was directly opposite the windows,
and above the gilt mantel was a huge Gainsborough
portrait of an ethereally beautiful woman with light

blond hair and a wistful smile. Isobel had been admiring the painting for some time before she realized it must be Lord Hartforde's late wife. She stepped behind the desk to look at it more closely. He had to have been terribly in love with this woman. She was holding a lily in one tiny hand. Isobel was convinced there had been no need for Gainsborough to improve upon the looks of his model.

Taking up her book, she settled down on the sofa with a sigh. After only a few minutes she gave in to temptation and took off her shoes and stockings to wriggle her toes in the soft wool of the carpet. She opened the book and was soon absorbed in the story. There was rather more cursing than she thought might be proper; it reminded her very much of the kind of conversation she had heard bandied about of an evening when she had stayed to supper at Faircourt's. She was nearly a quarter of the way through when her eyes began to feel heavy. She lay down on the sofa and continued to read until, finally, her lids drooped and did not open again.

She did not stir when the door opened and Lord Hartforde entered the room and seated himself at the mahogany desk. He opened one of the drawers and pulled out three heavy ledgers, and a stack of papers. He found a pen that satisfied him and, setting an inkhorn and plenty of extra paper by his elbow, he began sorting through the papers. Doing the estate's accounts was a chore he did not particularly relish, and he was always in a bad humor when he could put it off no longer. It was a job he usually left to an overseer, but he knew it was foolish never to check the accounts himself. He had been engrossed in his work for several minutes when a muffled thump startled him. He jerked his head up and glowered when he saw a blond head appear above the top of the sofa.

"What the bloody—" He took a deep breath and began again. "What are you doing in here, Miss St. James?"

Isobel turned around and looked at him, eyebrows raised in an offended expression. "And how pleasant to see you, too, Lord Hartforde." She stretched lazily. "I was reading, and I suppose I must have fallen asleep."

"I'm the only one who ever comes in here." He told himself he was irritated by her intrusion, but it also annoyed him to notice the breathless disarray of her hair. While she looked at him, clearly affronted at his sharp tone, it was especially infuriating that he could not tell if her eyes were blue or if there really was a purplish cast to them.

"If the library wasn't such a mausoleum, I confess I could have stayed in there all day."

"Indeed, you could have." He scowled when Isobel's head disappeared from sight while she bent to pick up her book.

"You have my most abject apologies for disturbing you, my lord, though I shall refrain from pointing out that I was here first." She brushed a few wisps of hair from her face.

"Do forgive me if I have disturbed your invasion of my privacy." He tapped his pen impatiently on the stack of papers before him. When she sighed and began to stand up, he said snidely, "Oh, don't go on my account!" He pulled out his penknife and focused his attention on recutting his pen.

"Why, thank you, sir. How uncommonly kind of you!" Her intention of leaving him to his work dissolved in the face of his unbearable rudeness, and she sat back down. "I do appreciate your letting me enjoy the view. 'Tis a lovely morning." She turned her back to him and opened her book. Her heart was pounding from the way those green eyes had made her stomach flutter in spite of her resolve not to let his extraordinary looks disturb her in the least. She frowned when she could make no sense of the words before her, and she turned the volume right-side up before she could find her place.

After a few minutes he threw down his penknife in exasperation. It was impossible to concentrate with her in the room.

"Am I turning the pages too loudly, my Lord Hartforde?" Isobel asked sweetly, turning around to find his attention focused on the point of the pen that he was attempting to recut a second time.

"Your sarcasm is wasted on me, Miss St. James." He glanced at her for an instant before turning back to his pen.

"Alas!" She stood up and walked over to the desk, still holding the book in her hand.

"Perhaps you'd care to do the accounts, then!" he suggested facetiously when she stood behind him and peered over his shoulder.

"I'd be delighted." She continued to lean over him.

"Are you quite finished?" he asked after a moment.

"Don't be absurd! Nobody could do figures that quickly." She reached around him and ran a slim finger down the columns of sums. "You're off one pound ten. Are these to be reconciled?" She pointed to the papers strewn about the desk. When he nodded, she put down her book to pick up the papers and, after neatly arranging them in a pile, began to sort through them.

"Perhaps you'd care for my chair?" But Isobel was oblivious to his sharp tone. She simply nodded and sat down in the chair he vacated for her. He looked at her book. "Ned Ward?"

"So?" she asked.

"Nothing." He shrugged, looking as though he were having trouble keeping a smile from his face. "But he was a Tory, you know."

"Even a Tory may write a book." She picked up his

pen and chewed on the feathers of the tip before posing
it on the page to enter a figure in the ledger. "Have
you another pen? This one seems to be cut down
rather too far," she said with perfect innocence, thanking him without the slightest change in expression
when he opened a drawer and handed her another.

He watched her for a few minutes before his temper
got the better of him. "This has gone quite far
enough." He put a hand on the page. "It isn't necessary to pretend any further. I apologize for my
rudeness. So be it if I am forced to change my habits in
my own home. I promise I shall no longer do the accounts in my study. From now on, I shall do them in
the scullery, where, I pray it, you are least likely to
disturb me."

"I assure you, sir, I know what I am doing. I am
quite good at mathematics. When I lived in New York,
I always did the accounts for my cousin Samuels."

"I've no doubt you Americans excel at sums," he
said.

Isobel regarded Alexander coolly. "Perhaps you'd
care to wager?" *Really,* she said to herself, *he is infuriating! Does he think me some empty-headed young thing?* It
did not occur to her he might think her offer an obvious attempt to get his attention. All things considered, it was well for him that it did not.

He was about to refuse the wager but thought the
better of it; it might be amusing to humor her. "What
have you in mind?" Imagine her insisting she could do
accounts! He smiled when he heard the amount she
was willing to give up on his behalf.

"A hundred pounds that I finish without an error."

"Done." He took the hand she held out for him.
"On your honor as a gentleman, Miss St. James?"

"Indeed, sir." She turned back to the ledgers and
took up the pen. She worked quietly, only rarely using
paper to do a figure. Alexander pulled up another chair

and sat down to watch her work. She wrote a fine hand, filling the page with neat columns of figures. It vexed him as he watched her that he should notice how she chewed on her bottom lip, which only called attention to the soft curve of her mouth. From where he was sitting, her skin looked perfectly smooth and her waist impossibly small, though, he thought, perhaps 'twas only because she appeared to have a tantalizingly well-shaped bosom.

She put down the quill and leaned back to stretch. "Julia was right. Ashdown Grey pays a tidy income." She was disconcerted to see him staring at the floor with an amused expression, and she followed his gaze to see what he found so humorous. She had stretched out her legs and her bare feet were sticking out from under the hem of her dress. Their eyes met when she said, "Don't tell me a worldly man such as yourself is overcome by the sight of two bare feet?"

"And pretty feet they are, Miss St. James," he remarked.

" 'Tis fortunate I did not expose my ankles, or you should even now be my slave!" She flicked her skirts over her feet as she spoke, trying to hide her embarrassment behind light words.

"Do tell me, Miss St. James, how came you to lose your slippers?"

"I took them off to walk on the rug."

"It would have been quite all right to walk on it with your shoes." He smiled at the flush rising to her cheeks.

"I know that"—she gave him a stern glance—"but it reminded me so much of home and my father and how I used to walk barefoot in his study. It made me want to feel the . . . it looked just as soft as I remembered the rug in Boston," she finished in a low voice, feeling completely ridiculous.

"And was it?"

"Yes." She cursed herself for letting him fluster her and she directed her attention to the papers on the desk. "I'm finished." She stood up. "Do you mind if I take the book with me?"

"By all means, Miss St. James, do." He watched her go over to the sofa to pick up her slippers and stockings.

"I shall expect prompt payment on our wager as soon as you determine you have lost," she said tartly as she walked out, draping her stockings over the crook of her elbow and wondering if there was even the most remote chance she might appear dignified.

Alexander stared at the door after she had gone out. Miss St. James was exceedingly unladylike, and if she acted that way with her father it was a wonder he did not take her to task for such forwardness. The infuriating little thing was apparently incapable of dissimulation, for most women possessing even half her wit were at great pains to hide the fact. He looked down at the neat columns of figures filling the pages of the ledger. He suspected it would be a waste of time to check her work. He shook his head. Ned Ward, indeed! If he wasn't careful, he thought, he would end by liking her a great deal more than was good for him.

IV

"Well," Julia said with a radiant smile, while she and Isobel waited for Alexander to come down and escort them to supper, "what do you think of it?"

Isobel handed back the letter Julia had given her to read. "I think Lord Burke is very much in love with you, Julia. But it tells me nothing I did not already know."

"He spoke to Hartforde the very day we left London! Charles was absolutely certain I was going to marry Allryn. Can you imagine?" She laughed gaily at the thought of being in love with Allryn. "Charles asked permission to write to me, and Hartforde came to Ashdown Grey to deliver the letter personally. And such a letter! He is ten times more romantic than I ever thought possible!"

Alexander appeared just as Julia finished speaking, without apology for having kept them waiting. Isobel looked at him expectantly, but he gave her only the briefest glance before offering his arm to his sister and leading her into the dining room. Some people, she thought, were too enamored of themselves to admit their errors graciously. She stuck her tongue out at the back of his broad shoulders as he went through the door in front of her. At precisely the instant she was demonstrating her pique, Alexander turned to look over his shoulder at her. He arched one eyebrow and shook his head in the manner of one severely put upon.

"Is everything all right?" he asked softly when he saw her to her seat. "I feared for a moment you must have been taken ill. I can send for a doctor, if you think it necessary."

"I am as well as possible, given the company, sir," she retorted, feeling herself go scarlet. What an insufferable man!

"So, Hartforde, I have asked Miss St. James to help me plan my engagement ball when we return to London," Julia said when he had taken his seat. She looked at Isobel and wondered at the high color on her cheeks.

"I've no doubt she is quite clever enough to make it a success," he said sourly.

"Hartforde!"

"I believe, Julia, your brother is in a bad humor because he found he seriously misjudged me today." She smiled a little smugly.

"Will you tell us, Miss St. James, how you learned

the accountant's trade?" He moved his head to one side as a footman placed a bowl of soup in front of him and glanced at Isobel before picking up his spoon.

"Is your memory so short that you've already forgotten I told you I did the accounts for my cousin Samuels?" Certain his voice held a note of amusement, she made an effort not to lose her temper. "Or did you think I told an untruth?"

He lifted one eyebrow, quite definitely suggesting she took herself far too seriously. "I believe I recall every word you uttered. If I seem incredulous, 'tis only because one rarely finds a woman of such masculine accomplishment as yourself, Miss St. James."

"Tell me, sir, is it your habit to be so insufferable when you lose a wager?"

Julia could only look on in amazement. She had never seen her brother in such a peculiar mood. He was always unfailingly polite to women, but here he was acting as though his fondest wish was to send Isobel into a rage. "Hartforde," she cut in as he was preparing a retort, "what is Isobel talking about? Is it true you lost a wager to her?"

Isobel glared at him before looking back at Julia. "We wagered I could finish his accounts without error. And I have won, have I not, Lord Hartforde?"

"I have not yet finished checking your work, Miss St. James," he said stiffly.

Julia decided it would be prudent to change the subject.

V

"Tell me about your brother's wife," Isobel said suddenly the next day when she and Julia were walking in the gardens before dinner.

"She's dead." Julia shrugged her shoulders.

"Yes, I know, but what was she like?" she persisted.

"She was blond, like you. And she had blue eyes, very light, not as dark as yours."

"I saw her portrait. She was beautiful."

"She was very beautiful." Isobel's heart dropped at Julia's words. "Every man she wanted fell in love with her. I remember she had a lovely smile."

"He must have loved her very much."

"No. He didn't. He might have at first. I was quite young when he married, so he might have loved her then; I don't know. Lady Hartforde was a selfish and cruel woman who did her best to make Alexander miserable. She never loved anyone in her life except herself, and she certainly never loved Hartforde! I hated her! I was glad when she died!" There was a brief uncomfortable silence. Then Julia continued. "There's nothing to be sorry for, Isobel," she said kindly. "What Hartforde needs is a woman who loves him. He was married to that witch for five years. What he needs is you."

"Julia, your brother doesn't even like me. Believe me!"

Julia only smiled in return.

VI

Three days passed without Isobel's seeing Alexander, except during dinner, when he was infuriatingly polite while he tried, generally with great success, to bait her on one subject or another. She finally mentioned to Julia that it was high time her friend return to Lord Burke before he despaired of her acceptance, but Julia merely gave a satisfied smile and refused to leave while things were going so splendidly.

On the fourth day, Isobel awoke well before seven. She lay in bed for several minutes staring at the canopy, annoyed that she was unable to fall back to sleep. She threw the covers back and dressed quietly. A ride in the fresh air was what she needed. After leaving word for Julia on the chance she was out of bed before she got back, she headed toward the stable, and while the groom saddled Boots for her, she played with the puppies. Her heart had gone out to the black-and-white one; it was by far the cutest of the litter. She liked it best because it was the biggest. She had a time convincing the groom to let her go out alone, but what she needed was the peace of solitude. Another groom helped her to mount and under a foggy gray sky she trotted sedately until she was well out of sight of the stable. The sidesaddle was uncomfortable and she was positive she would never get over the fear of losing her balance. "I'll be dashed if I continue to use this thing!" she said crossly to herself. When she reached a low fence of piled-up rocks, she pulled Boots to a stop. It was but the work of a moment to dismount and unfasten the hated contraption. Once she had the saddle off, it remained only to get back on the horse. But the voluminous skirt of her riding habit made remounting the patient animal impossible. She did the only thing she could do, short of taking off the habit (a solution to which she gave only the briefest of consideration); she pulled the back of the skirt between her legs and drew it up under the front of her belt. She managed to remount by climbing on a fence of piled-up rocks. The sensation of having her legs exposed to the air made her uncomfortable; she could well appreciate the practicality of a pair of breeches and she wished she'd thought to bring a pair with her. The thought that still someone might come along worried her until a good twenty minutes had passed, during which she did not see so much as a squirrel.

She kicked Boots into a gallop and whooped with exhilaration as the horse responded. When she finally drew up, both she and the horse were breathing hard. She reached down to pat his neck. "Do you need a

rest, old boy?" she asked breathlessly. She slid off his
back and stood looking at the fields. The rolling land
stretching out as far as she could see was an intense
verdant green lost at the horizon in a misty fog, and
the flowers dotting the fields made patches of color in
an otherwise solid green carpet. The sky was a gray
dome above her and it gave her the eerie sensation she
was the only person in the world, and that the world
existed solely of these fields and the low gray sky. She
let her skirt down and, because she wanted to feel the
grass under her feet, she pulled off her boots. After
stuffing her stockings inside the toes, she threw them
down to walk down to a meadow where bluebells
stood out from the green. The grass was cold but only
a little damp between her toes. It tickled her ankles as
she walked. She sat down in the middle of the meadow
and at last began to understand why her mother had so
loved the flower and why the man she would always
think of as her father had wanted to cultivate it. She
lay on her back, knees bent to face the cool sky, and
stared at the flowers around her. Her life had changed
so much since she had left New York, and she shuddered to think what might have happened if she were
still slaving away for Samuels. Philip would have accosted her again, and she doubted there would have
been anyone to stop him a second time. Now, she had
a father who, even if he didn't exactly love her, was at
least unabashedly spoiling her. And all she had to do to
secure her future was marry some nobleman who was
sure to measure the depth of his love by the size of her
fortune. She sighed and closed her eyes, forcing herself
to think of something else, anything else, besides being
married to someone who didn't love her and whom
she didn't love either. She began humming a tune,
adding instruments as, in her mind, the refrain devel-
oped. She began waving her hands in the air, con-
ducting the orchestra that was even now performing

her symphony. Just when the music had reached a crescendo and she was exulting at her triumphant symphonic debut, she was startled to hear someone calling her name.

Her eyes flew open to see the tall shape of a man standing a few feet away. "Oh, it's you," she said, her initial reaction to be annoyed that Lord Hartforde had interrupted her symphony. He was standing with his weight on one leg, hands crossed over his chest, with something—she couldn't ascertain what—clasped in one hand and a sardonic expression on his perfect features. She glared at him, but as she took in how the lean muscles of his legs were accentuated by his close-fitting riding breeches, it was hard to stop the rush of warmth that so often afflicted her when she looked at him.

"I was just trying to decide whose boots I had found." He held up the offending footwear. "I should have guessed it was you. Don't you ever wear shoes?"

His disparaging tone made her want to cringe, but she returned his cool stare. "What you think no longer concerns me, sir, and if I choose not to wear my shoes, 'tis no business of yours." She sat up and crossed her arms over her knees. "Here." She was thinking of New York and had half forgot Alexander was there. "I am free to do whatever I like. I don't have to work for anyone except myself! And 'tis so beautiful"—she waved an arm—"I could not help myself." Belatedly, she realized she must sound like a complete ninny. She looked away and told herself this arrogant, unpleasant, and unrelentingly handsome aristocrat would never think of her as anything but an annoying and brainless female.

"I am gratified you find my estate beautiful, Miss St. James. However, you might have hurt yourself, and I should hardly care to be responsible for any misfortune of yours." He walked down to where she was sitting and threw the boots at her feet. "Put them on," he demanded.

"But I don't want to," she said, and just to be perverse, she lifted a foot and wiggled her toes at him. "Though I must say your concern touches me deeply." She lay back down. "It's such a lovely day, do you not agree?" His eyes were very near the color of the grass.

"Put them on." He sounded distinctly annoyed.

"Look around you, Lord Hartforde! Does it not calm your soul to be surrounded by such beauty? Don't you ever want to feel the earth under your feet?" She realized her panegyric was having absolutely no effect on him, and she reddened. "How did you get to be such an old fogey?" she asked angrily. She snatched up her boots and told herself he probably knew full well how handsome he looked in his riding clothes. "You can't be so much older than I." She smiled as she said these last words, but it did not appear to improve his mood. Deciding, wisely, she thought, not to bother with her stockings, she pulled them out of the toes of her boots and surreptitiously let them fall to the ground away from his view.

"I'm thirty-one," he said finally, staring down at her with a look that told her she had better be quick about putting on her boots.

"Even such an advanced age as that shouldn't mean one cannot appreciate the beauty around him." She looked pointedly at him and started to pull on one of the boots. "You'd best look away if you do not want to see my ankles, sir. Remember, I warned you once before." Shrugging when he refused to look away, she pulled on the other boot.

"This old fogey seems to have escaped your siren call," he said wryly when she stood up.

"Well, I'm sure I've spoiled you for other women now." She saw he was smiling and she smiled back at him. Was it too much to hope he might actually be courteous for a change?

"Don't forget your stockings," he said. "You seem to have dropped them over there." He pointed.

Isobel glowered at him and stalked over to pick them up. "Just what do you expect me to do with them? I haven't any pockets!"

"I shan't be indelicate enough to suggest you put them on, so perhaps you had best give them to me." He held out a hand. "I'll see they are returned to you."

She thrust them into his outstretched hand and he folded them with a great show of delicacy before stuffing them into his pocket.

"Do you mind if I inquire about your saddle?" he said as he walked alongside her up the slight incline to where his horse was standing next to Boots.

"Oh. Well. It was in the way," she explained, wondering just how she might explain it without convincing him she was indeed the fool he thought her to be.

"Yes, but where did you leave it?"

"Over that way." She pointed vaguely in the direction from which she had ridden. "Have you seen Julia this morning?" she asked in the hopes it would divert his attention from the subject of the saddle, being fairly certain he was already not too pleased with her.

He shook his head. "Miss St. James, your attempt to change the subject is pitifully transparent. I shall not be so easily diverted from learning why you decided to ride without the benefit of a saddle. Did it break?"

"No." They had reached the horses and Isobel stopped next to Boots. "Well," she said, "I hope you have a pleasant ride."

He wrinkled his forehead and sighed. "I have no intention of letting you continue to ride alone. Perhaps in the colonies you were permitted to ride unescorted.

Such is not the case here. You shall please do me the kindness of accompanying me to the stable."

"I wouldn't dream of burdening you with my presence," she said, anxious for him to leave and increasingly doubtful he intended to do any such thing. "I'll be just fine, I assure you!"

"You are, without any doubt, the most difficult young lady I have ever had the displeasure of knowing," he said, bending to offer her his hand up. Isobel stared at him and he sighed and straightened up. "What is the matter?"

"I'd much prefer to ride back alone," she said, trying to think of some way of convincing him to let her ride back without him.

"Miss St. James, if you do not get on that horse this very instant, I shall put you there myself." He glared at her. "Have I made myself clear?"

"I rode astride," she said. She felt herself go scarlet when she realized there was no way she was going to avoid his seeing her legs dreadfully exposed as soon as she got on the horse.

"That is an inescapable conclusion, even to one as dim as myself." He cupped his hands and bent again. "What is the trouble?" He straightened.

"I won't do it!"

"Get on the damned horse, if you please!"

"No!"

"Then I'll put you on myself." He took a step toward her and his hand actually closed on her arm before she shook him off.

"All right, all right!" she snapped.

His expression changed to surprise as she turned her back on him and bent to pull her skirt between her legs and tucked the hem into the front of her belt. "What in the good Lord's name are you doing?"

"How else do you think I could get on?" she snapped.

"You never cease to amaze me," he said, bending once more to offer his cupped hands.

"Not so hard!" she cried as he heaved her upward. She would have fallen off if he hadn't suddenly grabbed her leg and steadied her. Her skin was burning where his hand grasped her thigh. She looked down at the fingers pressed into her stockingless skin; they were long and slender, and the nails looked freshly manicured. Her skin was tingling where he touched her and her stomach suddenly felt as though it were flipping over. A slow warmth spread over her as his hand lingered on her. His touch was—almost—a caress. When he lifted his hand she saw hooded green eyes that brought back the fluttering in her stomach in its full disturbing force.

"Your legs quite live up to the promise of your ankles, take it from an old fogey who should know," he said, running a finger lightly down the line of her leg. His mouth lifted at one corner when he saw her shiver at the contact. He turned away and she stared at his back, watching the play of muscles through his clothes as he mounted his horse in one fluid motion.

She kicked Boots into a gallop as soon as he was up. She had to do something to take her mind off the way she was still tingling from his touch. Alexander's bigger horse had no trouble keeping up as they galloped over the fields. She heard him shout when they reached the fence where she had left her saddle, but she ignored him and jumped the gelding easily over it.

"I didn't think I could stay on when he jumped! That was so exciting!" she cried as he rode up to where she sat on Boots. "I can't wait to do that again!" She was on the point of turning her horse around to do just that when he stopped her by reaching over to snatch the reins from her hands.

"Didn't it bother you that you might have broken

your neck, you little fool?" he snapped as he dismounted and held up his hands to help her down.

"It never occurred to me." She laughed, swinging her leg over the horse's back.

His hands tightened around her as he lifted her down and they lingered there, nearly circling her waist. His eyes suddenly darkened and, for a brief heart-pounding moment, Isobel thought he meant to kiss her. Her eyelids fluttered downward in anticipation, but he suddenly let her go. He grabbed the reins of her horse and walked quickly to where her saddle lay on top of the fence. While Isobel rearranged her skirts, he resaddled Boots. Then, with a deliberately expressionless face, he helped her back up.

They rode slowly back to the house, both lost in silence until Alexander asked abruptly, "How is it you're so different? Are all American women like you?"

She shrugged her shoulders. "I'm myself. It's the only way I know how to be."

"Surely you did not ride without a saddle in America?" He was touched at the sudden look of sadness that crossed her face. "Or did you spend your time doing the accounts for your cousin?" It was infuriatingly difficult to continue the indifference he had promised to feel towards her.

"I am doing my best to forget I ever lived in New York," she said. "I hated it there. I did not know how miserable I was until I came to England." The searching look he gave her made her stomach do flips again, and in self-defense she changed the subject. "Tell me how you got to be such a stern old man."

"A stern old man? On the contrary, I am a mature adult who knows better than to cross the bounds of propriety—even when I am alone."

"Is that the trouble? Have I offended your sense of propriety?"

"What if it hadn't been I who found you?" he chided her. "Another man might have had his way with you and there would have been nothing you could do about it. You should not have gone riding alone."

"But I like being alone."

"Miss St. James," he fixed her with an icy look, "that is hardly the point. The point is men have certain physical desires and there are such of us who will take any opportunity to satisfy them."

"Oh, yes, and then blame the woman for their inability to act civilized," Isobel retorted heatedly.

"You are being unfair," he said.

"No, I am being accurate. Life is more fair for some than for others, do you not agree, my lord?"

"Miss St. James, you are an impossible young woman."

"It has occurred to me, sir, that every time we start to get alone, one of us always says something unpleasant to spoil it." She thought to herself it was generally his lordship, but she charitably refrained from telling him so.

"What ever made you think we were getting along?" he asked mildly.

"I should have thought that you, of all people, would not resent a woman's having a mind of her own."

"What a charming child you are," he murmured.

She saw he was baiting her and for once she refused to rise to it, choosing instead to look away. While they rode in strained silence she thought about what he had said, and, grudgingly, she had to admit he was right. No matter how unfair it was, she would have been defenseless had someone come along and wanted to do her harm. She put her hand on his arm and, though he raised his eyebrows at her in that maddening way of his, she managed a smile. "I'm sorry, Lord Hartforde. You were perfectly right," she said contritely as they came up to the stable. "About the danger of being out alone, I mean. I apologize for being a brat and I take back what I said about your being a stern old man. Do you forgive me?" She gave him what she hoped was a charming smile as they rode up to the stable.

"Such an insult is not easily forgiven." He grinned at her and they both laughed when she stuck out her tongue at him. He lifted her off the horse and immediately turned his back on her to talk with the head groom. The two conversed quietly while Isobel sat down by the door to play with the puppies. They recognized her and scrambled playfully into her lap when she sat down. As usual, the black-and-white one demanded, and got, most of her attention.

Alexander nearly tripped over her as he walked briskly toward the door. She was sitting on the dusty floor of the stable, her legs folded under her. "What in bloody hell—Miss St. James, what are you doing on the ground? I damned near tripped over you!" he added when she looked at him as though she had no idea what he was getting so upset about.

"Look what I've got!" She held up the black-and-white puppy for him to see. "Isn't he darling?" She spoke more to the puppy than to Alexander, who looked down at the five others playing around her knees. She put down the dog and watched him run to his siblings, looking sadly after them for a moment. "I'm sorry if I was in your way." She held up a hand for him to take as she stood up. She brushed off her skirts and straightened up.

"You seem to have a talent for getting in my way." He was annoyed for thinking about how smooth her leg had felt, for the shock that had gone through him when she had put a hand on his arm, and, immediately after that, for the erotic picture she had just made, when playing with puppies, was not in the least erotic.

"Oh! Forgive me, my lord!" Isobel feigned horror,

clutching her face between her hands. "Shall I cut off my right arm? Will it make up for scuffing your boots? Do send them to me when you've changed and I shall have them polished for you."

To her utter amazement, he burst into laughter. "Miss St. James, you are going to make me admire you in spite of myself." He held out his arm. "Shall we go back to the house? I have a Rubens I should like to show you."

VII

The day before Isobel and Julia were to return to London, Alexander found her in the library. He cleared his throat. "Ah, there you are! I've been look-ing all over for you!"

Isobel looked up from her seat on the sofa. "Why? Did I do something to annoy you and now you want to berate me?" She smiled at him, glad that his resolu-tion to be pleasant to her had already survived three days.

"No." He made her a small bow. "I've brought you a gift."

"Well, it isn't big enough to be your Rubens, so just take it away." She made a shooing motion with one of her hands.

"How ungrateful you are!" he protested, as he walked over to where she was sitting and held out the basket he had been hiding behind his back. "Here."

She took the basket and, holding it on her lap, opened the lid. Her face lit up as she reached in and took out the black-and-white puppy. "Lord Hartforde, I'm speechless!" Her eyes were shining as she held the puppy to her cheek.

"For once," he said, turning a grateful eye upward. She put the puppy down on the floor and pulled out

the ribbon holding back her hair to trail on the floor
for it to chase.

She glanced up when he sat down next to her. When
he found himself looking into glowing blue eyes, he
felt a distressing pull of desire as he took in the soft
curve of her smile, and the golden hair falling loose
about her shoulders, framing her face. Her lips parted
and he found his gaze focused on them.

"This is the nicest thing anyone has ever done for
me," she said, lifting her arms to hug him.

"Don't do that!" He pushed her away. He had not
expected the sudden light pressure of her torso against
him to affect him quite as it did.

"Don't do what?" To his great relief, she sat back to
look at him with an exasperated expression. "You
mean hug you? Why ever not? If you insist on doing
nice things, you must expect to get hugged." She put a
hand on his arm and smiled at him.

"Such behavior is most unladylike," he said sternly,
hoping his harsh words would discourage another attempt. She looked so hurt he was instantly sorry.
"You are in sore need of some refinement," he said.

"I knew you'd say something unpleasant." She
sighed. "Well, I simply won't let you spoil this. You
may go to the devil, you old man!" She turned her
attention back to the puppy, which had let out an impatient yelp at being ignored. She bent over to shake
the ribbon, and the puppy took it in his sharp little
teeth and ran between Alexander's legs. She twisted
toward him and put a hand next to his leg to prop
herself up. Hardly aware that he did so, he reached out
to stroke her shoulder. Her skin was warm under his
fingers.

She quickly lifted her head. "Now, what?" She
frowned when his hand lingered on her shoulder.
"What are you doing?"

He felt a shock when their eyes met. She sat perfectly still as he ran his hands through her golden hair, pulling it away from her face. One long finger gently traced the outline of her lips, caressing her cheek. "Kissing you," he murmured, leaning forward until his lips were just inches above her own. "Surely you've been kissed before?" One hand held her chin, while the other gently reached around her waist.

"Once, and it was horrible," she said in a low voice.

He looked into questioning eyes and wondered if it could be true that she had been kissed only once before. She leaned toward him as he lowered his head to hers. He found it hard to believe. "You must tell me afterward if it was horrible this time as well." He closed the space between them. He was unprepared for the strength of his reaction when he felt his mouth on hers. He held her and thought her lips seemed unconscionably soft and warm. When he caressed her shoulders, her skin felt as smooth as the satin of her gown, and as he closed his eyes, the image of her slender legs as they had looked that day she had been out riding came to him. He remembered how soft her skin had felt just from that brief contact, and he wondered if it was possible for her to be as soft everywhere else. He deepened his kiss, his demanding tongue parting her lips, and he felt the heat of his desire beginning to overcome them both. He twined his fingers in her silky hair and his other hand pressed against her back to pull her as close as possible. Tentative arms wound around his neck, her slender body fit just so into the tightening circle of his arm, and the press of her against his chest as she began to relax against him was beginning to stir him beyond control. There was a familiar tightening in his belly and he bent her head back under the increasing pressure of his desire. He pulled away from her lips and looked into dark blue eyes to see the passion he had felt when he kissed her. His fingers were still tangled in her hair, so she was unable to move. "My God, Sarah," he said softly.

When Isobel felt Alexander's hands tighten their hold on her head, she leaned closer and wondered if it was possible to die from bliss. She didn't know what she should do with her hands, so she shyly put them around his neck; her fingers brushed his hair as they met at the nape of his neck. His tongue was slipping over her lips and, under the demand of his mouth, they parted. She didn't care if she had done the right thing, for his tongue darted gently into her, and she was lost in the slippery sensation. Timidly, she increased the pressure of her lips against his. In answer, his hand slid around to hold her face, while his other arm tightened around her waist. She was giddy with her response to his touch, she was drunk with the feel of him, the taste of him, the warm, musky, masculine smell of him. She couldn't believe what was happening—this was Lord Hartforde, one of the most powerful men in all of England, and the handsomest man she had ever seen in her life! Then she stopped thinking and gave herself over to the whirling, dizzying pleasure of his arms. He was pulling her close, his hands were touching her so gently, so intimately. . . . She was disappointed when he stopped, but, then, the look he gave her made her afraid that, for a moment, she had forgotten how to breathe. He was still holding her, his face so close to hers she could feel his breath on her skin. It was impossible that he should be looking at her this way with those extraordinary green eyes burning into hers, yet he was. She waited for him to speak.

Isobel shook her head free and had to take a shaking breath before she could say, "I don't know who Sarah is, my lord, but clearly you would prefer her company to mine."

The vehemence of his reply shocked her. "Sarah is a woman I liked just as little as I like you."

She bent to pick up the puppy before standing. "I should hate to think what would have happened if you actually liked me!" She whirled around and left him sitting alone.

Alexander winced as the door slammed shut. He leaned back against the sofa and closed his eyes. It had never occurred to him before that she did bear a slight resemblance to his dead wife. If he wasn't careful, Isobel St. James would wind herself around his heart the same way Sarah had, and he had sworn that would never happen to him again.

"What a swine that man is!" Isobel raged as she lay on her bed, staring up at the ceiling and wishing it would just crash down and put her out of her misery. The puppy snuggled against her side and pressed its wet nose to her fist. She could hardly wait to get back to London and be away from that hateful beast. She had gotten her wish; Lord Hartforde had kissed her at last. And she had never experienced anything like it; every inch of her body had felt on fire at his touch—still felt on fire! She was ashamed to think she might never have stopped him if he hadn't called her by another woman's name. But, why, if he wanted another, why had he kissed her? Because he was beastly, positively beastly! She groaned in misery. Just the recollection of his lips against hers sent a thrill through her. How could she ever face him again?

Chapter 13

Preston Hawes looked around his little room with disdain. These dreary surroundings, so distressingly far from the West End, were nothing compared with what he intended to have. He lit his last cheroot and sat down in one of the faded velvet chairs, his feet up on the table in front of him. An ember from the cigar fell to the carpet, where it burned yet another small hole in the wool.

Hawes maintained his rooms by exploiting the only two talents he had—his original profession of the law, much to his father's despair, not being either one of them. His first and most useful talent was artistic in nature. He could render practically flawless copies of any document he had in front of him. His facility was impressive, and that, coupled with his second talent for putting off his creditors, had gained him a reputation among a certain class as a man with prospects. In truth, the only thing standing between Preston Hawes and his prospects was his love for cards.

Hawes was able to make enough money copying documents—he never asked what was to be done with them when he finished—to keep his two rooms and make occasional payments to his tailor. His father sent him money if he pleaded with just the right words, but still he sometimes wondered if real success would always elude him. Patience he had in abundance, but luck was something that seemed to have deserted him lately. He finished his cigar and, carefully brushing off his one and only frock coat, went out to see if he could coax luck into smiling on him.

William Fordham leaned back in his chair, a glow of satisfaction on his face.

"One hundred pounds." Hawes frowned. He'd lost more money before, but he had never had such a consistent run of bad luck. This would put him in exceedingly strained circumstances. He shook his head ruefully and looked at the man sitting across from him. "Well, here you are." He handed over his note for the hundred pounds, smiling as he did so. His tailor would have to wait.

"You don't mean you haven't the money?" Fordham queried, his tone tinged with outrage.

"Not just this moment, I'm afraid. But I'm good for it. Ask anyone here and they'll tell you Preston Hawes always pays his debts."

"Eventually, I'm told."

"Quite. I do eventually pay my debts." He smiled nervously. He did not like Fordham's tone in the least.

"Tell me, Mr. Hawes, have you ever done any writing? Or copying, perhaps?"

"Oh, now and again," he said, relaxing into his chair.

"Could you copy this?" Fordham took a sheet of paper from his coat pocket and tossed it on the table.

Hawes unfolded the sheet of paper. "Of course."

"It will be in your interest to do your best work. If

it is good enough, I might just have a position for you."

"Really?"

"Yes. You seem like a gentleman to me."

The word "gentleman" sounded to Hawes like the name of a long-lost friend.

Chapter 14

With Bridget close behind her, Isobel walked purposefully into the jewelry store. The maid stood near the door waiting, while her mistress looked at the finery. Another woman came in and was waited on by a second clerk.

"How much is that?" Isobel pointed to a brooch.

"Fifty pounds," the clerk sniffed. Imagine having to ask!

"I need to spend exactly one hundred pounds, not a shilling more nor less!" Isobel said, giving the scrawny man a stony glance.

"Well, this bracelet is just about that." He picked up a delicate gold band set with several small amethysts and sapphires. He held it up for her to admire. "The finest workmanship, as you can well see, madam. The stones are of the finest quality and cut—"

Isobel interrupted him just as he was taking a breath to continue. "I'll take it," she said.

"An excellent choice, madam."

"You may send the bill to Lord Hartforde, at Hartforde House."

"Ah! A gift for the Lady Julia?"

"No," she said shortly. "You may send the bracelet to number five Albemarle."

"Very good, madam." The clerk kept his face expressionless, for he had no intention of offending Lord Hartforde's newest mistress. Neither did he miss the way Lady Shorington's ears pricked up at the young woman's instructions. No doubt all of London would know about this before the week was out.

"Thank you." Isobel nodded to Lady Shorington as she left.

In the days that followed, the bracelet would gain in value until it was whispered it had cost hundreds of pounds and that the purchase included earrings worth hundreds, a brooch worth thousands, and (only occasionally) a necklace of diamonds and emeralds that was nearly priceless.

Chapter 15

I

Isobel was often at Hartforde House because she was frequently out late with Faircourt, and Julia insisted on those occasions that she stay to supper. In addition, the two spent a great deal of time planning the ball to celebrate Julia's engagement to Lord Burke. Isobel was not unaffected by seeing Lord Hartforde so often, but she found it impossible to tell Julia what a fool she had been. To make matters worse, she never knew how she ought to act around him. She had meant to take her cue from his behavior, but he did not seem to be able to make up his mind from one day to the next how he would behave toward her. At first he was cold and distant, and when she got over her hurt at his unconcern, she affected a similar attitude, only to have him engage her in conversations that showed him capable of great solicitousness. When she got over her suspicion at his being so agreeable, he took to teasing her unmercifully. She discovered it was when she was most determined to be pleasant that he could be counted on to send her into a rage. She was often beside herself at his penchant for making her angry, but when he left her alone, she found herself near tears at his neglect. But it was the times he was pleasant that she found unbearable, because they only made her realize how fond she could become of him.

One afternoon he came into the drawing room, where she and Julia were busy choosing a pattern for Julia's gown. He apologized for interrupting them but said the engraver had sent over several samples of invitations and he was taking the opportunity to show them to his sister. Julia looked through the samples and declared she had seen a design in a magazine somewhere that she wished to compare to them.

"'Tis in my room." When Isobel got up to follow her, she said, "Stay with Hartforde, Isobel, I shall only be a minute."

She sat back down, confused because she did not know where to look or what mood to expect of him.

"Is there something the matter, Miss St. James? You seem all afluster."

"There is nothing the matter, sir." She raised her eyes to his and was immediately incensed at his smug look. She picked up one of the pattern dolls and devoted herself to its examination.

"Are you always so ill at ease with a gentleman?" he asked.

"I am never ill at ease with a gentleman, sir!" She put down the doll and stood up. "What could be taking Julia so long?"

"She hasn't been gone so very long."

"Indeed, she has!" There were a few moments of silence, while Isobel paced around the room.

"Have you named your dog?" he asked finally.

Isobel immediately flushed scarlet. He looked as though he had no recollection of what she could not forget. Every moment of that afternoon was burned into her memory. "Oh, yes," she replied when she was sure her blush had faded and she could face him again. "I named him almost immediately."

"Pray tell, what was your choice?"

"Why, my lord, I had you for my inspiration, so the choice was easy. I named him Beast." At that moment Julia came back into the room and Isobel was spared his response.

A week or two afterward, Isobel was surprised to receive from Alexander a letter and a small packet. Being too well bred to send any missive to her via the post, he had sent a servant to Redruth to give them to her directly. The servant thrust the letter and packet into her hands and, saying only that his lordship did not require him to wait for an answer, left before she could refuse to accept such an impertinent delivery. She knew she ought to send back the package and letter, but she found she could not. There was only one possible reason he would risk such a breach of propriety. He was hopelessly in love with her and the letter was a declaration of the condition of his heart. The packet had to be some token of his love—a lock of hair, perhaps. She opened the letter with trembling hands. The letter read:

My dear Miss St. James,

Enclosed you will please find the articles I promised to return to your possession. I would also enclose a bank draft in satisfaction of our wager, but a notice from a certain jeweler's was received here t'other day which appears to make that unnecessary.

The items returned were in residence in one of my riding jackets, and I do confess to you I had forgotten them until they were recently discovered by my valet, who is now convinced, no doubt along with yourself, I am an adventurer of the first degree. I have left him to this belief in consequence of my unwillingness to apprise him of the innocent manner in which I came by them, as I am certain the telling of it would not sound so innocent by half as it was in whole.

I beg your gracious indulgence to allow me to inform you that I personally supervised the laundering of the silken items herein. I assure you, you may wear them again without further ado on your part. I remain ever your humble, obedient, and, of course, beastly servant.

Hartforde

The day after she received his packet she had the misfortune of seeing the letter's author, and when he greeted her his eyes were sparkling with mischief. She summoned all her dignity and, taking her hand from his, said, "You have never been humble a day in your life, my lord, and I should never allow you to be my servant, even were I in need of another one. As for being beastly, the appellation must surely have applied long before ever I gave it to you. And furthermore, I would have you know, I threw them directly into the fire!"

Julia looked at the two of them and wondered why her brother looked as though he could barely restrain himself from bursting into laughter and why Isobel was turning a particular shade of scarlet. "Shall we go, Isobel?" she said, half afraid the young woman might do her brother some harm.

"Yes."

II

It was so obvious Julia was in love with Lord Burke and Lord Burke loved her back that Isobel could not help but feel a little envious. Whenever Julia talked about Charles, a dreamy expression came over her, and Isobel wondered what would it be like to be in love with someone who loved her back.

They were both determined Julia's engagement ball would be the event of the season. The two spent hours planning every detail. Julia rebuked her brother every time he complained of yet another expense.

"I shall only be engaged once!" she would say. "To think you would begrudge your only sister such a little thing!" Alexander would grumble good-naturedly and accuse her of plotting to ruin him, but he would always relent.

Isobel spent the day of the ball with Julia fretting over last-minute arrangements. The musicians arrived late in the afternoon after Julia had spent the previous hour agonizing over whether they would arrive at all.

"Oh, for heaven's sake! Would you stop all this worrying?" Isobel laughed after her friend consulted with her butler for the third time about the correct quantity of wine. "Everything is going to be just fine. I'm sure your brother has seen to it there will be food and drink enough; he'd not dare do otherwise! He knows you'd never forgive him if everything isn't just so."

"I only want this to be perfect!"

"I dread your wedding if this is the way you act at something as simple as your engagement."

At Julia's request, Isobel stayed with her while she dressed, but at last she warned Julia that unless she were to go, she would still be wearing her muslin day dress when the guests arrived.

"Send someone to get your gown so you may change here," she suggested. "Won't you please stay?"

"Oh, all right!" Isobel shook her head. A maid was sent to fetch her gown, and Julia penned a quick note begging the earl's forgiveness for keeping Isobel with her. Bridget arrived with the gown and a short reply from the earl, stating that he expected to dance with Julia in return for allowing his daughter to stay.

III

Isobel did not finish dressing until nearly eleven o'clock. As she walked down the hall she could hear music from the ballroom rising above the hum of conversation. She paused at the door, debating whether it was proper to go in unaccompanied. Several men immediately approached her and she frowned to see Lord Strathemoore was not among them. She had especially commissioned Julia to see that he was standing by so she might not walk in alone.

"Miss St. James, at last!" Lord Hartforde made his way to her side. "I was beginning to despair of your ever coming down. Gentlemen, my lords, I have the honor of escorting Miss St. James tonight." He took the hand she had not extended to him. "Don't be childish, Miss St. James," he whispered.

"I am not being childish!" she snapped, wondering how it was that just the sight of him had sent her heart pounding. Was she such a fool that she could forget for even a moment that she meant nothing to him? His light touch on her was warm, and she could not help remembering how those hands had touched her once before.

Alexander covered her hand with his and led her away from the crowd of disappointed men. Though he might try to make her think he was unaffected, he could not pretend to himself. Her wine-colored gown made her skin look as smooth as alabaster, only he could not help thinking that he knew very well her skin would be warm under his fingers. The burgundy silk swooping down from her shoulders to tuck into the V of her bodice barely covered what would have otherwise been an immodest amount of bosom. He had a sudden and forceful recollection of the way she had melted against him that day at Ashdown Grey. There was at least one difference between her and Sarah; his wife had never responded to him as passionately as Isobel had done. He smiled to himself; she had positively glowed when she caught sight of him coming toward her. She ought not to be so transparent. "I trust you remembered to put on your shoes," he said quietly as he led her across the room.

Isobel laughed, her smile lighting her face. She wished he were always so pleasant toward her. "Why? Do you think I should have worn them?" she teased, feeling a happiness out of all proportion to the occasion.

He drew in a sharp breath when he saw her smile. As they crossed the room, he bent and whispered into her ear, "You are breathtaking tonight, Miss St. James."

Isobel looked at him and realized just how badly she wanted his words to be true.

IV

"Who in heaven's name is that?" a tall, slender man dressed in gray and blue satin asked Julia. He had watched his former son-in-law offer his arm to a woman he had never seen before. She was quite pretty, he thought to himself, until she laughed at something Hartforde said. No, she was ravishing! The two looked besotted with each other.

Julia followed his glance. "She is Miss Isobel St. James, the earl of Chessingham's daughter."

"Ah! Unfortunately, I was out of the country when she arrived in London. I understand she has been quite a success." He stared at the two as they approached and tried to remember what else he had heard about her.

"Miss St. James," Alexander said when they reached Julia and the duke, "may I present you to His Grace, the duke of Mallentrye."

The duke bowed over her hand after Hartforde introduced her. His lips brushed the back of her hand and lingered there just a moment too long when she straightened up from her curtsy. He remembered hearing she was the by-blow of some affair of Chessingham's; the man had been quite notorious in his younger days. "'Tis a pleasure, indeed, to meet you, Miss St. James." He continued to hold her hand and was rewarded with a rosy blush. "It would be an honor to spend a day with you, miss," he said. "And may I be so bold as to tell you I have never seen a woman of such rare beauty as yourself?"

"It appears you may be, Your Grace," she answered.

"Are you an American, Miss St. James?" He reluctantly released her hand.

"I grew up in Boston and New York, Your Grace." She fingered her bracelet with long fingers, not meeting his pointed stare.

"America's loss is England's gain," he said with a gallant bow. The duke smiled coldly as Isobel was quickly surrounded by men who wanted to dance with her. His eyes never left her face unless it was to dip downward to the flesh pushing so enticingly against the neckline of her gown. She danced once with Hartforde, and in watching them the duke suddenly recalled someone's remark that this enchanting young woman had bought an expensive necklace and then sent the bill on to Hartforde. An interesting piece of information, if it was true. How amusing that Hartforde was so smitten with her! Would it have been so hard to have been even half as attentive to his wife? When Hartforde and the young woman finished their dance, the duke made his way to where they were standing with Julia and Lord Burke.

"Do you know, Miss St. James," he said, taking her hand when there was a pause in the conversation, "something about you reminds me of my daughter."

"Why, thank you, Your Grace."

"Sarah's eyes were pale, but her hair was as golden as your own. I'm surprised if Hartforde hasn't mentioned it himself."

"He means, Miss St. James, the late Lady Hartforde. I must beg to differ with His Grace. There is no resemblance that I can see," Alexander said stiffly.

"Well"—Lord Burke filled the uncomfortable silence—"there can be no disagreement that Miss St. James is a beauty."

"There is no disagreement about that," the duke said, "and I, for one, would be honored if she would dance with me."

Isobel took the duke's hand without looking at Alexander. "The honor is mine, Your Grace."

"Perhaps you would care to rest outside?" the duke suggested after only a few moments. "It is rather warm, and no doubt some cool air would be refreshing."

"Yes, Your Grace, it would be." She was grateful he had noticed her agitation and she fanned herself as they stepped out into the garden. He led her to a stone bench and sat down beside her.

"Will you think me rash if I say I have been completely overcome by your beauty?" His voice was hushed.

Isobel looked at him in surprise and stopped fanning herself. "I would think you rather silly for saying such a thing, Your Grace."

"But, 'tis true, I have, Miss St. James. You are the loveliest creature I have ever seen." He took her hand and raised it to his lips. "You are sublime beyond belief."

Isobel tried to pull her hand away, but he held it

fast. "Your Grace, you will embarrass me if you continue this," she said, becoming alarmed when he turned her hand over and pressed his lips first to her palm and then to the inside of her wrist. "Stop this immediately!" Apparently it had been a dreadful mistake to come outside with him, but it had never entered her mind he would suddenly act half his age.

"Don't be cruel, my love. I insist I am carried away by your beauty." He moved closer to her and wrapped an arm around her waist.

"You had better unhand me. I shall call out if you don't!" In answer, he laughed and bent his head to kiss her temptingly bare shoulder. "Let go of me this instant!" She tried to push him away.

He raised his head to look at her, his dark eyes devouring the pale expanse of skin above the décolletage of her gown. "Surely you realize how much more I have to offer you than he." His hand caressed her throat. "I am a much wealthier man." The words, calculated to offend, did exactly that.

"So much more to offer me than whom? What are you talking about?"

"You needn't play the innocent with me, my dear. All of London is talking about you and your lover. Had I but known what a beauty you were, I should have arranged to meet you much sooner." His arm around her waist tightened as she struggled to get away. "You are exciting me beyond my imagination—"

"Let me go!" Isobel was horrified. Surely he couldn't mean what he was saying?

"Hartforde may be better-looking, my dear, but I assure you I would be more generous. If it's jewels you like, I would shower you with them. If you were my mistress, my fortune would be at your feet."

Isobel was so scandalized when the duke's words sank in that she stopped struggling. "Hartforde?" *That swine!* she raged to herself. While he had been pretending to not care, he had been telling all of London about her loose behavior. She sagged against the bench, devastated to discover that Hartforde had such a low opinion of her.

"That's much better," the duke crooned, bending his head to kiss her, while one hand pulled at the bodice of her gown.

When she felt his fingers on her, she struggled to stand up. "Let me go!" she cried, twisting her head away from his lips, and pushing at his chest. To her relief, suddenly he did let her go. She jumped up from the bench so distraught she did not notice he was staring past her. "I assure you, you have made a grave mistake, Your Grace. I am not, nor have I ever been, Lord Hartforde's mistress, and for you to suggest such a thing is . . . is . . . why, it's simply appalling!"

The duke stood up and bowed to someone standing behind her. Isobel whirled around and saw Alexander. There was an amused expression on his handsome face.

"Perhaps you'd best leave, Your Grace. I don't believe Miss St. James desires your company after all." He spoke softly, moving aside to let him pass. When the duke was gone, he gave Isobel an offended look. "My mistress?" he repeated in an incredulous tone. "Would you care to explain what that little scene was all about?"

She sat down on the bench again, feeling nothing but relief now that the duke had left. "I should think you ought to know," she said at last.

"I'm afraid I am at a loss." He shrugged.

"You're the one who's been telling everyone that I, that you—that we—" She was too ashamed to continue. She blinked rapidly to hold back her tears.

"What are you babbling on about?" When she glared at him, he raised his eyebrows. "Oh, that!"

"A gentleman would have kept quiet. But, then, I should have known you are no gentleman."

"Miss St. James, I assure you, I have not told a soul about that little . . . peccadillo, shall we say?"

"Well, I certainly didn't! Perhaps you'd care to tell me why His Grace seems to think I am your mistress?" She bit her lip, embarrassed at the implications of what she had just said.

"What a ludicrous idea. Perhaps he meant only to flatter you, and you misunderstood."

"If the duke was flattering anybody, it was you!" she snapped. "And I don't believe I mistook his meaning. Of course, what's important is that he insulted you. Why, he told me you're stingy with your lovers." How dare he suggest she was making up the man's vile proposition! Her cheeks were still burning, only now it was due to anger.

"But I am quite generous to my mistresses!" Alexander put a hand to his heart, as though wounded.

"Oh, yes, it must pierce you to the quick to hear yourself slandered so cruelly. Never mind all of London thinks we are lovers, and that I am ruined because of it. If I were you, I would call him out for saying you don't treat your mistresses as well as he treats his!" She was nearly sputtering with fury.

"Are you sure he asked you to become his . . . lover?" He looked doubtful. "I expect he meant to be gallant but found himself carried away."

"Well, let me see, sir, if I can recall his exact words. He said although you are the better-looking, and of course I must agree, he would be the more generous, and that as his mistress, I should want for nothing. Tell me, do you think I misunderstood? Or have I over-reacted to a proposition commonly made in English society?" Isobel glared at him and then looked away, suddenly ashamed to meet his eyes and unwilling to let him see tears spilling down her cheeks.

Alexander sat down next to her and took her hand. "The duke believes, however mistakenly, that I was responsible for his daughter's unhappiness. After we were married, neither of us was very happy, and it's true I eventually gave up trying. I suspect he even blames me for her death."

"What does that have to do with telling everyone we're lovers?" She snatched her hand away.

"I've done no such thing. Mallentrye simply wanted to make trouble for me. And he's certainly succeeded. Isobel," he said softly, pulling her face around to his with his other hand. He found himself looking into eyes liquid with tears. Before he could think about what he was doing, he bent his head to hers. He could feel her trembling as he held her face with one hand, while his other hand moved to her back to pull her to him. He kissed away the tears escaping down her cheeks.

"No," he heard her say, but he did not want to listen to protestations. He moved his lips over her throat. He felt her try to push him away, but he raised his head and covered her lips with a kiss that demanded she give in to the desire he wanted to create in her. He groaned when he felt her arms around his neck and he leaned forward until she was pressed against the back of the bench, her body yielding to him. He grasped her waist with both hands, pulling her up against him. He was a fool to think he had imagined his feelings the first time he held her in his arms. He wanted this woman as he wanted no other, and she was returning his kiss with a passion that told him she wanted him just as badly. He knew he was being foolish, but while she was answering his desire so exquisitely it was difficult to think of anything else. His need for her shook him. He felt as though he could not get enough of the lips that were meeting his own increasing demand. When at last he pulled away, because if he hadn't he

would have taken her right then, he could only stare at
her for a moment before saying, "Isobel, this can lead
nowhere. I've already told your father I won't marry
again. In the name of decency, I ought to tell you the
same thing. For God's sake, you're not even twenty
yet, are you? How could you possibly understand? I'd
be taking advantage of you if I let this go any further."

"Let go of me," she whispered.

He told himself it was for the best when she left him
without saying another word.

V

The next day Isobel stayed in her room and made a
halfhearted attempt to read. Eventually she threw the
book down and just stared out the window overlooking the gardens. It was no use denying she was in danger of losing her heart to a man who had as much as
told her she meant nothing to him. She ought to have
slapped him, or struggled, or something—anything
except cling to him the way she had. She had been
powerless to do anything but stare into those moss-
green eyes. As soon as his hand touched her cheek, she
felt as though there was a slow fire spreading from
deep inside her, and she had wanted more. The humiliation of his disdain for her ought to cure her, but she
only wished she could make him like her better. It was
not only that he was beautiful; there were other men
almost as handsome who were ten times more agreeable. There was an electricity about him that had
drawn her to him from the very moment they met.
And they were very much alike; he sought power with
the same fervor with which she devoted herself to music. And it was that fervor that attracted her—that and
the realization that in spite of it, he never lost sight of
himself. She had already experienced the intensity of
his intellect, seen how he measured others until he was

satisfied he knew their worth, and she admired his ruthlessness in discarding the unworthy. Try as she might, she could not discover the difference between knowing the quality of a man and being in love with him.

She was surprised when Bridget announced Lady Julia was waiting downstairs for her. "Send her up here." She smiled thinly when Julia came in, unable to summon any enthusiasm at her visit. "It's terribly early for you to be up, isn't it? It's barely two o'clock," she said, making a feeble attempt at humor.

"You don't know, do you?"

"Know what?" She wandered over to another chair and plopped down dejectedly.

"Hartforde and the duke of Mallentrye are said to have had words last night," Julia said.

"Is that so?"

"Yes. I'm told a duel was barely prevented."

"Why did they argue?"

"I was under the impression you might tell me." Julia sat down on the edge of the bed and looked expectantly at Isobel.

"I?"

"Hartforde told me the duke had said something unpleasant to you."

"Oh, Julia, this is simply awful!" She stood up again and began pacing the floor at the foot of the bed.

"What do you mean, awful? Why, this is practically a declaration for you. I had no idea my brother could be so romantic as to fight over a woman! What in heaven's name happened?"

"The duke asked me to be his mistress."

Julia stared at her.

"Your brother overheard him." She leaned against the windowsill. "I won't regale you with the tale of my behavior, but I am quite certain your brother thinks I am as common as they come."

Well before the end of the day, everyone knew that a duel between Lord Hartforde and the duke of Mallentrye had been narrowly averted and, further, that Isobel St. James was reputed to be the cause of this latest rift.

Lord Strathemoore was not the only man, married or unmarried, whose heart sank to think the young heiress was spoken for. But, to the amazement of all and the gratitude of a few, Hartforde seemed deliberately to shun her.

VI

If Isobel had hoped Julia was correct when she interpreted her brother's actions as a declaration, she was destined for disappointment. In the days that passed, she rarely saw Alexander, unless Angelica Vincent, or occasionally some other handsome brunette, was on his arm. She told herself she did not care and almost convinced herself it was true. She decided if he was so unaffected, then she could at least appear to be the same. She turned her attentions to Lord Strathemoore; of all the men who were pressing suit, he was by far the best-looking.

Strathemoore's own fears were soon assuaged when it became evident Lord Hartforde was no rival as far as Miss St. James was concerned. Still, he felt glad to have persuaded her to ride with him in Hyde Park one morning, and although he was curious to know where she had been the day before, he wisely refrained from questioning her. He did not want to anger her when she finally seemed to be softening toward him. Her very aloofness made him long to be with her, and he considered it as a victory each time he succeeded in making her smile at him. She had been quite attentive to him of late, although it concerned him that she was so secretive about where she spent her time when she was not with him. She adamantly refused to satisfy his curiosity on the subject.

Strathemoore expertly maneuvered the carriage through the gates of Hyde Park, and though he seemed to have his attention fixed on the horses, he glanced several times at Isobel. She was wearing a rose-colored silk gown with elbow-length sleeves tied in two small bows at each cuff. Her dainty straw hat hid most of her face and he found himself admiring the smooth skin rising above the demure neckline of her bodice. She was obviously a modest woman and he sometimes amused himself by imagining what it would be like to awaken passion in her for the first time. He was convinced that under her almost prim exterior was a woman of great sensuality, and he wanted to be the first to discover it. He pulled into the line of carriages without so much as jostling a hair on her head and relaxed now that the horses would do most of the work. She did nothing when he let his hand innocently brush her shoulder, and it emboldened him to let his thigh press against hers. She blushed and looked away, but she did not move. He said something witty and was rewarded with a smile. That breathtaking smile of hers had been turned on him twice already during the ride, and if they had not passed Lord Hartforde and Angelica Vincent in a four-in-hand just as he was about to raise Isobel's hand to his lips, he would have considered the afternoon a complete success. Miss St. James's smile had turned to a frown as soon as Lord Hartforde's open carriage passed them. After that, James was sure Isobel had hardly heard a word he said to her. He found himself wondering if there was anything to the rumors circulating about the two.

"Are you in love with him?"

"In love with whom?" Isobel turned her head around to give him a puzzled look.

"Lord Hartforde. Who else?" He shrugged.

"In love with Lord Hartforde?" She tried to sound incredulous. "What a ridiculous idea! I loathe the man! He's nothing but an arrogant, hateful rogue!" She shut her mouth firmly when she realized she was in danger of protesting too much.

"It's just that you've been so awfully quiet since we passed him." Relieved at her response, he gave her a look he usually reserved for more experienced women.

"Why, Lord Strathemoore, I do believe you're jealous!" She put a small hand on his arm and turned her dark eyes to him.

"Of course I am. I'm jealous of any man who gets more of your attention than I do." Apparently he'd said the right thing, for she gave him another of her dazzling smiles and afterward seemed to hang on his every word.

Isobel was shocked when Strathemoore suddenly asked if she was in love with Alexander. As soon as he had said it, she knew it was true, even though she vehemently denied it. She panicked to think he might have guessed the truth. She wasn't foolish enough to think there was any hope for her where Hartforde was concerned. At least James cared for her.

Chapter 16

I

Isobel hurried home, clasping her arms to her chest for warmth. It was getting darker and colder by the minute. She and Faircourt had been at the rehearsal hall, working on the revision of her first long piece for fortepiano and violins, and it was nearly seven o'clock before she had even thought to look at the watch Julia had bought for her. The work was coming along so well she had been loath to stop, and it was only her desire not to worry Julia that made her leave. To make things worse, she had been unable to find a hackney cab, so she was forced to walk the distance to Albemarle Street, only it was no longer a brisk evening in March, it was a fully dark and cold night! She considered herself lucky it wasn't raining. She wanted only to get to Julia's and change into a proper gown and then go home to her own fireplace. It was easier, and safer by far, for her to change her clothes in one of the unused sections of Hartforde House. To risk being seen at Redruth while dressed as Ian Boxham was unthinkable. At least at Hartforde House Julia could be counted on to provide a rescue if it became necessary. She drew a breath of relief as she let herself in the servants' entrance, thanking the Lord she hadn't been set upon by thieves, or worse. She went through the kitchen and came out into the hall that passed a drawing room where a fire burning in the hearth looked too inviting to ignore. It was so bitterly cold her hands were still numb, and she held them as close to the fire as she dared. Next time, she thought to herself, she would see to it that she had an overcoat and gloves. Just as she was about to turn around to warm her back, she was startled to hear a voice behind her.

"You, boy! What's your name?"

Isobel whirled around, briefly confused, until she remembered she was still dressed as Ian. She suppressed a moment of panic before answering boldly, "Ian Boxham." She nodded her head toward the enormous figure that stood in the doorway. "I was only warming myself, madam."

"Who are you?" With her hands on her hips, Mrs. Peaslea's formidable bulk filled the doorway. "Why haven't I seen you before?" She had seen Isobel come in the servants' entrance and, suspicion aroused, followed her down the hall.

"I'm Emma Carlton's nephew, ma'am. The Lady Julia told me I might stop by of an evening to borrow some books." Emma Carlton was a former servant of Julia's, and Isobel hoped their agreed-upon story—in case someone should see her coming in the servants' entrance—was going to work. It had seemed foolproof when they had settled on it, but now, in front of Mrs. Peaslea, it did not seem so plausible.

"Milady isn't at home." Mrs. Peaslea enunciated each word and crossed her arms over the broad expanse of her chest as she gave her a suspicious look. It was a marvel the woman's hands could reach the distance that separated left from right.

"Then I'll just wait here until she can see me, madam, if you don't mind." Isobel tried to keep her growing panic from showing.

"Aren't we the high-and-mighty one, borrowin' books from the lady? Getting a bit above y'self, ain't you?" Mrs. Peaslea despised such eager and ambitious young men who did not know their proper place. A pleased expression came over her as she thought how she might take this young man down a peg or two, and teach him a lesson about honest work in the bargain.

"Lady Julia has been extremely kind in furthering my education. I would be in your debt if you would be so kind as to tell my lady I am here. I am confident that if you tell her I am here, she will see me, as she was expecting me this evening."

"Not so fast. Y'aren't above a bit of honest work, are you?" A smile pulled at the corners of her wide lips when she carefully emphasized the word "honest," h included. "I need someone to help his lordship. Mr. Peters is come down serious ill. I think you'll do as well as the next." She took a few steps into the room.

"But, madam—"

"You'll be paid for your trouble, if that's what's bothering you. Or do you think you're too good for the work your aunt did? Service 'tweren't too low for your aunt, I vow! Here he comes now!" She glanced over her shoulder. "Look smart for his lordship, do y'hear me?" With a quickness surprising in one of her bounty of flesh, Mrs. Peaslea reached out and grabbed Isobel's arm, pulling her out into the hall after her.

"Where is Mr. Peters, Mrs. Peaslea?" Alexander stopped when he saw the two of them. "I need him now." He was holding a thick packet of correspondence in one hand, and in the other he held a box Isobel supposed contained his seals. She surmised, therefore, that he was on his way to the room where he received callers, and that Mr. Peters was his secretary.

"M'lord, he's taken terrible ill. But Mr. Boxham, here"—she jerked a thumb at Isobel—"can do for you. He's Emma Carlton's nephew."

Isobel kept her head down, deathly afraid he would recognize her and frantically wondering where Julia had got to. If Julia didn't show up soon, Isobel was going to have to go with Lord Hartforde—either that or try to explain why a complete stranger had entered the house through the servants' entrance instead of the front door.

"Very well, then." He shrugged. "Come with me." He raised his eyebrows as Mrs. Peaslea gave Isobel a shove.

"He's a shy one, milord. It's due t'all them fancy books he reads," Mrs. Peaslea snorted as she gave Isobel another push between the shoulders.

"Come along, then."

Surely there could be no difficulty in acting as Lord Hartforde's secretary for a while, Isobel thought, as she followed him up the stairs. She prided herself on writing a good hand. How bad could it be? She would write out a few correspondences, perhaps seal a letter or two, and be on her way. She was behind him as they continued down the hall, so she could not see the thoughtful expression on Alexander's face.

To her great surprise they entered rooms that looked very much as though they were Lord Hartforde's private chambers. She watched him walk to a small desk where he deposited the letters and the box. He shrugged off his coat and held it out for her to take.

"Hang it up over there." He pointed vaguely at one corner. When she had complied, he stood in the center of the room, arms crossed over his chest. "I haven't seen you before. Have you been in service here long?"

"No, my lord. In fact, I'm not actually on the staff."

She did not like his curious gaze, and she prayed he intended to do something besides question her presence in his house.

"How unusual that you find yourself here, then." He raised his hands to his chin and, pressing the tips of his fingers together, gave her a speculative look. "Excuse me a moment." He stepped over to the bellpull and tugged it twice. A moment later a chambermaid came in and he instructed her to draw his bath, then dismissed her.

"Help me with these boots," he said when the girl was gone. He sat down in an armchair and held out his foot.

"Excuse me, my lord," said Isobel in a voice thick with a growing suspicion of disaster.

"Is there something the matter?" He glanced impatiently at his outstretched leg, then back up at her.

"Would you be so kind as to tell me what position is held by Mr. Peters?"

"Mr. Peters is my valet."

"Oh," she said.

"Come, come, young man, I'm not taking a bath with my boots on." He clucked impatiently while Isobel bent down. "You look familiar to me," he said as he extended his other leg to her.

"People say that to me all the time, my lord."

"Fascinating, Mr.—Boxer, was it?" He stood up and began untying his cravat.

"Boxham, my lord."

"Boxham."

"You're not going to undress, are you?" she cried, eyes widening with horror.

"It's customary to do so when one bathes, Mr. Boxham." He began unbuttoning his waistcoat. "Help me off with my clothes, will you?"

"My lord, I—"

"Is there something the matter?" He put his hands

on his hips and stared at her. "Something you feel you ought to tell me?"

"This is all just a dreadful mistake!"

"How so, Mr. Boxham?"

"I thought I was going to write letters for you. I didn't know you meant to undress! I came here to see Julia . . . I mean, Lady Julia, and then Mrs. Peaslea . . . well she saw me and—"

"Do you know," he interrupted calmly, "I am positively convinced I've seen you somewhere before."

"Yes, perhaps you have, but as I was saying, I came here to speak with Lady Julia, and your housekeeper somehow thought . . . well . . . it is entirely impossible for me to help you . . . I'm afraid it's simply been a mistake, and I do apologize for any inconvenience to you, my lord."

"Spare me your excuses, Miss St. James, I quite agree with you." He strode across the room to snatch his coat from the hook upon which Isobel had hung it.

She stared at him. "You knew who I was?" Anger quickly replaced her horror at her predicament.

"Of course." He thrust his arms into his coat.

"And you let me think you didn't know, that you were actually going to undress?" He shrugged and gave his attention to the buttons. "For what possible purpose? Just what did you mean to accomplish? Was it some sort of test?"

"I admit I was curious to see how far you might let matters go."

"Is your curiosity satisfied, my lord?" she snapped. "Tell me, what would you have done if I had not refused?"

"I should have concluded that your character was . . . base." He prevented what was obviously going to be a heated retort by raising his voice. "Surely, Miss St. James, I am entitled to wonder about the character of a woman who goes about dressed as a man." He waved a disdainful hand at her.

"Why do you give a fig about what I do?"

"You Americans are a frighteningly—"

They were both startled when someone knocked loudly on the door. "Hartforde! Is Mr. Boxham in there?" Julia's worried voice came through the door. "Send him out here this minute!"

"Mr. Boxham and I are just coming to the conclusion of a most interesting conversation, Julia. I'll send him out in a moment." He turned back to Isobel. "What possible reason could you have for wanting to masquerade as a man, Miss St. James?"

"It wasn't my idea. I write music—no, Lord Hartforde, I am a composer, and John Faircourt believes I have talent enough that he agreed to work with me. He's helped me immensely! It was his idea. He said if I performed dressed as a man, people would hear only my music, and he was right." She returned his intent gaze.

"I presume Julia knows all about this."

"She gave me the introduction to Mr. Faircourt. And she completely agreed with the idea that I change my clothes here. Father would be livid if he found out. He would never allow me to continue. All he wants is to see that I get married. Lord Hartforde, you're not going to tell him, are you?" She grasped his arm. "You can't tell him!"

He looked at her for a moment before answering. "It means a great deal to you, doesn't it?"

"It means everything to me."

"You needn't worry. I don't intend to tell anyone about your little masquerade."

"Ian Frederick Boxham is considered to be John Faircourt's brightest pupil." She bristled at his tone.

"Miss St. James, you are a very unusual woman, I'll

give you that. But I'm not at all certain I understand this peculiarity of yours."

She shook her head and smiled ruefully. "How odd. I thought if anyone would understand, it would be you."

"I think you had better go before Julia decides you are in need of rescue." He laughed at Isobel's wry expression. "Perhaps, my sweet little Euterpe," he said as she walked toward the door, "you might write a symphony in my honor."

She turned to face him before leaving. "I would if I thought you cared," she said.

"And what if I did?" he whispered as she shut the door after her.

II

"Isobel!" Julia ran to Isobel when she opened the door to Julia's room. "What happened? He didn't find out, did he?"

"No, he did not." The denial was automatic. "His valet is ill and he needed someone to polish his boots," she said sharply. "Mrs. Peaslea saw me and decided I'd do." She quickly began changing her clothes. "What time is it?" she asked. "Father must be wondering where I am."

"Nearly nine." At her frantic look, Julia continued. "Don't worry. I sent word that you were having supper here."

"Why, Miss St. James! What a pleasant surprise! I had no idea you would be supping with us tonight." Alexander smiled his most charming smile.

"'Twas a surprise to myself as well," she said, feeling a little suspicious of his good humor.

The meal was surprisingly gay. Alexander was at his most entertaining, and Isobel laughed in spite of herself. The conversation turned briefly serious when Julia mentioned the current talk of London: a pamphlet viciously attacking the King for his attempts to weaken the Prime Minister. "I've heard," Julia said, "that His Majesty intends to discover the author and exile him."

"George lives in fear of another John Wilkes," Alexander said, dismissing the subject. "But enough of that. After such an excellent meal, I find I am in the mood for music." He turned to Isobel. "Tell me, Miss St. James, do you not play the fortepiano? Would you favor us?"

"If you have your heart set on music, I cannot disappoint you, my lord."

"Excellent!" Alexander rose and escorted them to the music room, where he led Isobel to the fortepiano.

She sat down. "Have you something you'd like to hear?" She played a scale. "Mozart? Handel? Boccherini? I also know all the latest tunes."

"Play anything you like." He sat down and watched as she began to lose herself in the haunting strains of a piece he did not recognize. He had to admit she was possessed of no little skill. He closed his eyes, letting the music wash over him, its sensuous melody winding around him, touching his very heart as the last trembling chords echoed in the room. He opened his eyes to see her looking directly at him and for a moment he had the uncanny feeling he was seeing into her soul, before she looked down and began to play a popular tune that, until now, he had always liked. He said nothing when she finished playing, and at last Isobel colored and turned to Julia.

"It really is quite late." Her words were clipped. "Julia, would you be so kind as to lend me a servant to see me home?"

Alexander stood as he spoke. "I am going out this evening and should be more than happy to see you home first."

"That isn't necessary," Isobel said quickly.

"Nonsense. 'Tis no trouble at all."

"I recognize that tone," Julia said, looking from one to the other. "It means he won't take no for an answer. I'm afraid Hartforde is even more stubborn than you, if such a thing is possible." She, too, stood up. "You played wonderfully, Isobel. Now, if you will excuse me, I am going out myself a little later." She nodded at Alexander when she left, worried about what had really happened between Isobel and her brother.

III

"It seems silly to take a carriage just to go down the street," Isobel said as Alexander helped her in.

"It is for my convenience, not yours." He swung up into the seat across from her after telling the driver to take them first to Redruth. "I shall be continuing on after I drop you. I wanted the chance to speak with you privately. I'm afraid," he said after a moment of silence, "I owe you an apology."

"I believe you do." She drew her cloak tightly around her.

His eyes held hers in the dim light. "I apologize if earlier I failed to take your musical accomplishment seriously. Even I can identify genius when I hear it. That first piece was yours, was it not?"

"Yes!" Isobel was so surprised at his praise she forgot to be nervous at being alone with him. "Did you really like it?" The carriage rolled to a stop.

"Indeed, I did." Alexander signaled the driver to stay where he was. "Perhaps I understand your peculiarity after all." He was smiling at her, and she was powerless to look away, just as she was powerless to stop him when he unexpectedly moved to her side and bent his head to her mouth. Once again, she felt that dizzy sensation and she clung to him, wanting more, yet not knowing what it was she wanted. "Isobel," he groaned in her ear. His hands circled her waist as he took her lips in a soft kiss. His touch was making her head whirl and she heard his words through a fog of passion. She leaned against him as his hands stroked her throat. Dreamily she found herself looking up into green eyes darkened with desire. "What a trusting little creature you are," he said softly. "You are fortunate I am a man of honor, or else—"

"Or else what?" She smiled.

He reached across her to open the door to the carriage. "Or else"—he took a deep breath—"I would not be sending you home right now." He stepped down from the carriage to help her out and lifted her hand to his lips when she was standing beside him. "Will you permit me to call on you?"

"Whenever you like, my lord," she said breathlessly.

Alexander waved off his footman as he got back inside. As he sat, looking at nothing in particular, the walls of the carriage seemed to close in on him. He pulled down the glass and stared out at the street. Had he really asked permission to call on her? The words had just come out; it wasn't as though he actually meant them. An entanglement with Isobel St. James was the last thing he wanted.

Chapter 17

The night Preston Hawes lost one hundred pounds to Mr. William Fordham had turned out to be the luckiest night of his life. It was obvious Fordham was connected with someone of considerable influence, and Hawes was almost certain he knew who it was. The more he proved he could keep things to himself, the more money Fordham paid him for copying. And the more sensitive the documents got, the more he was going to ask for. Hawes sipped from his glass, smiling because at last he was able to indulge his taste for fine port.

He had been accepted at two clubs in London, but Brook's, more popularly known as the Savoir Vivre, in particular was a triumph over his undistinguished background. Nominally a coffeehouse, it was renowned for the high stakes and drinking that went on inside its hallowed walls. There was a steady hum of low voices coming from the men gathered around the gaming tables, punctuated now and then by moans of despair or words of encouragement, as was appropriate to the case. Winners there were never so vulgar as to shout. In its fashionable interior, the port flowed like water, and though food could be had, few bothered to leave the tables for it. They merely waited for the serving-men who scurried around to replace empty bottles with full ones. The fortunes gambled there each night were astounding. These aristocrats lost ruinous sums without so much as a blink, and it required all of Hawes's poise to seem unconcerned when thousands of pounds were bet on a single rubber. Of course, he didn't have enough money, not yet, anyway, to join the high-stakes games, but he enjoyed cards as much as the next man.

Lord Hartforde, with whom he sat now at the card table, was as good a gambler as he had ever met. Hawes had played with the marquess once before and had counted himself lucky to come out only a little behind.

"So, Mr. Hawes, any relation to the Manchester Haweses?" Hartforde asked conversationally as he dealt the cards.

"On my mother's side, Marquess," he lied.

For a time they were silent while they played. Hawes played badly. He could not help wondering what Lord Hartforde would do if he were to tell him everything he knew and everything he suspected. He wondered how much his information would be worth to a man who stood to lose everything.

Chapter 18

I

By the end of March, Isobel was devoting herself almost exclusively to working with Faircourt on their upcoming subscription concert at which her first symphony was to be performed. Up to this point, even her longer compositions had not been written for a full orchestra, and although Faircourt's opinion of the symphony was positive, when she heard the orchestra playing the work in its entirety, two of the movements sounded so dismal that she almost despaired of it. Only Faircourt's continued encouragement prevented her from giving it up.

Because she and Faircourt were rehearsing with the orchestra almost daily, Julia had insisted on Isobel staying at Hartforde House, and Isobel had gratefully agreed. It meant she would not be faced with having to make difficult excuses to her father regarding her whereabouts. The earl did not seem to care how often his daughter went out, or even where she went, so long as it was fashionable, but he made a point of asking about her outings so that he might offer his opinions on them.

At Isobel's suggestion, Julia had taken the precaution of explaining to Mrs. Godwaite that it would be necessary for Mr. Boxham to enter the house frequently because he was providing sample work for some vaguely-alluded-to project of great importance to her ladyship. If Mrs. Godwaite ever wondered exactly what the project was, it was not her place to ask questions.

Lord Chessingham was pleased enough at the arrangement; he thought Isobel was spending her time with society and in proximity to Lord Hartforde. In truth, Isobel's only reservation about staying at Hartforde House was due to her dread of seeing its owner.

After the night when the marquess had asked permission to call on her, Isobel had spent one entire week overcome with happiness, but as days went by without his appearance or sending so much as a note, her happiness turned to confusion, then resentment, and when she finally did happen to see him, the meeting was marred by a curious tension. His failure to call on her or explain his neglect went deliberately unacknowledged, and it had created a wall of reserve between them.

She generally woke up at eight and had a leisurely breakfast alone by half past. Julia, of course, did not arise until much later in the day. So far she had not seen Lord Hartforde even once during her stay, until one morning when he joined her at breakfast. To her great surprise, they got on quite well, but then she knew he could be charming when he wanted to be. Her triumph came the very next day, when he joined her again. She would never forget the look on his face when their conversation concerning Virgil was interrupted by the arrival of Lord Strathemoore, who had come to take her riding in Hyde Park. She jokingly

told Lord Hartforde it was only this interruption that
had saved him from having to admit her point. On her
way out, she wished with all her heart that he would
be stricken dead with jealousy. To think she had be-
grudged Lord Strathemoore this morning out!

II

   It was after ten o'clock one night at the beginning of
April when Isobel finally finished the last of the
changes in her symphony. Faircourt and the musicians
had long since gone home and she was alone in the
huge rehearsal hall. Her manuscript was full of corrections, but she was confident that when it came back
from the printer's this time the only changes necessary
would be corrections of the printer's errors. She
stretched, stood to gather the papers strewn over the
desk into a neat pile before putting them into her case,
then walked to the door, pulling on her coat all the
while. She called out to her coachman to bring around
the carriage and waited impatiently for it to come, for,
in spite of her overcoat and heavy clothes, she was
cold. The air felt heavy with moisture and she was certain it would soon rain. "To Albemarle Street," she
instructed when the coachman finally pulled up.
   The linkboy stifled a yawn as the door shut after Mr.
Boxham, and when the coachman climbed back up to
his seat, he pulled his coat closer about him. The light
of the linkboy's torch made a dim yellowish halo that
bounced with each trotting step he took.
   The exhaustion Isobel had been holding at bay all
day hit her as soon as she sat down. She told herself
that after a nice hot bath she would climb into bed for
some much needed sleep. Or maybe, she thought, as
her eyes began to droop, she would just climb into
bed; a bath could wait until the morning. It had been
an exhausting few weeks. She was working feverishly

to have the symphony perfect in time for the performance in May, just six weeks hence. The rehearsals
were tiring, but she never put down the baton without
a feeling of regret or without looking forward to the
next time, especially now that she was so much more
comfortable in front of the orchestra.

She was asleep when shouts and the sudden halt of
the carriage jolted her to wakefulness. There was more
shouting and then the carriage door was pulled open
and rough hands dragged her out onto the street. It
was dark and almost impossible to tell where they
were, but she guessed it was somewhere around Charing Cross.

"A bit young to be out so late, aren't you, lad?"
drawled the man who had pulled her out of the carriage.

Her coachman was lying on his back in the street,
his contorted face so still that Isobel knew he was dead.
She looked away from the dark pool of blood around
his head.

"Don't you know it's dangerous to be out so late?"
said another shorter and stouter man, laughing to himself as he spoke. There were five or six of them; all
were armed.

"I haven't any money, if that's what you're after."
Isobel was surprised her voice was not trembling with
the fear churning in her stomach. She clutched her
packet of music to her with one hand, and with the
other slid her fingers around the dagger she kept in her
pocket.

"'Tis a bloody shame if true, young fellow," said
the tallest of them, apparently the leader. In the dim
light cast by the carriage lamp she could not see his
features, except to tell he was dark-haired. "Surely you
have something of value." He stepped into the faint
circle of light emanating from the carriage, eyeing the
case she was holding. Isobel was shocked to see he was

a handsome man with a pleasant, friendly look at odds
with the threat in his stance.

"There's nothing in it except my music, of value to
no one but myself." As her fingers tightened around
the case, her only thought was that she would prefer to
die than risk losing her symphony.

"Do you believe him, boys?" There was a chorus of
no's from the group behind him. The man shook his
head ruefully. "The lads don't seem to believe you."
He took a step forward, reaching out for the pouch.

"One more step and you'll lose the hand!" Isobel
clenched the dagger in her fist and backed up against
the side of the carriage.

"Surely, whatever is in there isn't worth your life?"
the leader said and, with a lightning-quick movement,
leaped forward and twisted her arm around behind
her. Her numb fingers loosened around the knife and
she felt him take it out of her now-shaking hand. He
grinned as he took it and she found herself with the
point of the dagger at her stomach. "Perhaps you'd
care to rethink the matter?"

Slowly, she held out the pouch. The man took it
and, not taking his eyes off her, handed it to one of his
henchmen.

"He was telling the truth, George—'tis only paper!"
The ruffian sounded exasperated. They had all had
their hopes raised by the boy's fierce protection of the
case. He threw the pouch down in disgust. George
smiled wickedly and pressed the point of the dagger
into her stomach.

"What a bloody shame." He shook his head in disappointment.

"Do you remember the time we stripped old Geof-
frey Shoringham?" one of the men sniggered. The
memory was amusing, for it caused general laughter
among the group.

"All he had left was his peruke!" one called out.

George reached out and yanked on Isobel's hair. "This one hasn't—" A surprised expression came over his face as the wig came off in his hand. "What have we here?" He cocked his head at her. "Damme, 'tis a wench, lads!"

"Someone's coming!" The man holding the horses shouted the alarm.

Isobel struggled when George clamped a hand around her arm, and she held onto the door of the carriage as he tried to shove her inside. She cried out in terror before his hand covered her mouth. She screamed anyway when she felt a sharp pain in her arm.

III

Rupert Selwynn was headed for White's for an evening of cards when he heard a commotion down the street. He put his head out the coach window so he could instruct the driver to go around if there was trouble. He cursed when his carefully curled hair was bombarded by several large drops of rain. Just as he was pulling his head back inside, he saw that a group of men had surrounded a carriage and seemed to be in earnest conversation with a smaller man who had his back to it. The taller man reached out and pulled on the other one's hair. Surely, Rupert thought to himself, gentlemen might be left to settle their differences in peace. He was just on the point of telling his coachman to go another way when he heard a cry for help. To his horror, his driver suddenly shouted and whipped up the horses and they careened down the street toward the group.

"You fool!" Rupert shouted. "Stop this instant!"

The men scattered when they heard the carriage coming, and Rupert caught a glimpse of a frightened young man sitting on the street where one of the men had shoved him. From what Rupert could see, he appeared to be reaching for his hat. Rupert's coachman jumped down and ran toward the man who was now calmly placing his hat back on his head. As soon as Rupert was sure the men were gone, he started to step down from the carriage. It was raining in torrents now and he paused with one foot on the steps so he was still protected from the rain. At that moment, his linkboy arrived, breathless from running after the carriage.

"You all right, Mr. Selwynn?" he asked, panting, barely able to hold up the torch that, in any event, had been effectively quenched by the downpour.

"Make sure they're all gone!" Selwynn peered out into the dark and then swung his head back to the other carriage. His driver reached the man just as he was picking himself up and held out a hand to help him.

"My music!" he cried when he was on his feet. He pointed at a leather case lying where it had been thrown to the side of the road.

The coachman bent to pick it up and handed it to him.

"Oh, thank you!" he said as he hugged it to him. His hat perched on his head in a tilted, bedraggled mess.

"Are you all right, sir?" asked Selwynn's coachman.

"I think so," he responded. "What about my driver?" The coachman shook his head.

The linkboy came back to report that the gentleman's driver was dead, and he was about to go investigate the gentleman himself when Selwynn shouted at him, "Come back here!" He trotted back obediently. "Tell the gentleman he is welcome to any help he may need." The fact that the young man's carriage was a fine one was not lost on Selwynn. The boy nodded and picked his way back through the puddles forming on the road. A few minutes later, the young man sat down with a squish of his overcoat on one of Selwynn's fine leather seats. "Mr. Rupert Selwynn, at your service," he said.

"Mr. Ian Boxham," Isobel responded after a momentary silence. "Thank you, Mr. Selwynn. You have my most sincere gratitude." She brushed away the water dripping down her cheeks. "I do think they meant to do me harm!"

"What can I do to help you, Mr. Boxham? I'm afraid your driver has suffered the worst." He was about to add he would lend his postilion as a driver, but he was interrupted.

"I've got to get home! Can you take me to Albemarle Street?"

"Albemarle Street?" Rupert was suitably impressed.

"Yes, number ten Albemarle Street."

"I'd be delighted to take you there."

"Oh! But what about my coach?"

"I'll have my postilion drive it back." Before Boxham could object, Selwynn leaned out the window and gave the instructions. "Well, Mr. Boxham," he said after he had pulled up the window, "very few men can call number ten Albemarle home."

"I'm staying there only for a few days."

IV

The butler pulled open the door of Hartforde House and Mr. Selwynn smoothly filled in the silence that elapsed when the boy said nothing. "Tell my Lord Hartforde that his guest, Mr. Boxham, has been robbed, but he is quite safe now."

The butler looked nonplussed and was about to answer when a voice behind him saved him the trouble.

"Mr. Boxham?"

Selwynn was sure he saw the young man wince at the sound of Lord Hartforde's voice.

"And Mr. Rupert Selwynn." Lord Hartforde
stepped into the entranceway.

"My lord." He bowed. "I happened to be on the
scene just as Mr. Boxham was being robbed. He gave
me to understand he is your guest, and as his driver
was killed and his linkboy fled, I offered to see him
home in my carriage. I've had my postilion drive the
carriage back." He pulled out his watch and looked
surprised at the lateness of the hour. "'Pon my word!
'Tis past eleven! If you will excuse me, my lord, I have
an urgent appointment. Good evening."

"Thank you, Mr. Selwynn!" Mr. Boxham said fervently as Rupert turned to go. "You saved my life. I
shall not forget it."

"Mr. Boxham, would you be so kind as to come
with me?" Alexander's face was tense and his green
eyes were dark with an emotion Isobel was convinced
meant no good for her. "Smatherson, please take Mr.
Boxham's coat and send a bottle of brandy to my
rooms."

"Yes, milord." His expression was blank while he
helped Isobel struggle out of her sopping-wet coat.

Alexander got a firm grip on her arm.

"Let go of me!" she snapped, vainly trying to pull
away from him.

He held her firmly by the arm and propelled her forward. "You're coming with me, you little witch!" he
hissed.

"You are quite mistaken, my lord, I am not going
anywhere with you!" She planted her feet resolutely
but found herself being pushed along anyway. He kept
a tight grip on her shoulder as he guided her up the
stairs to his rooms. "I don't think you're being quite
the gracious host to force me into your rooms," she
said snidely when he had closed the door behind them.

"You may go, Peters. I won't be needing you anymore tonight." When the valet was gone, Alexander

turned to Isobel. "It isn't as though you haven't been in here before," he remarked. He saw her flush at his words and an amused smile came to his lips.

A servant arrived with a bottle of brandy and two glasses soon after them. He took the tray and set it down on a table, then locked the door when the footman was gone. He filled the two glasses and handed one to Isobel, waiting until she had sipped from the glass before saying anything. "Miss St. James, would you be so gracious as to tell me what were you doing out so late?" He seated himself in the only comfortable chair in the anteroom. His mouth was set in an angry line as he gave her a cold stare.

"I fail to see how it's any of your affair, Lord Hartforde," she retorted, pulling off her hat and throwing it onto one of the chairs, where it landed with a slap. She was tired and wet and getting colder by the minute. He had to know she was longing to sit down, not to mention that she needed some dry clothes. She remained standing because it would suit her just fine if she fainted dead away from his shocking treatment. She pictured his lordship bending over her prostrate body after she had finally fainted, her sopping-wet clothes staining the expensive rug beneath their feet, his face ashen with distress as he clasped her limp body to his breast.

"It is my affair," he said, "when you are visiting my house and you endanger your life in such a reckless fashion. I have a duty to your father to see you are safe here, however unwelcome a guest you might be." He sipped from his glass.

"I am not your guest, Lord Hartforde, I am here at your sister's invitation." She took a deep swallow of the brandy and barely managed to suppress a cough as the liquor burned down her throat.

"Whether you are here at the invitation of my sister, or anyone else, does not make the slightest difference.

Must I remind you I can forbid your presence here? This is my house and it is on my sufferance alone that you are permitted to carry on this ridiculous game of yours." His eyes swept disdainfully over her.

She didn't respond to his spiteful words; instead, she drained her glass and held it out to him. He refilled it without getting up from his comfortable seat. "Sir, I apologize for endangering your reputation as a gracious host." She took another gulp of the brandy before continuing. "You force me to admit the truth. I asked those ruffians to stop me and, yes, I planned for my driver to die in my defense so I might be robbed and killed myself. Why, as soon as I saw them, I told them they ought to rob me. I was a fool to think you wouldn't find me out. But, I promise your lordship, the next time I am set upon by thieves, I shall endeavor to do so as far away from you as possible. And should things go well, I won't be so unlucky as to be rescued." She swallowed half the contents of the glass and blinked as she suddenly began to feel the effect of the brandy. She gulped most of the rest of the glass.

"Don't compound your errors by becoming drunk," he said dourly.

"I don't see how it's any concern of yours." Really, she thought, he had no right to talk to her as though she were some sort of errant child!

"It is if I have to carry you to your bed. You are trouble enough sober."

Isobel took a step past him, heading for the bottle, only to have him stop her by grasping her forearm. "My lord, I have had about as much of your shocking rudeness as I can take," she said as primly as she could. "I am cold, I am tired, and in case you haven't noticed, I am dripping water all over your lovely carpet. If you won't allow me to change into some dry clothes, I shall catch my death, and rest assured, I shall see to it the full blame for my demise is placed on you. Now, are you going to let me alone, or not?"

"My dear Miss St. James"—he did not let go of her arm—"I am not stopping you from changing out of your clothes. Be my guest! There is a dressing gown over there." He pointed with his free hand. "But, I do insist that you not drink anymore. You have had quite enough."

"Then may I suggest you let go of me, my lord? Where may I change?" she asked after he complied.

"Here is perfectly all right with me," he said.

"You may go to the devil, sir!" She drained her glass and held it out until he took it. If his lordship wanted her to undress in front of him, then he might just as well have his wish. And if he so much as laid a hand on her she would bring the house down with her screams. She strode over to where a dressing gown was draped over a chair and began working at the buttons of her frock coat. She let if fall to the floor and in another moment had shrugged out of her waistcoat. At the last minute, she found that, in spite of her intention to humiliate him, she could not undress in front of him, so she took the dressing gown and walked past him into his bedchamber.

"Blast it, woman!" He jumped up from his chair and in two strides was at her side.

"I thought you said I might get out of my clothes," she said, taking a step backward when he reached her.

"You should have told me you were hurt."

"What?" She followed his glance to her arm and was surprised to see that blood stained the sleeve. "Oh," she said softly. "What are you doing?"

He grabbed her arm and when she looked up at him she felt her head swimming. Whether it was from the sight of blood on her shirt or from his being so close to her, she did not know.

"Your arm needs to be looked at. I can call a physic, if you insist, but I rather expect you would prefer the staff should not find out about this." He raised his eyebrows at her and then continued, not having expected an answer. "Now, just be quiet for once, would you?" He shrugged off his own coat and threw it on a chair. Guiltily, she noticed he was dressed to go out; he had obviously taken a great deal of care with his appearance. She felt a stab of jealousy as she thought he had probably been on his way to see Angelica Vincent. She knew she was staring at him, but she couldn't seem to look away. "Sit down," he ordered.

"Where?" She didn't like the way he addressed her as though she were a servant, and, really, couldn't he be even the least bit sympathetic? After all, she was wounded! She looked at her arm and suddenly felt the throbbing all the more acutely.

"Anywhere!" He pushed her down on the bed and scowled at the look of resentment on her face. From the sideboard, he retrieved a bowl of water, and on his way back to her, he picked up a chair. He pulled her upright from her supine contemplation of the folds in the canopy. Lines of worry creased his forehead, and she sucked in her breath as he gathered up the material to tear the shoulder. "Hold still!"

"It hurts," she moaned. And really, now that she could see the blood, it did hurt, like the very dickens.

"Would you rather I take it off?" he asked sarcastically.

"Yes!"

Sighing, he went into the other room, then came back with one of the glasses and the bottle of brandy. He splashed some into the glass, drank it himself, then refilled it and handed it to her. He began undoing her cravat as she drank, and when their hands briefly tangled he gave the sigh of one whose patience was being sorely tried. He waited for her to empty the glass be-

fore finishing the job and pulling open the neck of her
shirt. The wound was impossible to get at without
pulling the shirt off at least one side of her. Isobel sat
with her eyes closed, while he tried to pull the other
half of the shirt down over her exposed torso.

"It would appear, milord, that modesty cannot be
effected without risking my strangulation," she intoned while opening one eye to see if he had appreciated her wit. He had not.

"Sit here." He stood up to change places with her,
turning her sideways on the chair as he began to dab at
her arm with the cloth he had dampened in the bowl of
water. She winced in pain. "You look ridiculous with
that thing strapped to your belly!" he snapped, jerking
his head toward the pillow tied around her stomach.

"All right, then." She struggled to get the rest of the
shirt off, while keeping her other arm still. Using her
good arm, she managed to undo the fastenings that
held the pillow to her. "I hope I don't offend you now,
Lord Hartforde." She threw the pillow away. To her
amazement, she discovered she was having trouble sitting up straight and she wondered if, just perhaps, the
brandy might have gone to her head. She watched him
bending over her arm, fascinated first by the shape of
his jaw, then by the pulse beating in his neck. She
wanted to trace the firm lines of his face and she
flushed when their eyes met briefly. With sudden clarity she remembered the way his lips had once taken
hers.

"Be still, damn you!" He dabbed some more at the
wound, softening his touch when she gasped in pain.

"It's rather close in here, don't you think?" she
asked as he wiped away the remaining blood. He did
not bother to respond. "How odd. It barely hurts
now." She looked down at her arm, puzzled that it
should be so, since not five minutes ago it had hurt like
the devil.

"It's all the brandy, love," he said gently. "I don't think it's very deep, just a scratch." He folded her cravat into a strip and wrapped it around her arm.

She looked down at the neat bow he tied. "Will I live, then?" She looked at him and thought he was more beautiful than the drawing of Michelangelo's David she had once seen. She blushed at the direction her thoughts were taking. Really, it was far too hard to concentrate!

"Yes, I think so," he said, making no attempt to lift his gaze.

"What a disappointment it must be to you." She flushed anew as she realized where his gaze was fixed and how very little of her shirt was covering her body. Mortified, she pulled at the material and crossed her arms over herself, not taking her eyes off the floor until he stood up to fetch his dressing gown.

"Here, cover yourself if you feel that modesty is suddenly necessary." The expression on his face was an odd one, though she could tell it was not anger. She grabbed at the dressing gown he tossed at her. It slid off her lap onto the floor.

"I don't annoy you on purpose, Lord Hartforde," she said in a small voice. She was remembering, however unwillingly, the way he had touched her, the play of his muscles under his skin, how his lips on hers had made her giddy.

"I know you don't." He drew in a deep breath as she picked up the garment, watching her struggle to find the top of it. She had grabbed it by the hem, and if he hadn't been so exasperated he would have thought her expression comical. "If you don't cover yourself, Miss St. James, I won't answer to the consequences," he warned.

Her face went scarlet with shame when at last she had to shake the dressing gown to find one of the sleeves. She rose a little unsteadily as she thrust her good arm through it. She was gingerly doing the same with her other arm when he reached out and yanked it closed. He expelled a sharp sigh, suddenly aware he had been holding his breath. She swayed and he was still grasping the material in his hands when she put her hands to his chest to balance herself.

"You would find me more than you bargained for, Isobel," he growled when she did not move away from him but continued to stare up at him.

"Would I?" she whispered. She wondered again if she was drunk, she felt so wonderfully light-headed! But she didn't care if she was, because at that moment all she wanted was for him to kiss her. When she leaned against him she felt his heartbeat quicken, the proof of his desire. His eyes seemed to darken at her words and she felt a thrill go through her as she saw the answer to her question. Slowly, almost reluctantly, he lowered his head to hers, and when she lifted her face to his, he groaned. Her befuddled mind knew only that he was responding to the pressure of her hands on the back of his neck by leaning forward and kissing her urgently, his lips firm and demanding against hers. She felt a giddiness overtake her and she relaxed against him. Surely this was as close to heaven as it was possible to get without actually going to the trouble of dying. Her head swam as he picked her up and carried her the few steps to the bed. Nothing could be more like heaven than to have this man kissing her. She wanted it to go on forever.

"I would give anything, Isobel, if I could just stop thinking about you," he said fiercely as he pulled off her shoes and hose. His fingers trembled as he pulled open the dressing gown to unbutton her breeches and pull them off her.

She meant to protest at what he was doing, but suddenly his warm hands were stroking her bare legs, moving up to capture her aching breasts, and when he gently pulled the heavy silk robe off her, careful not to hurt her arm, she shivered as cool air whispered over her nakedness. He was crooning her name in her ear and then his tongue ran wetly down her throat to linger at the top of her chest. His hands moved over her, his fingers pressed into her, his clothes scraped her skin and sent little shivers up to center in her belly. She let out a ragged breath when she felt his fingers on her breasts, brushing lightly over her nipples until she could think of nothing but his touch. She moaned when his hands moved away from her breasts, only to gasp at the sensation of his lips replacing his hands. She opened her eyes and focused her attention on Alexander's golden hair. The thought that this was wrong began to penetrate her fogged mind, but somehow, it was hard to believe it when she felt as though she might melt right into the bed from the pleasure of his touch. She had once believed she could never be tempted to fall, and now she was finding out how enormously, wonderfully wrong she had been. Her head was spinning and all she could think of was how thoroughly he overwhelmed her. He trailed kisses up to her throat, and when he finally covered her lips with his, she felt all the tension go out of her as she gave herself up to the pleasure his hands were creating in her. Nothing mattered except that she was in his arms. . . .

Alexander was surprised at how tense she was, and he was equally surprised when he suddenly felt her relax. He deepened his kiss as she moaned and arched herself against him. He gently ran his tongue over her teeth and then into her mouth, and his kiss became one of triumphant possession. She was his and he meant to take her as she had never been taken before. His hands stroked her gently rounding breasts, and when he felt her becoming taut under his fingers, he bent his head to a nipple. He felt a visceral spark fanned into flame by her groaning response to his touch. He reached up to pull off her ridiculous man's wig, loosening her hair until he could twine his fingers in the golden curls that spilled over the bed-cover. "I've wanted this for so long. . . . You know that," he whispered into her ear, tracing its delicate outline with his tongue before taking her mouth again. His hands stroked down her sides before moving over to the triangle between her legs, covering her for a moment before he sat up and, eyes locked with hers, began to unfasten his clothes so he could feel her against him without the nuisance of any covering. A smile pulled at the corner of his mouth when he saw that her eyes never left him while he undressed, though they briefly dropped downward when his breeches and underclothes dropped to the floor. He slid next to her on the bed and pulled her on top of him, throwing one lean leg over hers and groaning at the feel of her warm skin on his. She seemed to weigh practically nothing, yet when her breasts pressed against his chest the weight of her was nearly unbearable. He could taste the brandy on her mouth as she kissed him, her hair falling like a golden veil around their heads. His hands pulled her waist tightly against him and he arched his hips so she would feel the hardened length of him pressing into her. He continued kissing her, marveling, while his hands searched her curves, that any woman could be as perfectly shaped as she was. She moved her hips against him in answer to the pressure of his hands on her. Still holding her, he rolled over to press her into the soft mattress. She seemed not to know what to do with her hands, and because he was mad to have her touch him as he did her, he placed them on his back. "Touch me, Isobel," he ordered softly. Her fingers lightly stroked his shoulders, then, so slowly it was almost a torture, traced the muscles of his back down to his waist. "You are perfect," he groaned, lowering his lips to a breast. He heard her gasp as he lightly bit one nipple, then the other. "A moment, love," he said softly

after she tried to pull him back when he got up to douse
all the candles but the one on the bedstand. Her skin
gleamed palely in the darkened room. He ran a finger
down her long legs, watching the shiver that followed
his touch. "I've dreamed of you often, Isobel," he said in
a low voice, "but the reality far exceeds my imagination." He bent to kiss her again, and when she pulled him
down to her and curved against him he found the passion
he was arousing in her was more powerfully erotic than
the passion she wrought in him, and soon he could not
tell the difference.

Tentatively she ran her hands over Alexander's sweat-
slickened body. Hard muscles tensed and relaxed under
smooth skin as he touched her in ways that made her
quiver. She hadn't known he wanted her to touch him
until he placed her hands on his back, and now she could
no longer think; she was caught up in wave after wave of
spiraling pleasure. His fingers were probing her and she
cried out his name as she felt as though she were suddenly, deliciously, falling from an immense height. His
breath was warm on her face and she was relaxed completely when she felt him move over her, his thighs
between hers, hard against her own smooth skin. His lips
brushed hers and then he was kissing her, his chest
pressing her back into the bed. She felt him probing
between her parted thighs, and, because she was aching
with unfulfilled need, she was willing, anxious, to do
whatever he demanded of her. She felt she would do
anything and let him do anything. At this moment, she
would have trusted him with her life. She could think of
nothing but him and how often she had dreamed of him
whispering her name and kissing her until she was senseless. Her entire being was concentrated on this moment,
on his hands and lips touching her, the feel of his body
on, over, and next to hers, the texture of his hair, the taste
of him, the sound of his whispered endearments. She felt
his hardness thrusting inside her and she was suddenly

and painfully surprised at the sensation. He continued to push and she squeezed her eyes shut against a searing pain. She tensed, biting her lower lip when his hips jerked forward again. At last she could bear it no more and she tried to make him stop, but he had such a firm grip on her waist as he pushed once more that she could not twist away from him. She cried out in pain and then he was filling her body so intimately that when he cursed at her she could not keep back the tears crowding behind her tightly shut eyes.

The feel of her silken body against his was too much; he could wait no longer. He shifted until he was on top of the smooth, sleek figure moving under him so that he half-thought he might erupt just from the pleasure of it. She was so completely relaxed when he parted her thighs and began to slide himself into her that he was surprised at how awkward she was at helping him to accomplish it. When he met resistance his desire was so overpowering that he did not realize he was the first with her until he had thrust once more. And then it was too late. He was inside her before her cry of pain could stop him. "Bloody hell!" he heard himself say. He was dimly aware he had ruined her, but right now, when he was so close to fulfillment with a woman he had wanted for such an achingly long time, it never occurred to him to stop. "Hush, love," he whispered, tasting salty tears when he kissed her cheek. "I promise you, I won't hurt you anymore." He cursed again, but this time it was from the quivering pleasure of moving inside her. She was hot and slick and so damnably and enticingly tight around him that he felt his world quickly narrowing to just that one area of joining. The thought that she was a virgin and that he ought to be gentle completely left him as an overpowering passion began to take over his body, and he wanted nothing except what their joined flesh promised him. His kiss was one of possession until he felt the

beginning of a shuddering climax. Involuntarily, he
hoarsely repeated her name. There was nothing but him
and her and his aching, pulsing inches of flesh demanding
to be satisfied. When the torment consuming him finally
ended in a shattering release of his entire being into her,
his fingers dug into her shoulders until at last he could lie,
breathless but quiet, on her bewitching body.

Isobel lay tense and sobbing when Alexander cursed
at her. The heady exhilaration was gone. He had hurt
her and she was not inclined to believe him when he
told her it would not hurt anymore. She felt his lips
brush her cheeks and then he was cursing again and
moving inside her. He kissed her, taking her lips with
a tenderness that almost made her forget the pain. His
head was bent over hers, and when she heard the passion in his voice as he called out her name, she opened
her eyes. A thrill went through her when she saw the
intensity of his expression. His lips were parted in a
panting curve and she saw him catch his lower lip between his teeth and then heard him groan. "Oh, my
love," he said with a hoarse sigh. She looked between
them and saw his ridged abdomen rising and falling
against her belly. The pain was forgotten, fading into
the back of her mind as he took her head between his
hands and kissed her again. His lips found her shoulder
and she felt his teeth on her, gentle. He threw back his
head and then his eyes opened and he looked at her
while he moved in her. His hands gripped her shoulders and she could not look away from the vulnerable
passion she saw in him. Then his fingers were tightening on her and she felt his body shuddering and she
held him close while he cried out her name.

"Ah, Isobel," he murmured as he moved off her and
lay beside her. After a moment he turned her tear-
streaked face to him. "Wait," he said, getting up from
the bed. He made his way to the water basin. Taking a

towel lying next to it, he wet it and cleaned himself off. He wet it again and went back to the bed and gently wiped away the blood staining her thighs. "I never thought—I did not expect to be the first," he said, at a momentary loss for words when he began to appreciate the consequences his rashness might have for the both of them. "I could not stop." He shook his head. "I should have once I knew you were . . ."—a pause—". . . but, my God! I was mad for you!" As he looked into her darkened eyes, he thought to himself it would be sheer folly to continue with her. He took her hand. "You should have told me. I would never—" He stopped because he found he could not say what he knew to be an untruth. "What have we done?" He shook his head when she sat up. He leaned forward, intending only to kiss her cheek, but instead he groaned as his arms went around her and he buried his face in her hair. "Isobel, no," he said roughly when he felt her hands on his thighs. He pushed her away and lay back on the bed, willing his body not to respond to her touch. Surely, he told himself, he had imagined the sensations she had aroused in him. She was nothing more than an infuriating young girl whose naïveté and willfulness had momentarily made him forget thirty-one years of good breeding. He tensed when he felt her hand on his belly, but her lightly brushing fingers sent shivers through him. She bent to kiss him, and even though he knew he should push her away, the flesh of her waist curved so deliciously to slim flanks that he opened his mouth under the gentle pressure of her lips to let her slip her tongue inside, to let her kiss him passionately, touching all the surfaces of his mouth. He felt himself responding to her caresses and he almost pulled her back when she put her hands on his chest and pushed away from him.

"It excites me to touch you this way," she said as her hands moved caressingly over him. "I want to touch you. . . ." She kissed his nipples, running her hands over his arms. The effect was electrifying. He closed his eyes as she softly kissed his face, then trailed light fingers down the ridges of his smooth, muscled chest. "I want to know all of you." She kissed his stomach and moved down to his legs. She kissed the insides of his thighs and he no longer wanted to stop her. Her lips were searching for and finding every sensitive area of his body. He could no more have stopped her than he could have stopped breathing. She began to kiss his belly, sliding down to kiss his hardening member, and when her mouth slid over him, he groaned. She looked up, her face darkened by shadows.

"Don't stop!" he gasped, and pushed her head back down. She pressed her lips to him and as she ran her tongue down the length of him he reached down and tangled his fingers in her hair. He felt her take him in her mouth and he groaned again, pressing her head down. Her tongue was wet and hot on him, sliding around him, and her hands on him brought him to a shivering climax. He cradled her in his arms, slowly stroking the smooth curves of her. He forgot the short moment ago when he had promised himself he would not touch her again. Now, though, he was not so desperate for her that he could not take the time to make her desperate for him. He kissed her neck, her shoulders, her breasts, and slowly moved down to the junction between her legs and began to kiss her there, using his tongue as she had used hers on him moments ago. She cried out when his hands stroked her, and as soon as he felt her release, he pulled himself up and trailed kisses back up to her parted lips. "You are mine," he whispered as he slowly entered her, eyes fixed on the face that had been haunting his dreams. She wrapped her arms around him and her breath began to come in pants and it was hot on his cheek and he was caught up in the moment, lost in the whirling storm of passion she was creating in him. This time, their bodies sought each other, fitting together with a perfect sweetness that took his breath away. He propped himself up on his elbows, just above her shoulders, his hips moving, thrusting, and he was filling her, sliding, pushing into her deeper and deeper. She was throbbing around him and he found himself swept up in a burst of ecstasy that ended only in an abandonment so intense he barely heard their cries of passion as he felt his seed empty into the body moving so exquisitely beneath his.

Isobel clung to his slick shoulders, feeling his muscles bunching and relaxing, and then she could think no more, could only cry out when she felt herself swirling, fluttering, searching for something only his body could give her. With her arms tightened around him, she heard him urging her on, dimly, telling her to give herself to him. And she did, in waves of crashing pleasure, until they were both breathless and consumed by it.

Later, he heard her whisper his name. Her voice was shy and he pulled her close because he wanted to have her next to him.

"Yes, love?" he said into her hair, breathing in its sweet fragrance.

"Are you sorry . . . about this?"

"My own, it should never have happened," he said. But he was not sorry. No doubt it would have been better if they hadn't, but he half thought their joining was inevitable. Now that it had finally happened, it would be possible to get her out of his thoughts and dreams and return to his formerly peaceful life. He kissed her shoulder and pulled the covers over their sated bodies.

"I'm not sorry," she murmured.

Chapter 19

I

For several long sleepy moments when Alexander awoke the next morning he believed he was in his rooms at Arlington Street and that the woman next to him was Angelica Vincent. Pulling her against him, he savored his impression of a night well spent. He buried his face in her hair and kissed the back of her neck while his hands began a slow exploration of her body. Through the grogginess of what had been a deep sleep penetrated only the observation that Angelica seemed to have lost weight. His lips moved down to the top of her shoulder and his tongue made a lazy circle on her warm skin. He heard her moan softly and felt a rounded derrière press against him. He opened his eyes just enough to see by the clock across the room that it was going on five o'clock. The room was bathed in a dim light, creating a soft golden aura around the pale hair spread out over the pillow. It took only a minute or two for his sleep-heavy mind to register that he was not at Arlington Street and that the woman in his arms was not Angelica Vincent. His recollection of exactly how he had spent the night and with whom he had spent it was suddenly painfully clear. It was, of course, impossible to comfort himself with the thought that she had known exactly what she was doing. He frowned when he remembered some of the things he had said to her. He vaguely remembered meaning every word at the time. He shook her shoulder.

"Are you awake?" he questioned softly. The servants would be up soon, and if he didn't get her into her own bed, there was going to be hell to pay. He hoped to God she wasn't going to make a scene. He shook her again and prepared himself for the worst.

"I'm awake," she said, turning to face him.

He was touched by the uncertainty he saw in her eyes and he reached between them to take her hand and bring it to his lips. He breathed a sigh of relief to see she obviously intended to follow his lead. "How's your arm?" He suppressed the sudden tender urge he had to embrace her and tell her she was beautiful, no matter how true it was.

"'Tis a little sore," she said softly.

The makeshift bandage had long ago slipped off and he was glad to see no signs of redness about the wound. Really, it was not so very deep. "You'd better get dressed," he finally whispered, still holding her hand. "I've no doubt the servants expect to find you in your own bed." He was sorry when she took her hand away and sat up to swing her feet off the bed. He spoke quietly as she gathered her clothes. "You know, of course, your father's fondest wish is for there to be a match between us." He looked away from the disturbing sight of her, taking refuge in his sharp words. "It so happens, I don't care for blondes, no matter how rich they are. I only hope to God I do not have to marry you after all."

"Be quiet, sir, and help me! My arm's too sore to button these damned things."

He sat up and looked at her. "It would be all right if you called me Alexander," he said as he watched her struggle with her clothes. He was about to help her when she uttered an oath and stepped out of the breeches.

"Oh, never mind!" she said in disgust. "Even if I got them buttoned, I'd probably never get them off. You'll have to go get me a wrap. Bridget should have left one lying on my bed."

He sighed and got out of the bed to pull on a dressing gown of his own before walking barefoot out into the hall. He came back with the garment a few tense moments before Isobel had decided he must have been seen going into her room. After giving it to her, he sat back down on the bed.

"Thank goodness you're not totally useless!" she said as she put on the wrap. When he laughed she walked over to where he sat on the edge of the bed. "So, Alexander, what makes you think you might have the ill fortune to have to marry me?" She looked at him searchingly before she shook her head. "Oh. I see. You're quite mistaken if you think I intend to force marriage on you. And anyway"—she gave a smile that looked bitter for a moment—"I should never marry a man who does not like me."

"I was thinking more that nature might force us." And, although he could see she hadn't understood him, all he could think about was how perfect her body had felt against his. Without thinking, he reached up and pulled her to him, pushing his hands inside the thin silk wrapper and holding her hips. "We were together, love, so many times last night. . . ." His fingers were pulling gently on the triangle of hair between her legs. He was amazed he could still want her with such an aching need.

"I only thank God I am not a brunette or a red-head—or I should be dead of it!"

Alexander's laugh was low. "Are you never at a loss
for a retort?" He untied her wrap and pushed it open,
sighing when, with a shrug of her shoulders, it
dropped to the floor. He brushed his fingers over her
before pulling her head to his so he could kiss her. She
returned his kiss with an abandon that brought a familiar sensation to his belly. He deepened their kiss when
he felt her hands on his chest sliding lower, caressing
him until he could stand it no longer. He pulled her
back onto the bed and let his hands explore the curve
of her waist down to her buttocks before raising her up
so he could enter her slickness. He held her against his
chest, letting her move on him. "Perhaps I was mistaken about my preferences in women," he hissed into
her ear.

II

When she shut the door softly behind her, he lay
back and stared up at the canopy. The bed was still
warm where she had been. He was acutely aware that
nothing had been done to prevent disaster, and though
he knew they ought never to lie together again, he still
found himself thinking of a next time. His thoughts
drifted to the silken perfection of her body, the deep
blue of her eyes, and how he had felt to hear her calling out his name. He closed his eyes and gave in to a
feeling of pleasant exhaustion. He knew he ought to
marry her, but he did not want to be married again,
not just yet. In a year's time, perhaps. And if, in a
year's time, he still felt the same way about her, was
there really any reason why he should not consider re-
marrying?

How weak was Alexander's resolve not to repeat
their folly was demonstrated by his giving her the key
to the private entrance to his rooms. He told her it

would be safer for her to use his private staircase rather than the servants' entrance, and every evening she rehearsed with Faircourt and the orchestra, he found some excuse to wait for her. One night, though, she went to a ball given by the duke of Portland that he had declined to attend. He arrived just in time to take her home. Another time, during the day, by pure chance he spotted her leaving a building near the Haymarket. He recognized her because she was wearing his old frock coat. He made his coachman stop while he leaned out the window and hailed her. "Mr. Boxham, is it not?" he called out.

"Good afternoon, Lord Hartforde!" She made him a nice little bow.

"My carriage is at your disposal, Mr. Boxham, if you would care to have me drop you somewhere."

"You are too kind, my lord." She stepped up into the coach when Alexander signaled the footman to open the door for his friend Mr. Boxham. He immediately pulled her onto his lap and they made cramped but abandoned love while they drove back to Albermarle Street. The driver had pulled open the door not seconds after Alexander had finished buttoning Isobel's breeches. They walked over to the Duke of Albemarle Publick House and drank enough ale to float a ship before making their exhilarated way back to number Ten. That night, Alexander came to her room.

On the day before she was to return to her father's house, he unexpectedly found her in one of the parlors playing a game of solitaire. Her head was bent over the cards in a study of concentration, and he had been unable to resist walking quietly up behind her and surprising her with a kiss on the slope of her shoulders. "I will go mad if you do not come to my room at once," he growled into her ear. And so she had.

Chapter 20

I

When Isobel returned to her father's house, Alexander told himself it meant the end of an affair he hadn't really been having anyway. He did not believe he would continue to want her if she wasn't around so constantly. It surprised him not a little to find he was mistaken. Other women no longer satisfied him. The event always fell short of what he sought, and he was left worse off than before. When he began dreaming of Isobel and that bedazzling body of hers about a week after she had returned to Redruth, he decided it was high time he did something about it. His mistake had been in not making it perfectly clear they were not having an affair and she must not expect an offer of marriage from him unless there were any unfortunate consequences from their madness. He convinced himself it would be just as simple as all the other liaisons he had ended.

He found her in the gardens. She smiled at him uncertainly, and he realized with a pang of remorse that she had been hurt by his silence. He sat down when

she moved over to make room for him on the bench.
"Good morning, Miss St. James." He kissed her hand.
Just seeing her made him want to be with her again.
Surely he would forget her after a while, just as he had
forgotten other women.

"Miss St. James?" She raised her eyebrows at his serious expression and took her hand away from him.

"Isobel, to continue our . . . alliance would only be
irresponsible on my part." He did not expect the
scornful look she gave him. "Surely you can see we
would be an ill-matched pair. You know, of course,
about my late wife? Let it suffice to say the experience
of marriage is one I wish never to repeat, and I cannot,
in good conscience, offer you less." He meant to tell
her that if he had got her with child, she could expect
him to do right by her, but she sighed as though bored
and interrupted him.

"My lord, you are always saying unpleasant
things—when I am not in your bed, that is," she
added.

"Isobel, you deserve—"

"I deserve better than you. I deserve not to be
treated so commonly!" She stood up. "Would you be
so kind as to leave me now?"

"Isobel—"

"My lord, I do not like you any more than you like
me. Let us part on that understanding. I've had ample
time to think in these last few days, and now I understand that night was merely an aberration, the result of
my disgraceful drunkenness, of which I think you
must agree you took equally disgraceful advantage. As
for the rest of it, it would be best if we do not examine
it too closely, lest we come to some unpleasant truths.
I think we might both be thankful that it is over.
Now, you will surely understand when I ask you,
again, to go at once." When she saw he intended to say

something, she repeated her words. "At once, my lord."

"As you wish." He stood and bowed. She was only telling him what he had meant to say himself, and he wondered why he was angry instead of relieved.

II

When he was gone, Isobel burst into tears. He had forgotten her existence just as soon as she left his house. Alexander cared no more for her than some common street girl. And to her undying shame, she had let him treat her like one. She told herself she would not waste another thought on a man who cared so little for her. She had given herself shamelessly to a man who had dazzled her senses. She thanked God she was no longer naïve enough to hope he did care for her. Whenever her thoughts turned to him, she would force her mind elsewhere. But she could not stop her dreams. Isobel began to see Viscount Strathemoore more often, this time actively encouraging him.

Some two weeks later, she had to send Strathemoore a regretful note declining their early morning ride in Hyde Park, as she was ill. She assumed her indisposition was in consequence of her unhappiness and expected it to pass.

Chapter 21

"No, my lord, you may not come inside." Isobel put a hand to his chest to keep him at arm's length.

"You are breaking my heart," Strathemoore said, one arm reaching out to circle her waist and pull her to him.

"I'm quite convinced you haven't a heart to be broken, Lord Strathemoore." She laughed.

"Are you sending me away without even a kiss to sustain me until tomorrow?" He affected a look of despair that made Isobel sigh and shake her head at him.

"Yes." She pushed him away, but he tightened his arm around her waist. "My lord," she scolded, "you forget yourself!"

There was a short silence while James pressed his lips fervently to the inside of her palm. He had kissed her once before at a masquerade ball, only to be rewarded with a stinging slap for his forwardness. It was days before she had consented to see him again. He chose not to press his luck quite so far this time. "Until tomorrow, Miss St. James," he whispered.

Isobel stood at the door after he had gone. He was nice and she was sure he cared for her. Only once had he crossed the bounds of propriety and tried to force himself on her. As soon as his lips met hers, she had thought of Alexander and it was enough to bring her to her senses. Why was it that Alexander's kisses made her giddy, while James's only made her frantic to get away? she wondered. He was nearly as handsome as Alexander, and, unlike him, James was always attentive and unfailingly polite. She was certain he meant to propose; he was beginning to drop hints to her. So far she had pretended to misunderstand him. She wasn't sure yet she wanted, or even ought, to encourage him in that direction. She was fond of him, but she did not love him. And she felt nothing of the passion that was there with Alexander. Why couldn't she forget the man, as he had so obviously forgotten her? She sighed and drew off her gloves and nearly ran into Alexander as she stepped into the hallway.

He grasped her elbows. "Good afternoon, Miss St. James." His eyes were hard as they met her startled look.

Her knees suddenly felt weak and she was disconcerted to find she could still be so affected by him. "How nice to see you, Lord Hartforde." She pulled away from him, hoping she sounded anything but pleased to see him. "What are you doing here?"

He grasped her arm again. "Why are you wasting your time with Strathemoore?" He didn't really care, he said to himself, but she was showing remarkably poor judgment.

"The prince was busy today." Did her skin have to tingle from his touch?

"Strathemoore is in the process of running through a considerable fortune." *This is not jealousy*, he thought, *she just needs to know what kind of man Strathemoore is.*

"He is very obliging." Why did his eyes make her want to throw herself into his arms?

"I can assure you that that obliging profligate," he sneered, "sees only the size of the marriage settlement he expects!"

"Unlike yourself, Lord Hartforde, my Lord Strathemoore is always a gentleman when he is with me." She stared pointedly at the arm he gripped so tightly. "And he has promised me he will give up gambling." She took a step back when he released her and rubbed her arm where his fingers had left faint red marks. "And I do believe he almost means it," she added wryly.

Alexander only snorted in response, a little embarrassed then at his heated reaction to seeing her with Strathemoore.

"Why are you here?" she repeated.

"I had business with your father." In fact, he had had a time convincing the earl they should meet at Redruth instead of at Brook's.

"I trust you had a pleasant conversation." She attempted to brush by him, but he grasped her arm again. "What is it?" She gave him an exasperated look.

"Are you always so impossible?"

"If I didn't know better"—she managed to sound bored—"I'd say you were jealous. Now, I suggest you let go of me before I summon the servants and have you thrown out."

"Jealous? Of Strathemoore? That's ridiculous!"

"You've seen my father, so why don't you go?" Isobel jerked her arm free and walked away, leaving him, she thought, standing in the hallway. She walked haughtily away, holding back her tears until she was in the privacy of a nearby sitting room. She had just thrown herself into a chair when Alexander came in after her. "Do me the courtesy of leaving me," she said. "I have no wish to talk to you."

"I don't intend to leave just yet." He crossed the room and stood firmly in front of her chair.

"If you don't go, I shall call a servant!" She jumped up and would have reached for the bell had not Alexander prevented her.

"Isobel, we must talk."

"I have nothing to say to you! And after all this time, I find it hard to believe you have anything to say to me." She looked away from him, mortified at how close she was to throwing herself into his arms.

"Isobel." He said her name very quietly, bending over her. She wanted to resist, but she was powerless to deny the longing his nearness was creating in her. She was never sure afterward who it was who closed the space between them. All she remembered was her arms around him and his lips covering hers in a kiss that made her cling to him all the tighter for its tenderness. For one wonderful moment, he was kissing her back. Then, suddenly, he pulled away.

"Isobel," he whispered, taking her hands between his. "This is not why I came." As much as he wanted her, it was unthinkable.

"Then, why? Why are you here?" Her eyes were shut tight against her tears, but she felt the tension in his hands, around hers.

"I want my life to be free of entanglements. I am far too set in my ways to change now."

"And I am only an entanglement?" She pulled away from him.

"You would be if I let you." He reached out to touch her cheek. "I'm sorry if I've hurt you," he whispered.

Alexander was back at Hartforde House before he realized that he had not asked the one question he had set out to ask her. He sat down at his desk, waving off his secretary, who was approaching with a handful of letters. He was most certainly not jealous! The sole reason for his disquietude was that he was tired of London. "Bloody hell!" he said to no one in particular.

Chapter 22

I

Julia came into the drawing room, where Isobel was sitting on an overstuffed sofa with a book lying abandoned in her lap. She walked over to her and, with a rustle of her skirts, sat down. "Dearest Isobel." She took her friend's hand and held it in her lap, her palm resting on top in a protective manner. "You've got to stop moping around like this!"

"Good morning, Julia." She smiled thinly. "How are you?"

"As fine as can be!" She grinned. "And you?"

"I've a terrible headache today," she said in excuse for her gloom.

"If I didn't know better, I'd say you were lovesick," Julia teased, thinking it would be a relief when she and Alexander were married, and shaking her head when Isobel failed to give even the faintest of smiles. "But you're much too levelheaded for anything so frivolous as love!"

"I am not in love with your brother!"

"What a shame. You two would be such a splendid

match." Julia had always done as much as she could to encourage Isobel and her brother, though it was ever a tricky matter because he had so often accused her of trying to foist her friends off on him (she had never done any such thing) that now he was doubly shy where her efforts for Isobel were concerned.

"Julia, what are you plotting?" Isobel didn't like the speculative way her friend was chewing on her lip.

"I came by to tell you that I am going to Sussex for a few days. I am in need of a respite from London. I was going to ask if you would come with me, but I can see you are not up to the trip."

"I think not, Julia." She sighed and picked at her skirt with nervous fingers. "How long will you be gone?"

"Oh, a few days." She stood up. "Shall I give any message to Hartforde?" Her concern was rewarded with a sour look.

"He's at Ashdown Grey?" She hated herself for the feeling of relief that flooded over her; it was business at Ashdown Grey that explained why she had not seen Alexander in so long. Or had he gone to Sussex to avoid her? For a moment, she considered going with Julia, but she steeled herself against such weakness. She refused to humiliate herself for any man who thought of her as an entanglement.

Julia hid a smile at this evidence of Isobel's lovelorn condition by concentrating on adjusting a bow on her sleeve. When she glanced at her friend again, her face was impassive. "Well, I really must be going. The carriage is waiting for me." She hugged Isobel. "What you really need to do is sit out in the air. Promise me you will?"

"Perhaps you're right." She sighed when Julia kissed her cheek.

II

"I know why you're in such a foul mood, Hart-forde." Julia shook her spoon at him during dinner on the second night after her impromptu arrival at Ash-down Grey.

"And why is that?" The smile he gave his sister did not reach his eyes.

"Because you've been cooped up here too long, that's why." She took a small bite of her veal. "You should be in London. Lord Dunsmire is giving a masque next week, and Lady Dunsmire tells me they have hired a circus all the way from India!"

"I can do without your concern, thank you," he glowered.

"Well, there are certain people in London who miss you." She fixed him with a meaningful stare.

"If you mean Miss St. James, I do not appreciate your misguided attempts at matchmaking," he said sharply, giving her another scowl. He was annoyed to see her look of surprise.

"Isobel?" She raised her eyebrows. "Why should you think I meant Isobel? I was speaking of Mrs. Vincent. I saw her at Mrs. Hughton's at-home, and she spoke about you at great length. I should add also that Lady Donbarton is busy telling anyone who will listen that your absence from London has to do with some dark conspiracy or other." She paused and took a sip of wine. "Though, now that you mention Isobel, we are all expecting the announcement of her engagement to Lord Strathemoore. He is so obviously in love that we shall all be quite relieved when he has finally spoken to Lord Chessingham. I'm afraid he shall be simply unbearable until her father consents to the marriage. I never thought the man would fall in love quite so hard, but he has." Julia was pleased to see her news had its intended effect, though Alexander quickly masked the start it had given him. She changed the subject. "You know, I thought I was tired of London, but I find I am already refreshed. Perhaps I shall return tomorrow."

Chapter 23

Isobel sat very still, letting the reality of how irrevocably her life was changed sink in. When Bridget had first delicately mentioned the possibility that she was with child, she had told herself it was impossible. It couldn't happen to her when there was so much going on, so many important things she had to do. Now she gently closed the medical book that had confirmed her disaster. She wanted to shout that it was unfair, she had plans for her life, it couldn't be true.

She could still see the way Faircourt had strutted around the room when he told her his news. It was not long after the subscription concert and he had been full of their success. "I think," he had said proudly, "I may say in all candor that you have arrived."

"What is it?" She had been smiling at him.

"Here." He handed her a letter.

"From the duke of Mallentrye?" Of course she had instantly recognized the seal pressed into the blood-red wax. It broke with a satisfying crack and she had eagerly read the letter; the heavy paper had felt so solid in her hands. The duke was giving a reception for the King and he wanted to commission a lengthy piece from Mr. Ian Boxham.

"Congratulations, my girl!"

"I've got to get to work! I've got only a month!"

That day she had thought herself on top of the world.

She moved the book aside and, picking up pen and paper, began to write:

My Lord Hartforde,

You must believe me when I say I would not write to you unless it was necessary. However, I have the misfortune of informing you that our misalliance has had a disastrous consequence. It is likely—nay, my lord, 'tis *certain*—I carry your child.

I am—
Isobel

She blotted the letter and, after directing it, went to find someone to deliver it to Ashdown Grey. Whether Alexander wanted entanglements or not, he had them now. But, for the first time in her life, she had no control over what was going to happen to her, and she hated it with all her heart.

Chapter 24

I

Alexander was in his study, feet up on the desk, feeling very nicely, thank you, when the butler knocked and timidly opened the door. "What is it, Brosham?" he snapped.

"A letter has arrived, your lordship."

"From whom?" He motioned to him to hand over the letter.

"From Miss St. James, I believe, milord."

Alexander waved the letter under his nose. She hadn't even bothered to perfume her first love letter. "Miss St. James?" He humphed. "I'll show you what I think of her!" With that, he turned and tossed the letter into the fireplace behind him, watching as it slowly blackened and finally caught fire. "She means nothing to me!" He splashed more liquor into his glass and swallowed it in a gulp. "You may go now," he said, not taking his eyes off the portrait of his late wife.

The day after Isobel's letter arrived, Alexander told the butler to close up the house and gruffly informed his valet they were leaving the next day for Hart-fordeshire.

II

"Heavens!" Peters said quietly when he came in the next morning to help Lord Hartforde dress. He stepped to the window and pulled open the curtains, letting the early morning light fall on the chair where his lordship was still sprawled. His clothes were rumpled, his hair untied and falling down to his shoulders. Peters shook his head when he bent to pick his coat up from the floor, where it had been tossed. His lordship smelled more than a little of brandy. He folded the garment over his arm and rang the bell, giving quiet instructions to the servant who appeared a few moments later. "Good morning, my lord," Peters said when he heard a groan from the chair.

"Good God!" Alexander sat up and covered his face with his hands. "What time is it, Peters?"

"Half past six, sir."

There was another groan from the chair. "I need a bath, Peters."

"I've taken the liberty, my lord."

At half past nine, just over two hours into the drive to Hartfordeshire, they stopped to rest the horses. Alexander paused as he was stepping up into the carriage. "To London," he said.

"My lord?" the driver repeated.

"You heard me. To London."

Chapter 25

I

Strathemoore's eyes widened in appreciation as Isobel came down the stairs. She was wearing a dress of ivory-colored satin with a neckline that scooped daringly low. Two rows of delicate ivory-colored lace trimmed the cuffs at the elbows, narrowing to a point at the edges. Her only jewelry was a double strand of pearls at her throat. Her hair was pulled back in an austere style, serving only to enhance the simple elegance of her gown. She blushed as he bowed, brushing his hat just inches off the floor.

"Good evening, my lord." Isobel held out her hand, pleased with the impression she seemed to have made on him. His lips brushed her fingers, and, when he did not immediately release her, she pulled her hand from his grasp.

"You are a vision tonight!" he exclaimed, his eyes lingering on her. His fingers lightly brushed the top of her shoulder as he helped her on with her wrap. "I shall be the envy of every man alive."

"Really!" She laughed, tapping his chest with her fan.

"You look ravishing." He bent his head and quickly brushed her shoulder with his lips as he moved to her side, watching anxiously for her reaction to the liberty he had taken.

"You are a rascal," she said.

When they arrived at the opera house, Strathemoore saw with pride that Isobel had the attention of every man in the place. He was sure each wished he was escorting the lovely (and someday to be rich!) Miss St. James. He knew they made an attractive pair, and he was elated that she had encouraged his attentions. Feeling inordinately happy, he took her arm and led her toward his box, taking care to go the long way around.

"May I get you anything?" He hovered over her as she sat down.

"No, thank you," she said, looking around distractedly until she realized Strathemoore had said something to her. She was beginning to regret that she had agreed to come; his familiarity was making her uncomfortable. "I'm sorry. What did you say?" Why couldn't she keep herself from thinking about Alexander, blast him?

"I was saying I heard Mr. Boxham play at Lord Sheffield's the other day. He was quite spectacular. I've heard he is something of a musical genius," Strathemoore repeated his comment. "One of England's few."

"I didn't know you had ever heard of Ian!"

"Do you know him?" He frowned to hear her use the name so familiarly.

"Yes. Rather well." She laughed at his expression of chagrin and took his hand. "Why, my lord! Dare I think you are jealous? Ian cares for nothing but his music—of that you may rest assured! Besides, he is no-where near as handsome as you."

Strathemoore raised her hand to his lips. "You flatter me no end, Miss St. James, and I hope you will continue to do so for a long time to come." He held her hand between his. "Isobel—I hope I may call you Isobel—perhaps this is not the right time, but it no longer matters to me. I can't go on like this. Please!" To Isobel's horror, he suddenly went down on his knee.

"My lord, get up, everyone will see you!"

"I don't care. Isobel, will you do me the honor of becoming my wife?"

Chapter 26

I

Alexander sat alone at a table at Brook's nursing his third drink and scowling furiously as he did so. All of London was talking about how Lord Strathemoore had proposed to Miss St. James at the opera, of all places! It was the first thing he'd heard upon his arrival at Hartforde House. Servants were a notoriously talkative bunch. With a sudden and dire need for a drink, he had headed straight for St. James's Street.

He refilled his glass, angered because he couldn't make up his mind what to do; he wasn't even sure why he had come back to London. All he knew was that he was thoroughly annoyed with Julia; he considered this whole miserable affair to be her fault. He lifted his glass and swallowed half the contents. He hoped to God Isobel had accepted Strathemoore so he could stop thinking about her. He wanted to congratulate her on her marriage to such a capital dunce and then forget her once and for all.

"Well, good evening, Lord Hartforde!"

He was surprised to see Strathemoore standing

stiffly at his table. "Do sit down. Have a drink with me." He motioned for a footman to bring another glass to the table.

"How long have you been back?" Strathemoore sat down across from him and gave him a friendly smile.

"I've only just arrived." He filled the glass set down between them, then topped off his own.

"Not playing cards?" he asked.

"Not in the mood, I suppose."

"Then what brings you back to London?" He raised his glass to Alexander and took a swallow.

"Nothing in particular."

"Oh." He leaned his forearms on the table. "I've been losing all my money to Fistersham. It'll be nice to lose it to someone else for a change."

"Why so melancholy, Strathemoore?" The image of him making love to Isobel filled his mind and he drained his glass again.

"You know, I expect, I had reason to be glad when you left." Alexander said nothing at this. "I thought it would give me a chance with Miss St. James. I expect you also know she was quite taken with you."

"Ah, yes," he snorted. "But my sister gave me to understand some weeks ago that an announcement was expected any moment." Alexander felt his stomach churning and told himself it was from all the drink.

"I'm afraid not. Lord Chessingham was delighted, but she refused me." He shook his head ruefully.

"Well, perhaps she merely expected you to ask her again," Alexander suggested, attributing his sudden elation to all the drink on an empty stomach.

"She refused me in no uncertain terms. Had me thrown out the second time. Really quite hysterical. Would never have asked if I'd known she'd be so upset at it." He pushed his glass in a little circle on the table-top. "I should have expected it; she never looked at me the way she did you. Anyway, I've gone and gotten myself engaged to Miss Parkston now; she's got a few thousands." He emptied his glass and held it out to be refilled. "She's a damned fine woman, Hartforde." They both knew he meant Isobel. "And you're a fool if you can't see that."

II

"Why so quiet, Miss St. James?" Lady Donbarton demanded. "'Tis unusual you are so silent." Lady Donbarton was a staid woman of forty who refused to admit she had long ago lost her looks. She was wearing a far too youthful gown of yellow velvet that only served to make her complexion sallow. She had on such a thick layer of powder her wrinkles looked etched in stone. It was an interesting fact that Lord Donbarton was notorious for the extreme youth he sought in his mistresses.

"I was attending to the conversation, Lady Donbarton." Isobel smiled at her while thinking to herself she was a bilious old busybody who ought to be more careful of what she ate if she didn't want to come dangerously close to resembling a certain sea fish.

"Do you know"—she lowered her voice because Julia was sitting just a few seats away—"I have heard that Lord Hartforde is the author of those notorious pamphlets and that the King will exile him if only it can be proved true."

"Since it will never be proved, I see no reason to speculate on the matter, Lady Donbarton."

Lady Donbarton snorted at this obviously prejudiced retort. "And I've heard there is proof," she said, with a vicious look. "Everyone, even Donbarton, agrees Lord Hartforde's absence from London is highly suspicious."

Isobel was sorry indeed that she had let Julia persuade her to attend this afternoon tea. Just hearing that

silly woman mention Alexander's name brought back
her nagging fear that he was not going to come for
her. It was getting harder and harder not to give in to
her panic at his long silence. She closed her eyes; he
was going to come. She could hear the sound of
voices, punctuated by frequent laughter. He had to
come. Someone was playing the fortepiano, and very
badly at that. She concentrated on the music. It was
Bach, but played with little feeling for tempo or delicacy. When she opened her eyes again, Lady Donbarton had turned her attention to someone else. She tried
to find Julia, but she had changed her seat. At last she
saw her, sitting on a couch on the far side of the room
talking earnestly with another woman. From where
she was sitting, Isobel could see Julia's face suddenly
brighten. Though she could not hear her, she saw her
say the single word "Hartforde."

She could see his eyes sweeping the room, but still
she did not move. She was paralyzed by the fear that
he wasn't really looking for her. Someone was still
playing the fortepiano; she could still hear people talking and laughing. It seemed so incongruous when her
whole life was hanging in the balance. When he finally
saw her she could not move or breathe or look away;
she could only wait for him to reach her side.

"Isobel," he whispered.

"To Arlington Street," Alexander instructed his
driver. He handed her up into the carriage himself,
then quickly climbed in after her.

She looked up at him, and he reached out and ran a
finger along the line of her jaw. Even that brief contact
made her shiver. He bent forward and gathered her
into his arms. She leaned toward him. "I was beginning to think you were never coming," she whispered.

"I'm not that big a fool," he said.

The carriage came to a stop and Alexander held her

hand while they got out. They were met at the door by a servant who quickly hurried to take their things. "Bring a bottle of champagne to the drawing room. Then you may go," he added softly as the man took his coat and held out a hand for Isobel's wrap.

"Very good, my lord."

Isobel stood examining a large globe of the world until the champagne arrived. "That will be all," Alexander said when a servant opened the bottle and set it down in a bucket of ice.

Alexander filled two glasses and handed one to Isobel, who was slowly turning the globe. He raised his glass and his green eyes held hers as they sipped.

She sat down on a sofa and Alexander joined her there. She drained her glass and held out the delicate crystal for him to refill. She stared into the glass, seemingly fascinated with the rising bubbles. "I love you," she said quickly, turning to watch his painfully beautiful face as her finger traced a line from his knee up to the top of his thigh, then down the inside of his lean, muscled leg.

"I know you do," he said. She heard his sharp intake of breath when she lightly ran a finger down the front of his breeches. He caught her hand in one of his and brought it to his lips.

"I was afraid you were going to marry Strathemoore"—he looked up at the ceiling for a moment—"and I had to stop you."

"No," she said, "I would never have done that." She looked up into his eyes, which darkened when she freed her hand, and again traced a line up his thigh.

"Be careful, Isobel, you might make me lose control," he said, smiling when he felt her fingering the row of buttons at the right of his hip.

"Could I do that, my Lord Hartforde?" She strug-

gled with the last button and worked a small hand inside the flap of material.

"You might." He took a deep breath as she leaned
closer, his eyes lowering to the alabaster skin above the
neckline of her gown, then going back up to the blue
depths of her eyes.

"Isn't that why you brought me here?" Her voice
was husky. "To make you lose control?" She had succeeded in unfastening the buttons at the other side of
his hip, and after that she did not need him to answer.

He held her head, groaning when he felt her tongue
on him. She seemed to know just when and how to
touch him, to tighten her lips around him, to surround
him until he was moaning for his release, and when it
came it was like nothing he could remember. His arms
snaked out to pull her onto his lap, and he took her
mouth in a hungry kiss while his fingers loosened
her hair, until it tumbled in pale golden curls down her
back. Twining his fingers in the silky mass, he stroked
her cheek and throat with his other hand. "You be-
witch me," he whispered into her ear. He felt her
tremble when he began to kiss the swell of her breasts.
He wanted nothing more than to make her cry out for
him, to make her hunger for him as he hungered for
her, to feel her quiver under his touch. His arm circled
her waist, while with the other he reached to remove
her slippers. He heard them hit the carpet with two
muffled thuds. The flickering in his belly started to
build and spread outward as his hand moved under her
skirts to slide along her slender legs and pull away her
stockings; the delicate silk fell to the floor with barely a
whisper. She gasped when his fingers spread over her
naked flesh. "I want you, damn you!" he hissed as he
swept her up in his arms and covered her lips in a
bruising kiss. "You and no other," he whispered. He
fumbled to fasten at least one of the buttons of his
breeches before he gathered her into his arms and car-

ried her into a small bedroom where he set her down on her feet, slowly sliding her down against him. He turned her around and began rapidly undoing the hooks of her gown. There was a swish when he pushed the silk off her shoulders and watched it fall to the floor. Her petticoats and corset followed, until he could hold her against him to stroke the curves of the body that had been so often in his thoughts. He stood still when she turned in his arms and began to unbutton his waistcoat. His clothes quickly joined hers on the floor.

"I want you now, Alexander." He heard her hoarse whisper as he pushed her back onto the mattress and began to explore the curves of her body. He crooned her name as he slowly slid into her. He lifted his head and looked at her, his eyes burning as she caressed the muscled ridges of his back, down to the narrow hips that pressed against her. She cried out when she felt him moving inside her. He touched her, stroked her, moved in her, watched her eyes, her face, and listened for the moans that told him his touch aroused her. He was aroused when she was aroused, and when he felt her increasing reaction, he felt it as though it were his own. He wanted to possess her completely, utterly, so she could love no other. Shudders of exhilaration swept through him when he felt her tightening around him and he began moving his hips with hers, letting her guide them until he had to give in to the demands of his own body, that was her body, that was the two of them. A fierce feeling of possessiveness took over him when he held her head in his hands and looked at her and saw how his passion was mirrored in her eyes. That she was so aroused by him was more important than that she aroused him more than any other woman with whom he had ever been.

"Isobel, my own," he heard himself saying over and over, until he was senseless to everything but her wet,

slick body scorching him as she took him with her to a
soaring ecstasy that caught them both up in a dizzying,
whirling climax that at the end left them clinging to
each other.

"In a year"—he reached to stroke her hair—"we can
marry in a year," he said.

"In a year?"

"I'm sure your father would not mind a long engagement." He sat up and swung his feet to the floor.

"But, Alexander!" Isobel sat up, too, and watched
the muscles of his smooth back flex and relax as he sat
on the edge of the bed and groped for his breeches.
"We can't wait that long!"

"Why in God's name not?" He threw his breeches
back on the floor and twisted to face her.

"I thought my letter made that perfectly clear."

"Ah, yes. Your letter."

She looked at him through narrowed eyes. "You did
get my letter, didn't you?"

"Yes, I did." He paused guiltily. "But I'm afraid I
never read it."

"And still you came after me?" she asked in a wondering voice. The ribbon holding back his hair was
askew and she reached up to pull it out tenderly. She
leaned forward to press her lips to his and bury her
fingers in his sandy hair. "Alexander, we can't wait to
marry because I'm carrying your child."

Their eyes met, and for a long moment Isobel
wasn't sure what he thought. Then he gathered her
into his arms and just held her, and for the first time in
weeks everything was right in her world.

Chapter 27

I

Alexander could have wished his meeting with Lord Chessingham had been even half so easy as procuring the special license. He had thought to marry in London; the earl had given his consent to the union— there had been no choice in the matter—but he was vehement in insisting that the marriage take place away from London. "You might," the earl had said sternly, "at least oblige me by going about this discreetly. Surely you can keep her out of London until after the child is born."

Their respective solicitors met and in only two days a satisfactory contract was drawn up. In addition to some properties in Norfolk, the earl settled on Isobel the astounding sum of one hundred thousand pounds. It gave hope that there might be an eventual reconciliation. It was such a fantastic sum that Alexander could only believe Chessingham had not quite hardened his heart against his daughter. It was unusual for the groom's solicitor to be advocating on behalf of the bride, but Lord Chessingham had evidently instructed his attorney to agree to whatever might be proposed regarding the disposition of the money. As it turned out, Alexander saw to it that the entire hundred thousand was set aside for Isobel, with five hundred a month pin money.

When Alexander told Julia he was to marry Isobel, she made no comment except to congratulate him on finally showing some good sense, and to insist upon attending the wedding. However, she questioned Isobel at great length, and when she had finished scolding her for not confiding in her, she ended by exclaiming, "He should have married you immediately!"

"Julia," Isobel said, "if I have learned anything about your brother, it's that he was very much in love with his first wife and she hurt him terribly." They were sitting in the gardens behind Redruth, and Isobel, looking a little drawn, smiled at Julia. "Though he'd never admit it, ever since then he's been afraid of loving someone that much a second time. I think maybe he does love me that much, and I think it frightened him. I only pray that I never do anything to hurt him."

"You won't, I know it, Isobel, because you love him and Sarah never did."

"I just wish this was all over! Father won't talk to me, and if you hadn't come to see me, I'm sure I would have spent this entire day without speaking to a single person."

Julia hugged Isobel. "Don't you worry. You're going to be happy for the rest of your life."

Alexander and Isobel did not see each other until the arrangements were completed and the marriage contracts could be signed. He felt a pang when he saw how pale she was. She did not look well; there were dark circles under her eyes, and when he sat down next to her she clutched his hand tightly.

"Father won't even talk to me," she said plaintively when they were finally alone. "He said that I've disgraced him."

"Give him time," he told her. "He'll feel differently when you come back after having the baby." He kissed the top of her head. "We're to be married day after tomorrow at Ashdown Grey. We'll stay there until after your lying in." He continued even though she was sitting up straight, dark eyes wide. "It's close enough that Julia can visit, so it's not as though you won't have company."

"Alexander, I can't stay at Ashdown Grey, not yet!"

He saw by the look on her face they were in for an argument, and, to forestall it, he sighed and said, "Why not, Isobel?"

"Because in two weeks I am engaged to conduct a specially commissioned piece for the duke of Mallentrye."

"Mallentrye?" he asked with a scowl.

"Alexander, listen to me, the King is going to be there. It's the most important performance of my life and I refuse to miss it—I can't miss it. I've been working so hard! Don't you even think of preventing me, Alexander!" she cried when she saw him shake his head.

"I was only going to say that I shall have to send my acceptance after all."

"Afterward, Alexander, I will stay anywhere you like."

"You are an impossible woman."

It took nearly the entire day to reach Ashdown Grey, though it included a lengthy stop to rest the horses and have a meal at the town of Wadhurst. The sky was just beginning to darken when they reached the outskirts of Ashdown Forest, and by the time they were at the front gates the chestnut trees were long shadows on the drive.

Alexander firmly held Isobel's elbow as he escorted her inside. They paused in the entrance hall just long enough for a footman to appear with a candle to light their way. The butler stood in the hall until long after Lord Hartforde had disappeared up the stairs, a smile on his thin lips. More than once during his lordship's last stay at Ashdown Grey, he had been sorely tempted to give notice, and he would have, if he had not been sure he would eventually come to his senses and marry the girl.

Isobel and Julia sat up most of the night talking. When Julia finally got up to go to her own room, she hugged Isobel. "I know you're going to be happy," she said.

"I know we will, too."

II

The witnesses to their marriage were the mayor of the nearby village of Horsham and a local squire, one Horace Falls, who, unlike the mayor, had the tact and presence of mind not to make any comments about hurried weddings. Neither the mayor's snickering nor the Reverend Paxton's stern and disapproving look could mar the happiness of the day. Isobel did not care what anyone thought. She was marrying the man she loved more than anything in the world.

*   *   *

Isobel rested her head on Alexander's chest when they were finally alone in his room at Ashdown Grey.

"Well, Lady Hartforde," he said, bending his head to kiss her cheek, "I'm sorry this has been such a strain on you." He looked into her eyes and was lost in their dark depths. "I can't believe I've been such a fool about you," he whispered. The moment his lips touched hers, he felt a familiar spark of desire center itself in him and begin to spread slowly outward. He pulled her closer to him and began, cautiously, to explore the depths of the passion that seemed always to be there to bind him to her. It felt so right to have her in his arms again. It was a heady feeling he was at a loss to explain or understand. She was there, with him, and now he could touch her as he had been longing to since . . . since the last time they had lain together. He picked her up to carry her to the bed, and then when he was next to her, he kissed her again. He wanted to kiss her just to see if he would ever tire of it. He kept thinking to himself, *We are married!* The words shocked him, but it was a shock that made him drunk with her and with a passionate joy that made him softly croon her name when he reached to touch her. He pulled her upright as his mouth slid down her throat, his fingers feverishly working at the fastenings of her dress. He whispered her name, his longing for her, and of how he wanted to touch her.

Just as feverishly, she was unbuttoning his clothes, pausing to pull his shirt off so she could slide her hands down the ridges of his belly. He pushed her dress off her shoulders and down to the floor, never taking his eyes from hers as he removed the rest of her clothes. When she was naked before him, he pulled her to him, running his hands down the smooth length of her. "You are beautiful," he said in a hushed voice. He sucked in his breath when he felt her hand on his breeches.

"I want you," she whispered. "I want you forever."

"And I you." He had never meant anything more in his life. There was no reason to hurry, no reason to check that he had locked the doors, no reason to hold back or muffle his cries for fear of being overheard. He had all the right in the world to make love to his wife.

*   *   *

Much later, Alexander sat propped up on the pillows watching Isobel sleep. He moved uncomfortably and shifted so her head lay on his thighs. She sighed and settled her head in his lap, one small hand warming his leg through the sheets. He stroked her cheek as she slept. How must she have felt when there was no answer to her letter? he wondered. As he looked at her, he wondered what it was about marriage that had so frightened him. Isobel could never be held up as an example of a proper young lady; her single-mindedness about her music was impediment enough to that. It was a shame, he thought, she was not a man, because her music was as good, better even, than any he had ever heard. He could easily admit he preferred an intelligent woman to a stupid one, but Isobel's intelligence was most masculine in its perspicacity, though—Lord!—he enjoyed their conversations. She had a sparkling wit, but an unfortunate willfulness. But, then, she had not had a conventional upbringing. She'd told him enough about America for him to know Jonathon Rowland had loved her dearly, and the Samuelses had made her life a hell. It was hardly surprising that someone with such an extraordinary upbringing should turn out to be such an extraordinary young woman. He only knew he did not want her to go back to London; he did not want her anywhere near the duke of Mallentrye.

III

They spent only two more days at Ashdown Grey before returning to London and Hartforde House, where, to avoid gossip, it was given out that Isobel was visiting with Julia. Very little time remained for Isobel to work on her composition for the duke, and though she threw herself into her work with a frenzy, she and Alexander seemed to grow even closer. He attended one of the rehearsals, much to the surprise of Faircourt, who, when he saw Alexander come in and quietly seat himself, whispered to Isobel, "Be on your best behavior, and you may have yet another patron!"

"What do you mean?" she asked quickly, frowning at his interruption.

"I mean, the marquess of Hartforde is sitting not twenty feet away at this very moment!"

"Good afternoon, my lord," Faircourt said after he had left Isobel to approach Alexander. "It is an honor indeed to have you here. Mr. Boxham has asked me to express his deep gratitude for your kindness in coming."

"I have been following Mr. Boxham's career with great interest."

"You display an excellent ear for music, my lord."

"I should like very much to meet Mr. Boxham. Do you think it possible?"

"Of course!"

"I look forward to it. And now, I should like to hear the music." It was unsettling to watch Isobel; this was a side of her he had never seen before. Several times he heard her exasperated voice rising above the music. At last she stopped the orchestra and strode over to the fortepiano.

"Like this!" She played several bars. "Slow, then slower, but, for God's sake, it's not a funeral march!"

When she finally put down the baton, Faircourt bustled up to her and, putting a hand on her shoulder, said, "Lord Hartforde wants very much to meet you. Be on your best behavior!" He waved a finger under her nose as he repeated the admonition.

"Really," she whispered to Alexander after Faircourt had made the introductions, "we ought to tell him."

"A pleasure to make your acquaintance," Alexander said. "Here is my card. You may call on me whenever you like. Perhaps"—he glanced at Faircourt—"I shall commission a piece from you myself, Mr. Boxham."

"Perhaps several?" Isobel said, pretending not to see Faircourt's horror at her boldness.

"Yes, I think several would be in order."

"Well," Faircourt said to Alexander, "it seems Mr. Boxham is going to be very busy. The duke of Mallentrye has also expressed interest in commissioning more work from him. He was here just yesterday and he was pleased, quite pleased, with what he heard."

"No doubt he was," Alexander said sourly.

"Why didn't you tell me Mallentrye was there yesterday?" Alexander demanded later that evening.

"Because I didn't think it was important," Isobel said.

"I don't want you to have anything to do with that man."

"I can't help it, Alexander. After all, he commissioned the piece. It's no surprise that he came to a rehearsal."

"I don't like it, Isobel," he snapped. "Does he know who you are?"

"Of course not."

"How many times has he come?"

"I don't know! I don't really pay attention."

Alexander's bad humor ended as quickly as it started. "I'm sorry," he said. He pulled her to him. "I'll be glad when this thing is over and we can leave London."

Chapter 28

Isobel arrived at the duke's shortly before the guests began arriving. It was not until she had spent about half an hour making sure the musicians were ready that she began to feel nervous. She paced the music hall until she heard a commotion that could only mean the King had arrived.

Faircourt nudged her. "Surely there is no harm done if you go take a look."

Isobel looked at him gratefully. "I hope it takes my mind off my nerves!" she said.

It was easy to find the room where the King was receiving. The duke's house was an old one, with most of the rooms connected to one another by doors so that one might walk the length of the house without going out into the hall. She found that she had an almost unimpeded view of the King from a small anteroom. She stood quietly, watching as he greeted the guests. He was not very tall, and his bright satin suit did not look well on his stocky frame. Mallentrye stood next to his chair, laughing dutifully at His Maj-

esty's occasional witticisms. The King suddenly
frowned and the duke bent to say something to him in
a low voice. She followed the duke's glance. Her heart
leaped when she saw Alexander, handsome in plum-
colored satin. He towered over the other men in the
room, and his bow to his sovereign was as gracefully
executed as any man could hope. To her surprise, the
King's greeting was curt; that he was for some reason
displeased with Alexander was all too evident.

Isobel's attention was riveted on the duke's cold
smile as he watched Alexander retreat. The expression
became a sneer when a short man with sharp dark features tapped Mallentrye on the shoulder. The duke
bent to the King again, obviously excusing himself, for
he followed the other man into the anteroom. She had
no desire to see the duke, and she was about to leave
through another door when the duke's words riveted
her to the spot.

"Hartforde's here after all, Fordham. Have you got
it?"

"Of course, Your Grace." Fordham's voice was
gravelly.

"And you've taken care of Hawes?"

"Yes, I've taken care of Hawes." The sentence ended
in a chilling laugh. Something about their tone kept
Isobel from leaving.

"Let me see it. I want to make sure you haven't bungled the job." She heard the crackle of parchment
being unfolded, then silence. "Excellent," the duke
said. "When His Majesty sees this, Hartforde will rue
the day he was born. Do you have the seals?"

"Yes, Your Grace."

"Then take this to my study and see that you finish
the job properly." The door shut behind the duke with
a bang as he left to rejoin the reception. There was a
softer repeat of the sound when Fordham left the
room.

Isobel stepped out into the hall in time to see Fordham disappear around a corner. Heart in her throat, she followed him. She had to get her hands on that document. She stood outside the door to the room Fordham had entered, uncertain what to do. At last she took a breath and went in.

Fordham jumped at the sound of the door's opening; and frowned at the sight of young Boxham, the composer. He was sitting at a desk, and he let go of the seal he was pressing into the wax spreading out over a slim packet. "Get out of here!" he snarled.

"Oh, dear me," Isobel said. "This does not appear to be the musicians' room."

"No, sir, it does not, does it?" Hastily he pushed the packet into the desk and closed it.

"Do forgive me, sir. I had no intention of disturbing anyone." She laughed and bowed.

"It's quite all right. No harm done." He relaxed at her abashed expression and stood so she would be prevented from seeing what he did with the seal.

"Do you think, sir, that you could point me in the right direction?" She smiled sheepishly. "I've simply no idea where I am."

He gave gruff instructions and she gave him another clumsy bow. "I knew I oughtn't to have drunk so much. Thank you, sir, for your kindness."

She had to wait for what seemed an eternity before she heard Fordham leave so she could slip back into the room. When she opened the desk she thought for one horrible moment that he had taken the letter with him. She looked frantically through the papers and finally found it, tucked away under a pile of other documents. She sat down in the chair, surprised to recognize the seal as Alexander's. The wax was still warm and she managed to separate it from the paper without breaking it. The letter inside the parchment wrapping was on plain paper, and when she unfolded it she almost believed she was looking at Alexander's bold writing. When she finished reading the two paragraphs she understood what the duke had meant. The brief letter purported to be from Alexander and it outlined a plan to garner enough support in the House of Lords "to bring George to his knees and have myself named Prime Minister." She was about to throw the letter in the fire when she stopped. She had a better idea. The sound of voices brought Isobel out of her intense concentration and into a panic of activity. She quickly replaced the letter and did her best to put the papers back in their original order. She was fairly certain that the duke did not intend to show the letter to the King until much later in the evening. With a silent prayer that she was right, she slipped out into the hall.

She made her way back to the reception hall and stopped one of the duke's footmen, instructing him to bring her paper and pen. As soon as he returned with the required materials, she found an empty room and sat down to compose an entirely different document.

"There you are!" Isobel jumped at the sound of Faircourt's voice. "Mr. Boxham, this is no time to be writing letters!" he cried when he saw what she was doing. "Come along, supper's almost over!"

"In a moment!" She waved the paper in the air until it was dry. After folding it carefully, she tucked it away in her frock coat.

"Congratulations, Mr. Boxham!" Faircourt slapped Isobel on the back.

"'Twas well received, I think." She took a deep breath and looked around at the crowd of well-wishers, searching for Alexander. This was no time for him to disappear; she had to warn him.

"What did the King say to you?" somebody asked.

"He was very charming and complimentary."

"Bravo, Boxham!" someone else shouted.

"Will you excuse me?" She bowed nervously. If she couldn't find Alexander soon, it would be too late. She was certain the duke would not show the King the forged letter until he was ready to leave, but His Majesty was beginning to show signs of boredom.

At last Isobel decided she could wait no longer. Making her way back to the duke's study proved to be more difficult than she anticipated. Everyone wanted a word with the new young composer, but at last she escaped the crowd to find herself alone in front of the duke's study. She listened at the door, and when she was satisfied there was no one there, she went in. With trembling hands she opened the desk and removed the duke's letter. The seal had hardened and she began to loosen it gently from the paper with the tip of a penknife. Every noise seemed amplified and several times she froze with fear at the sound of footsteps going past the door. She wiped a film of perspiration from her forehead and continued working at the seal. "Hell and damnation!" she swore when a small piece broke off the edge. It seemed to take an eternity, and when she was finally finished, her shoulders were aching from the effort. Slipping out the letter, she replaced it with her own. She blessed the servant who had left several candles burning, and, though the underside of the paper was unavoidably blackened when she held it inches above the flame, at last the wax was softened enough to reseal the parchment wrapping around the letter. If it wasn't examined too carefully it might pass for a fresh seal.

She heard voices, and her heart gave a sickening leap when she recognized the duke's voice. There wasn't time to make sure the original letter was burned, so she thrust it into her waistcoat. She quickly closed up the desk and replaced the candle on the mantel. The moment she stepped through the door, someone had her by the shoulders, slamming her against the door-way.

"What the devil were you doing in there?" the duke hissed, his face perilously close to her own.

At almost the same moment the duke grasped her, Alexander came around the corner. All Isobel could see was his shocked expression as he saw the duke holding her by the shoulders, pulling her so close they were almost touching.

The duke twisted around when he heard footsteps. "Get the hell out of my house, Hartforde!" he snarled.

"With pleasure, Your Grace."

She called out to him, but he never turned back.

"So, Mr. Boxham," the duke snapped, "would you care to explain what you were doing in my study?"

"Please, Your Grace." She shook herself free from his grasp. She brushed off her jacket and looked at him as though insulted. *I am going to be sick,* she thought. "I was not actually in your study, though I freely admit I was headed there. These rooms all look alike from the outside."

The duke's expression relaxed, and he stepped back a little. He would probably have let her go if Fordham hadn't come along.

"What's he doing here?" Fordham cried.

"You know him?"

"Of course he knows me!" Isobel interjected. "Even the King knows me today. How wonderful to see you again, sir." She nodded at Fordham.

"He was in here earlier, Your Grace."

"I think, Mr. Boxham, we'd better talk." The duke took her arm and, opening the door, pushed her inside. "Check the desk, Fordham." He jerked his head at the desk. "Tell me, Mr. Boxham, how is it you know Hartforde so well?"

"He has commissioned several works from me,

Your Grace, and his lordship is not, as I have discovered, a man to stand on ceremony." She purposely kept a bantering tone, hoping Mallentrye would be disarmed by it.

"It's here," Fordham said.

Please, don't look at it too closely, Isobel prayed silently.

"Give it to me." He held out his hand but merely glanced at it before putting it in his pocket. "Mr. Boxham, I find your manner insulting. You have let a small success go to your head. However, I will send you away with some advice. Don't depend on Hartforde's patronage; you will find it short-lived, indeed. Now, please be so good as to leave my house."

"You are too kind, Your Grace," she said, consoling herself with the thought that the duke was soon to present the King with a highly confidential letter that would prove to be an offer to purchase a racehorse. It would be some time before he gained the King's ear again.

Isobel did not bother to make her excuses to Faircourt. She went directly to the line of cabs waiting in front of the house and threw a handful of shillings at the first driver, promising him more if he got her to Albemarle Street as quickly as possible. She sagged against the seat, fighting off a nauseating panic. "Please, let him be there," she said out loud. But he wasn't there, and, though she waited all night, he did not return.

Chapter 29

I

Isobel waited five miserable days before a letter finally arrived. Tersely worded, it instructed her to go to meet Alexander in Hartfordeshire.

It was still dark when Isobel was roused with difficulty. She ate only a few bites of one of the rolls Bridget had set out. Even more than most mornings, she had no appetite; just the smell of food made her stomach roil. Bridget pressed her to eat more and was rewarded with a killing glance. They had to wait only a few minutes for the arrival of the five men hired to see them along the route north and then they were on their way. Isobel looked askance at the heavily armed men; they had been paid handsomely to see there were guns and shot enough to discourage even the most desperate of highwaymen.

They left well before six in the morning. Though Bridget made a few attempts at conversation, Isobel sat in a corner of the carriage and stared resolutely out the window at the lightening horizon.

The ride north was a miserable bone-jarring journey over muddy rutted roads. Bridget had given up trying to draw her mistress out. They just sat in silence as the minutes slowly passed. They stopped every hour or so to change horses, and more than once Isobel took the opportunity to find a private place to retch. They were able to make good time; by noon they had traveled nearly fifty miles. They stopped twice for meals and both times Bridget had to make sure Isobel ate. Both times Isobel dreaded getting back into the carriage to continue that nauseating rolling and her constant battle with her stomach.

"Just be happy it hasn't rained or the trip would be nearer two weeks than one," the driver said as he helped her back in after a stop to change horses.

They traveled quickly, stopping at inns where Isobel got very little sleep during the six nights they spent on the road. On what proved to be their last day out, they stopped for a fourth change of horses, and Isobel was so weak that, this time, she did not have a chance to make it into the small public house. Doubled over at the side of the road, she waved Bridget's hands away.

She was back in a moment with a tumbler of water. "Here, Lady Hartforde." Bridget pressed the water on her.

"We can stop here for the day, milady," the driver said, his voice edged with concern. "We can make the trip to Hartforde Hall tomorrow."

"Are we close?" She held out her hand and Bridget helped her up.

"Two or three hours." He shrugged.

"Please, let us go, then. I am sick to death of traveling. I want to be done with it!"

"I doubt you are up to it, Lady Hartforde."

"Please! I don't want to spend the night here. I want to sleep in a real bed and eat real food and have a real bath!" She could not keep the wavering note from her voice. *I want to see Alexander, to explain to him,* she thought.

"Yes, milady," he said softly. He picked her up and carried her back to the coach. When he put her back inside, she leaned back into the corner of the seat and gave Bridget a wan smile that was meant to be reassuring. As soon as the horses were changed and the men gathered, they left.

Isobel felt her eyes drooping, and though it seemed incredible that she could sleep through any small part of the bouncing, she balled up her wrap and, putting it between her cheek and the side of the carriage, closed her eyes.

II

"Wake up," someone was saying, while gently shaking her shoulder. "At least move your head! My leg's asleep." She was jostled some more and she struggled to sit up. "We're here."

"Where?" She looked around, trying to shake off the effects of her exhaustion.

"Hartforde Hall."

"Oh," she said, as the door to the carriage was opened, and a footman held up a hand to help her out. "But it's practically a castle!" she cried when she stepped down. The hall, built of a dull grayish stone, had no fewer than six turrets. Two rose up on either side of the massive front doors, and the other four stood toward each of the four corners. The walls between the towers were crenellated all around, and there were two domes rising up from the middle of both north and south wings, with a third dome in the center. The multi-paned windows at the ground level were narrow but rose until they were even with the top of the front doors. The windows of the first floor were wide, while the rest of the windows were narrower and, like those below them, had not yet been converted to the increasingly popular sashes.

"Not so long ago, it was a matter of necessity to be well protected from the Scots," the driver said, while Bridget reached into the carriage to get her cloak. It snapped in the breeze when Bridget shook it out before putting it around Isobel's shoulders. The hedges and lawns were neatly manicured and there was a circular pool with an algae-covered nymph rising up from the center. They were met at the door by the steward, who looked surprised when he saw Isobel.

"You may inform the staff that Lady Hartforde is unable to meet them today but will do so tomorrow morning," Bridget ordered imperiously. "She shall be having supper at eight tonight. Nothing heavy, just some soup and perhaps some chicken."

"Is my husband here?" Isobel asked.

"No, my lady. He's not expected to return from the Continent for several months."

Chapter 30

In spite of Alexander's determination that the Continent should cure his wretched condition, he was constantly tortured by the image of Isobel locked in an embrace with the duke of Mallentrye. She had lied to him. The duke had clearly known who she was. Not even Paris could distract him from his misery.

He returned to London in time for the opening of Parliament in October, and although he threw himself into his work, he managed to remain isolated, seldom going out and rarely consenting to see anyone. The only social function he attended was his sister's wedding, and he made himself scarce even then because Julia insisted on questioning him about Isobel.

He met Angelica Vincent purely by accident one afternoon but he discovered she no longer held even the slightest attraction for him. She was surprised when he left not half an hour after arriving at her apartments. "But, my lord!" she cried out. "Everyone knows you had to marry her!" It unnerved him that she had so easily divined the reason for his leaving and he scowled at her. "It doesn't mean you can't be with a woman you do want," she cajoled.

"I married the woman I want," he responded, without even thinking.

"Don't tell me you're in love with that American?" She stared at him openmouthed. She must have seen the answer on his face, for she had burst out laughing. "Go on, then, go back to your little wife!"

The first thing Alexander did the next morning was to visit his solicitor to inquire about beginning a proceeding for divorce. But for some reason he never went inside the office.

Chapter 31

As the days passed and her child grew inside her, Isobel became more and more unhappy. It was awkward to sit down and nearly impossible to get up without help. Her ankles would sometimes swell so she could not even walk out to the garden without discomfort. As the weeks passed into months, she was less often nauseated, but still the simple task of washing her teeth made her quite ill. Eating was unpleasant for though she might feel ravenous, after only a few bites her stomach was uncomfortably full. She was beginning to think she was going to be with child for the rest of her life.

She had finally taught herself not to think about Alexander; she half believed she would never see him again. If it wasn't for her music, she was sure she would go mad. At least what she wrote while she was in Hartfordeshire seemed to have benefited from her melancholy. During her enforced solitude, she had written a third and fourth symphony. They were by far her best works, but she had to wonder if they would ever be performed or whether they were doomed to grace only the inside of her leather case.

The increasing discomfort of her pregnancy finally began to slow her down. Whereas during October she had written some five pieces for fortepiano, in addition to completing a violin concerto, during November she wrote only one: a piece for cello and orchestra. By mid-December she had ceased writing altogether.

Isobel was sitting in the back gardens, pretending to read while a cooling breeze gently turned the pages of the book lying abandoned in her lap. Bridget was hovering over her, constantly asking if she was comfortable, if there was anything she could get her, when she only wanted to be left alone. For a moment she thought she heard the faint sound of hooves clattering on the cobbles of the front drive and she listened intently for a few minutes, straining to hear. What if it was Alexander instead of one of the servants? What if he had finally come for her? She resolutely put away the thought. He was never coming back. It was quiet, there was nothing to hear, and certainly nothing to hope for. She settled back in her chair and pulled her cloak around her shoulders.

"Come inside, Lady Hartforde," Bridget said, "it's getting cold." She wished there was something she could say to make her smile. She was becoming concerned at her mistress's deepening depression. Isobel did not eat nearly enough these days. Bridget hoped, as she helped Isobel stand up, to coax her into eating a little extra at supper that evening.

They walked slowly—Isobel did everything slowly these days—to her room, where Bridget insisted that she rest. She agreed only because it meant she could be alone. It seemed to take forever for the babies to quiet down enough for her to sleep.

"My lady!"

Someone was trying to make her wake up, and she did not want to.

"Lady Hartforde! Wake up. He's here."

Isobel opened her eyes.

"He's here and he wants to see you now."

Chapter 32

One of the men Alexander hired for his trip to Hartfordeshire was a short, stocky man, by the name of
Jack Wickenstand, who kept a pistol tucked into the
waistband of his breeches. His skin was pockmarked,
and when he grinned there were two gaps where teeth
had formerly been. He was addicted to snuff and was
frequently required to wipe his nose, a task he accomplished by using his sleeve in the place of a kerchief.
His hair was longish and ill kempt, but he spoke tolerably well and knew how to handle a gun. To a man,
Wickenstand's companions thought it odd a cove so
recently out of the Fleet could have come by the grand
snuffbox he made such a show of twirling about.

Chapter 33

I

"Tell Lady Hartforde I wish to see her in my study immediately," Alexander instructed the steward curtly as soon as he came in the Hall. The several days' coach ride to Hartfordeshire had not improved his sour temper in the least. Anger seemed to be his only defense against his infatuation with Isobel. He had almost let himself fall in love with that woman, and she had betrayed him! He refused to have a wife who cuckolded him. He had been that road once before and he had no intention of being so foolish a second time. He meant to put a quick end to whatever insanity it was that had made him think there was no need for an immediate legal separation.

After spending some time in his rooms, he went directly to his study and paced until Isobel was announced. He was struck by how pale and drawn she looked. It was late in the afternoon and he realized she must have been sleeping. Her eyes were dark with fatigue and he steeled himself against the sudden tenderness he felt when he saw her. It was difficult to keep from rushing to her side when she grimaced and placed her hands on her stomach.

"I am sometimes kicked to distraction!" she murmured.

There was no telling how long she had been carrying on with the duke. "I have something to tell you," he said. He seated himself behind his desk and clenched his hands into fists. The thought of her with the duke filled him with such a rage he was completely unable to see the matter in a calm light, though he thought he was being perfectly rational. His very calmness was proof of his clearheadedness.

"I'm listening." She shrugged her shoulders.

"Am I the father?" It was only one of the fantastic accusations he had come up with to feed his anger since leaving her.

"Of course you are!"

Before she could give vent to the anger he saw his question had caused, he asked in an acid voice, "Are you quite certain?" The scene was unpleasantly familiar. He had gone over it in his head time after time, he knew exactly what she would say, and he knew it would be nothing but lies.

"I've never been with the duke, Alexander. You never gave me a chance to tell you what you really saw." She sat down, holding a hand to her back, as though it suddenly pained her. There was something very much like panic in her eyes and he took it as a sign of her guilt.

"I know what I saw. You forget, madam, I have had this experience once before. I will not be the fool twice. You are no more capable of fidelity than she was."

"But I'm not Sarah! If you weren't afraid of loving me, you could see that."

"I came here only to tell you I am petitioning Parliament for a divorce."

"Will you just listen to me for a minute?"

"I've told your maid to start packing your things. You're to leave here at first light tomorrow."

"The duke had—"

"There is nothing more to discuss," Alexander snapped. He could feel his anger fading and he desperately wanted her to leave before he gave in to his insane desire to take her into his arms. More the fool he, if he did; it would only be so she could hurt him again.

Isobel struggled to stand up. She was too tired to fight, too certain that it would make no difference if she tried. "Do you know something, Alexander? For months I've been praying you'd come back. I was going to tell you what you really saw, but I can see now how silly that would have been. I don't think it's worth the trouble. You've proven how stubborn you are. You've won," she said as she closed the door after her.

By the time she was back in her room her anger had cooled only a little. "I'll show him what he's lost!" she cried out to the room. She pulled the duke's letter out of the leather case where she kept it and went back to Alexander's study.

"Read this." She tossed the letter on the desk. "Fortunately, when the duke caught me leaving his study, he did not know I had taken this." She wheeled around and walked out of the house, too angry to think about where she was going. She stopped for a moment, then began walking down the shaded drive.

It was not long before her anger was gone, replaced by the familiar numbing depression. Lost in its misery, she did not notice the glorious evening. The sun was setting and there was no breeze to chill the air. It had rained early in the day and the air still had that particular cleanness about it that followed a rain. She was just too tired to care. Let him get his divorce. As soon as her child was born she would go as far away from him as was possible, even back to Boston. She stopped and gasped in pain as the muscles of her abdomen suddenly tightened. She took a deep breath when it was over. She continued walking, so engrossed in her plans that she did not notice she was being followed. A man was carefully keeping pace with her, using the huge trees for cover. When she stopped at the end of the drive to straighten her hat, he stopped, too.

II

After Isobel left, Alexander sat in his study wondering how he had let that woman get so close to him that she could hurt him so. He stared at the letter, picked it up, fingered it. He knew what he had seen. There could have been no mistaking it, could there? He opened the letter and read it twice. It was nothing but a pack of lies, and not a very good forgery at that. He remembered the curt greeting the King had given him, how for weeks previous there had been whispers about his political aspirations. Whispers that he had ignored. It dawned on him that, of course, the duke had intended to show the letter to the King. He knew very well what His Majesty would have done if he'd seen it.

Alexander found Isobel's maid busy sorting out her clothes and packing them away. "Where is Lady Hartforde?" he asked.

"She's gone for a walk, milord."

"Thank you."

"Milord?"

"Yes?" He stopped at the door.

Bridget took a deep breath before she spoke. "You can't mean to make her leave, my lord. She's too near her time to be going anywhere. She'll have the baby in the carriage!"

"Lady Hartforde is not going anywhere."

"Yes, milord." She smiled and gave a sigh of relief.

Alexander wasted several minutes looking for Isobel in the gardens before he finally asked one of the servants if he had seen which way she had gone. He started down the drive and was about to call out for her when the glint of a small gold box lying in the dirt caught his eye. He stooped to pick it up and, as he straightened, he finally saw her, standing forlornly at the bottom of the drive. He dropped the box into his pocket and was breathless by the time he caught up with her.

III

Jack Wickenstand was elated when he saw Lord Hartforde coming after his wife. Quickly, he checked the powder in his pistol. He waited until the marquess had caught up with her and the two were standing still in the middle of the drive. He leveled the gun and, as soon as he had a clear view of Hartforde's back, pulled the trigger.

"Leave me alone," Isobel said when Alexander reached her side. She turned and started back to the house. "You've said quite enough already."

"Isobel—" He grabbed her arm. He saw her eyes widen in surprise at something behind him, and he was half turning to look when she pushed him away so violently that he landed hard on the ground at the same time he heard the sound of a pistol being fired. The bullet meant for him hit Isobel instead.

Chapter 34

I

Alexander paced outside Isobel's room waiting for the doctor to emerge. In exasperation the physic had finally ordered him to wait outside. "I assure you, my lord, I will do an even better job if you would be so kind as to pace out in the hall." He shook his head when Lord Hartforde finally closed the door behind him. He turned back to his patient. He had dealt with bullet wounds in the past when he was in the army, and he had dealt with countless childbirths, but never had he been faced with both in the same patient. He shrugged off his jacket and, after rolling his shirt-sleeves out of the way, turned his attention to the more threatening of the conditions. It was fortunate Lady Hartforde was unconscious, because he doubted the wisdom of giving her opium while she was so close to her delivery, and probing for the ball would be easier if she wasn't thrashing around.

Alexander took in the doctor's grave expression as he came out and his heart sank. "She's not dead!"

The doctor shook his head. "I'd be obliged for a drink, my lord." His lordship looked as though he could use one, too.

"A fine idea." Alexander took the doctor's arm and propelled him down the hall to one of the drawing rooms. The physic sat down with a sigh and sipped the brandy offered him. "Is she going to be all right?" Alexander asked anxiously.

"In all honesty, I cannot hold out much hope for her survival. There is every indication her lying-in will be difficult. It is my guess it had started before she was shot." He shrugged. "Regardless of her wound, I could not be optimistic. If there is anything fortunate about this, 'tis that the bullet missed her heart. Otherwise, I'm afraid she'd have died even before I arrived." He sipped from his glass. "My lord"—he sighed—"I have a difficult question to which I must know your answer."

"What is it?"

The physician saw that Alexander had anticipated the question, and he took a deep breath. "'Tis more than likely I can save only the mother or the child. You must tell me, which is it to be?"

"You must save them both!" Alexander propped his elbows on his knees and covered his face.

"My Lord Hartforde"—the doctor leaned forward to put a hand on his arm—"I must have your instructions in this matter."

Alexander lifted a tortured face to the doctor. "I could not live if she dies."

"You have two sons, my lord." The doctor closed the door behind him as he stepped out into the hall, where Lord Hartforde had been pacing the entire night.

Alexander grabbed the doctor's arms. "And Isobel?"

At the grim look on the doctor's face, Alexander gave an agonized shout. "I told you to save my wife!"

"She still lives, my lord." He stopped Alexander from bursting into the room. "But I would be damned to hell if I did not tell you her hold on life is precarious. I do not think she'll live 'til morning."

II

Worry was etched on Alexander's face as he stood at the side of the bed looking down at his wife. Contrary to the doctor's dire prediction, Isobel had not died, but she was nearly as white as the linen upon which she lay. She had been unconscious for three days, during which time Alexander had rarely left her side. The physic still would not say she was out of danger. She was so deathly pale even the doctor agreed that to bleed her might well kill her. Alexander reached down to wipe the beads of sweat from her burning forehead. Tenderly he brushed her hair away from her face.

She opened eyes, bright with fever. "I'm going to die, aren't I?" she asked in a faint voice.

Alexander sat down on the bed and bent to kiss her forehead. "You won't die. I won't let you die," he whispered.

"I'm so thirsty," she complained. There was a pitcher of water on the bed table and he reached for the glass next to it and filled it. She drank from it before saying, "Thank God you were not killed." Her eyes drooped closed for a moment, and when she opened them again, she looked at him and whispered, "Don't worry, I'll leave here tomorrow." She fell into a fitful sleep, and when she opened her eyes again she struggled to sit up but could not. "Where are my babies?" she cried plaintively.

"Hush, love, our boys are fine." He put his hand gently on her arm.

"Something is wrong with me. I feel so hot." She closed her eyes for a moment. When she opened them again it was as though she were seeing him for the first time. "Oh, it's you," she said. "Don't worry, I'll leave in the morning." She drew in a harsh breath. "I'm just too tired to go now." She closed her eyes just as the maid came into the room.

Bridget put a hand to her forehead and, taking in Alexander's worried look, said, "She's a strong woman, milord."

"She's so hot!"

"'Tis the fever." She pulled the covers back over her. "I'm afraid the wound's infected." She shook her head and turned to Alexander. "Perhaps you should get some rest, my lord. I'll call you if you're needed."

Alexander shook his head. "I won't leave her!" The fear that she would die filled him with such desperate panic he did not notice the tears filling his eyes until he lifted a hand to his cheek.

III

Isobel often dreamed Alexander was in the room, holding her hand, and once she thought she saw tears in his eyes. She shook her head; he was only waiting for her to die.

"I won't die just to save you the expense of a divorce!" she said to him once. "I'm just too tired to go now. . . ."

Another time she saw him raise a cloth to her head and she was convinced he meant to smother her. Her screams brought her maid running.

"He's trying to kill me! Make him go away! He wants to kill me!" she sobbed wildly.

One night, after a day when her fever had lessened

to an extent where she could take some broth, she could not fall asleep. When at last she closed her eyes, she was bothered by disturbing dreams. In one, she was in the gardens at Redruth, Alexander was calling her, and she turned, stretching her arms to him. "I love you," she told him when he was just about to take her hand. His radiant smile disappeared and he pulled out a pistol and leveled it at her heart. She screamed at him to stop, but he pulled the trigger anyway. He threw the gun to a waiting servant, and, when he walked away from her, he was holding the twins in his arms.

She sat up, disoriented and damp with sweat. She was convinced Alexander meant to kill her, and the only thought on her feverish mind was to escape. The maid who was supposed to be watching over her was asleep in her chair, and Isobel moved as quietly as possible to avoid waking her. She hastily pulled a gown from the wardrobe and dressed herself. Her fingers trembled as she struggled to fasten the buttons. She did not notice the spot of blood that appeared at her chest as her struggle reopened the wound. She found a small valise and stuffed more clothes into it. "I'll be damned if I spend another night under his roof!" she muttered to herself. She sat down on the bed to rest; she did not understand why she was so bone-tired. She swayed dizzily when she stood up, but she made it halfway to the stairs before she needed another rest.

She was partway down the steps when she saw him. He was so handsome, she thought; just to look at him made her heart break. She laughed at herself; it was ludicrous to think that she could still love this man. She was hopeless when it came to Alexander, Lord Hartforde. She pushed back her shoulders and gripped the banister as she continued to descend. She held her head high as she went. She didn't have to be a fool and let him see how she felt!

"Isobel!" Alexander cried out when he saw her. "What in God's name do you think you're doing?" He moved quickly up the stairs, reaching out to grasp her.

"I'm following your instructions. You've probably got your divorce by now, and so I'm leaving. I don't intend to die just to convenience you, Alexander." Her words had a pleasingly dramatic ring to them and she smiled at the effect she imagined they were having on him. She let go of the banister so she could brush past him, and as soon as she did, her knees buckled when her legs refused to bear her weight and she tumbled down the stairs.

Alexander shouted for help as he ran down the stairs to where Isobel lay in a crumpled heap. He cradled her in his arms. She was ghostly white. When he rose with her in his arms she seemed to weigh almost nothing. "I'll never divorce you," he whispered, "not ever!" But she had lost consciousness and did not hear him.

Two days afterward, Isobel opened her eyes to see Bridget sitting in a chair drawn up close to her bed. "How are you, Lady Hartforde?" Bridget asked when she saw Isobel was awake. She leaned forward to press a hand to her cheek.

"Better, I think," she said. "How are my babies?"

"They are very fine, beautiful boys!"

The next day, she sat up in bed to sip the broth Bridget pressed on her. "I feel much better today," she told her with a weak smile.

"Lord Hartforde will be glad to hear that, my lady!"

Isobel frowned. "Yes, I've been here too long." She sipped the last of the broth. "I want to see my boys today."

"Shall I bring them to you for a visit?"

"Yes." She shifted so Bridget could pick up the tray.

"I'll be back before you know it!" Bridget paused at

the door. "I think Lord Hartforde would be pleased to see you. Shall I call him?"

"No! I never want to see him again!"

Bridget did not understand what had happened between them; she'd never seen a man so in love with his wife. Whatever had happened to make him leave her in the first place was obviously over, but now it was Lady Hartforde's turn to be stubborn. She shook her head sadly as she walked down the hall to the nursery. When she and the wet nurse brought the boys to Isobel, Bridget held one of the twins while Lady Hartforde held the other.

She smiled foolishly at Bridget. "They are perfect, aren't they?" She held out her hands to take the other, disguising a wince of pain when holding her son hurt her. She played with them for nearly an hour until she could no longer convince Bridget she wasn't being taxed by lifting them so often. She kissed each one on the head, then watched as they were taken out of the room by the wet nurse. It would not be too soon before she could take her sons and leave.

She had no way of knowing it was solely the doctor's advice that she should be left alone that kept Alexander from insisting she see him.

Isobel refused to believe Bridget's ridiculous story about the time her husband had spent nursing her back to health. "He only wants me to get well enough to leave!" she snapped, tired of hearing Bridget repeat the ludicrous tale. She had had her heart crushed once too often by that man, and nothing—absolutely nothing— would convince her he cared for anyone but himself. She might still love him, but she had at last recognized her foolishness for what it was. She might be many things, but she was not so mentally unbalanced as to subject herself to the pain of his presence.

"Why would he want you to leave, Lady Hartforde!" Bridget exclaimed. "Why, any fool can see he's in love with you. And I know you love him."

"He thinks I betrayed him with another man! I could not leave here fast enough to please him." Isobel looked at Bridget as though she expected her words to silence her at last.

"I don't believe it," she protested.

"No doubt he's been hoping I'd die and save him the trouble of the divorce."

"Oh! Surely you don't think that?"

"Believe me, my Lord Hartforde made his feelings for me perfectly clear. Now, I won't listen to any more of your silly chatter about a man whom I loathe!"

IV

Isobel sat in her room staring out the window where she had a view of the fields stretching out past the stable, watching a lone rider head out to the north. She recognized Alexander's broad shoulders even from such a distance. As she watched him, it struck her he had yet to send word about how soon he expected her to leave. She saw no reason to wait until he threw her out. He might rule her heart, but he did not rule her mind. She knew he was going to a hunt at Squire Walters's and he wouldn't be back until quite late. She jumped up from her chair, quickly packed a valise, and found Bridget to tell her she was going for a walk. She didn't want her to go into one of her speeches about Alexander; it was easier to tell her the small untruth. She went to the nursery and found the wet nurse sitting with the twins. She was a young girl whose own child had died not long after its birth.

"Lady Hartforde." She nodded.

Isobel picked up one of the twins; he gurgled happily and waved two perfect little fists in the air. "What is your name?" she asked the wet nurse.

"Molly Westlake, milady."

"Are you up to a trip to London, Molly?"

"Of course, milady."

"I'll have the carriage brought round in half an hour. Will you be ready to go?"

"Yes, milady!"

In half an hour they were on their way to London. It began to rain the second day out, but before it had rained hard enough to slow them down, they had reached the better roads closer to London. Eight days later, they arrived in London. Isobel took rooms at a small inn and immediately went to sleep, exhausted by the trip. It was two days before she finally felt well enough to go out, and the first thing she did was pay a visit to Julia.

Julia's face lit up with pleasure when she saw her sister-in-law. "Why didn't you tell me you were coming?" She threw her arms around Isobel and hugged her tightly.

"Well, Lady Burke, how have you been? Have you forgiven me for missing your wedding?"

"Never mind me! Tell me how *you've* been. How are the twins? Hartforde writes us that the boys are two little angels. When are you bringing them to London?"

"They are angels," Isobel said, but Julia wondered at the hint of sadness she saw in her smile. "I brought them with me."

"Isobel, whatever happened between you two?" Julia asked. "Why did he leave you for so long?"

"What does it matter, Julia? Things are no different now. I'm sure he's waiting impatiently for our divorce to be granted." Isobel felt the corners of her mouth pulling downward as she tried to hold back her tears.

"Divorce? That's nonsense!"

"The only reason he came to Hartfordeshire was to tell me he was petitioning for divorce. When he got there in December, he ordered me to leave Hartforde Hall, and if I hadn't had an accident, I'd have been in London at Christmas! And I was still with child then"—she was sobbing now—"and he was throwing me out! He wouldn't listen to one word I had to say. The truth meant nothing to him! He was so anxious to have me gone. He doesn't love me and I could not stand to be near him one more day!"

"What accident?"

"I had an accident a few weeks ago. 'Twas nothing serious. I was abed a few days, that's all." Isobel shrugged.

"Is that why you're so thin?" She wondered how it could have been nothing when she was reduced to nearly skin and bones. "I don't believe Hartforde is going to divorce you. He does love you—I know it!"

"He doesn't, Julia. Don't you think he would have told me if he did? And, anyway, if he doesn't divorce me, I shall divorce him. If he wants so badly to believe I betrayed him with the duke of Mallentrye, then so be it!"

"Mallentrye? What about him?"

"It was at the duke's concert. Do you remember all those pamphlets attacking the King? And the rumors that Alexander was responsible for them? You know if there was any proof, the King would have exiled him. Well, the duke had a letter—forged, of course—that would have implicated Alexander. Never mind how I found out about it. I stole the letter and the duke caught me coming out of his study, and then when Alexander came along, all he saw was the duke holding me."

"And he could only think of Sarah." Julia was beginning to become very angry with her brother. "But surely if you explained it to him—"

"He would not listen to me! Don't you think he would have if he loved me even a little? I love him with all my heart, Julia, but I want nothing more to do with him!"

V

A day or so after Isobel visited Julia, she made a trip to Alexander's solicitor. She sat waiting in an uncomfortable chair until Mr. Avery came into the room and apologized for keeping her waiting for even the briefest moment.

He bent over her hand. "What may I do to help you, Lady Hartforde?"

"No doubt you know, Mr. Avery, that Lord Hartforde intends to divorce me. In fact, it is my understanding the process has already begun. It is quite impossible for my children and me to stay at Albemarle Street, as I'm sure you can well comprehend. My request is really quite simple, and it is that you advance me a sum sufficient to allow us to stay in London until such time as my lord has obtained the divorce."

"Lady Hartforde, Lord Hartforde has said nothing to me about a divorce!"

Isobel paused. "Well," she said at last, "you may take my word that it is imminent. I imagine he will be in London shortly to discuss it with you. And, if by some comedy of errors, he forgets to bring it up, you may be assured I intend to divorce him!"

"I am not at all convinced of the case, Lady Hartforde. However, I see no reason not to accommodate you for the moment. Perhaps it would be more convenient simply to have your bills sent to me? Your husband has been exceedingly generous in giving you a monthly allowance of five hundred pounds. I see no difficulty in having his banker disburse that amount to you immediately. I might add, Lady Hartforde, that Lord Chessingham was also exceedingly generous." He looked down at Isobel as he spoke. "If it is true you will divorce, you would be well advised to secure your own counsel."

"I think, Mr. Avery, that five hundred pounds will be perfectly adequate." Isobel waited patiently while he wrote out the name and direction of Alexander's banker, and instructions on how to locate his office. "How much did you say my father gave him for me?"

"I didn't. But as you ask, your jointure amounts to one hundred thousand pounds."

The next afternoon Isobel moved to rooms at the St. James's Hotel in Jermyn Street and had soon hired a maid and purchased a fortepiano.

She used up nearly one hundred pounds for the fortepiano and the cost of delivering it to the hotel, but she was mightily pleased when at last it was settled in the second of the three rooms she had taken. As soon as she was divorced she intended to move into a house, but until then she thought she would be quite happy at the St. James's. As soon as she was up to it, she would call on Faircourt, but she wasn't ready for that just yet.

When she sat down at the fortepiano, she was dismayed to find that she played badly. After an hour she gave up and sat staring at the keys. The depression she thought she'd left behind engulfed her, paralyzing not only her fingers, but her heart as well.

Chapter 35

I

Alexander's heart wasn't in the hunt and twice he considered giving it up and going back to Hartforde Hall. But later he was persuaded to take some port with Squire Walters and the other huntsmen before heading home. He was chagrined to find when he was ready to leave that the night was pitch-black. A thick fog obscured the moon, so it was impossible to attempt the ride home, and he found himself forced to spend the night at Squire Walters's. He was oblivious to the blatant looks the chambermaid cast his way, and when he slept he dreamed of Isobel. He rose at half past six and waited impatiently for his horse to be brought around. He left his thanks for the hospitality and his regrets for leaving so early and was on his way by seven o'clock.

He had been at Hartforde Hall for only two or three hours before a flustered Bridget was ushered into his rooms. He took one look at her anxious face and felt his stomach tighten. "Is Lady Hartforde all right?" he asked.

"I don't know, milord!"

"What do you mean, you don't know?"

"She's gone, milord! She left yesterday and took the boys with her!"

II

Alexander did not reach Albemarle Street until early in the morning some twelve days later. It had rained almost every day and the roads had very nearly been impassable. He was delayed two days when his carriage lost a wheel, but one day was saved when, on what proved to be his last night on the road, the rain cleared and a full moon enabled him to travel all night. For some reason he had expected to find Isobel at Albemarle Street, and he was disappointed she was not there. It was far too early to ask after her anywhere else, or he would have left immediately to look for her. He ate a quick breakfast while trying to decide where to begin his search. At half past nine, he decided he'd be dashed if he could wait until ten, and he walked to Redruth, where he was forced to wait half an hour before Chessingham would see him.

"Good morning, Hartforde." The earl gave him a look that told him he had better state his business and be on his way.

"Has Isobel been here?" he asked.

"If she had, I'd have turned her away. You know that." Though Chessingham had no intention of forgiving her, he was having a time forgetting how much he had come to care about her.

"Do you know she damned near died after taking a bullet meant for me? And that she's made you a grandfather twice over?"

Chessingham flushed. Whether it was with anger at Alexander's hard words or from the effect of the news they imparted, it was impossible to tell. "Well," he said after a pause, "why the devil has she left you? She's married now, and her place is with her husband."

"We had a . . . misunderstanding. 'Tis my fault she's gone—just as 'tis my fault she got with child."

"No, 'tis a man's nature to try and a woman's duty to resist until the act is sanctioned by the Church of England!" He turned away and looked engrossed in the fire.

Alexander recoiled from the bitterness behind the earl's words. "Yet, sir, I'd wager you've had mistresses in your time and never gave a thought to their souls, nor your own, either. I take your leave"—he bowed to Chessingham's back—"and I pray both your heart and your mind are opened before it is too late." He was striding out of the room when the earl's soft question stopped him.

"Is she all right, Hartforde?"

He turned around. "No, she is not."

As soon as he got back to Hartforde House, he ordered the carriage and set out for Berkeley Square.

III

"Yes, she was here, a day or so ago," Julia told him. "Hartforde, I do not think she is well, and she was completely distraught! She told me you had ordered her out and that you are suing for divorce. I said I did not believe her." Julia's voice rose in outrage at her brother. "It isn't true, is it?"

"Is that what she said?" Alexander sank down in a chair.

"Among other things. She also told me about the duke, and, though I know it is not my concern, I am making it my business. You are a fool, Hartforde! You have been less than a gentleman when it comes to a woman I consider my best friend. Perhaps some part of the blame rests with her, but I suspect, brother, you can be overwhelmingly convincing when it suits you. I was appalled enough to discover you seduced her while she was at Hartforde House." Julia colored but continued: "If you were going to be so despicable as to not marry her immediately, it was at least your duty to ascertain the consequences. I truly think I might never speak to you again. My God, when I think about what you have done to her—"

"Julia, I know—"

"As for the duke," she interrupted him, "I wish you had killed that despicable man! You will listen to the truth: Isobel saved you from disgrace. How could you believe she would have anything to do with him?"

"Julia, listen to me," he said sternly. "I know about the duke and I know that what I saw wasn't what I thought it was. I don't know why I've been so bloody bullheaded when it comes to that woman, but, though I admit you are right to berate me, you are also right that it is not your concern. The primary concern must be finding her, not telling me I am a fool for not realizing sooner I am in love with my wife. She is not yet recovered from her wound." He jumped up from the chair and began pacing.

"Wound?" Julia reapeated.

"An attempt was made on my life, and in pushing me out of danger, she was shot."

"Shot? She was shot?" Julia sat down on the sofa. "My God, Hartforde, I would never have let her leave here if I'd known!"

"She is not at Hartforde House, nor is she at Redruth. If she isn't here, I don't know where to look for her."

"She told me she was at the Cressington Inn. You must go to her and straighten out this wretched affair. If I hear from her, I'll send word to you immediately. Now, I offer you the suggestion you start by telling

her you love her." She put a hand on his arm. "I believe she loves you still, but I warn you she might succeed in putting you out of her heart. I shall pray it is
not too late for you."

"And I as well."

IV

Alexander came into his room and collapsed into a
chair, splaying out his long legs and sighing gratefully
when Peters bent over and removed his boots. He had
gone directly to the Cressington Inn, only to discover
that Isobel had departed just the day before. She had
left no word about where she was going. He sighed
and closed his eyes. He was so tired it was entirely
likely he would fall asleep where he sat. Tomorrow,
first thing, he would go to Faircourt to ask if he had
heard from her, and if he had no luck there he would
go to his solicitor and have him set about finding her.

"No word from Lady Burke, milord?" Peters asked,
concern more in his tone than in his expression.

"No," he replied. "Draw me a bath, Peters."

"Yes, m'lord." He went out to order the bath. While
the water was being brought, he moved to the armoire
to hang out his lordship's clothes. After the tub was
full, he helped Alexander undress. "Milord?" Peters
said over his shoulder, pausing at the door with his
arms full of Alexander's clothes.

"Yes? What is it?" He was reaching for the soap.

Peters thought he looked tired. The strain of these
past days was beginning to show in the look of fatigue
around his eyes and the tense set of his mouth. "You
won't be going out tonight, milord?"

"No, Peters. I shall stay in tonight."

The valet was relieved to hear him say he would be
at home that night. He turned back to brushing out his
lordship's frock coat and was suddenly reminded of

something he had found in the pocket of another of his lordship's coats. He pulled out a dressing gown, and when he went back to drape it over a chair so it would be within his master's reach, he said, "I've brought your snuffbox, milord. It's in the trunk with your other gear. Do you want me to unpack it?"

"Snuffbox?" Alexander paused from soaping his chest to look up. "You know I don't take snuff, Peters!"

"There was a snuffbox in your blue coat, milord, the one with the black lining? You wore it the day milady—"

"Unpack it." He quickly finished his bath and put on the dressing gown. Peters returned with the snuffbox and handed it to him stiffly.

He frowned as he remembered the day Isobel had been shot. Quite frankly, in all the excitement and terror of that day, he'd completely forgotten about finding the thing. The search for the would-be assassin had been unsuccessful until one of the coachmen wondered out loud where Wickenstand had got to. By the time they realized he had stolen a horse, Wickenstand was long gone. Alexander turned the snuffbox over in his hands, a curious expression on his face. It was a finely made box of enameled gold depicting the duke of Marlborough's victory at Blenheim and it belonged to the earl of Donbarton.

"I shall be going out tonight after all, Peters," Alexander said thoughtfully, all trace of exhaustion gone from his eyes.

V

Alexander arrived at Brook's at ten o'clock. Unless Donbarton was already with his mistress, the chances were excellent Donbarton would show up at the club. He was an inveterate gambler who often claimed to be at a loss when deciding between the seduction of cards or his mistress. Alexander took a table and toyed with the glass and bottle put before him. He had not been much active in London society since his marriage and he found himself having to put up with a great deal of fuss about the recent birth of his sons. Congratulations were offered, toasts to Alexander's health and to the health of his sons were proposed, and he was forced to listen to several lewd comments about the beauty of his bride and one or two about the rapidity with which she had given him an heir. Alexander took the banter in the spirit in which it was meant, and it wasn't until he saw Lord Donbarton come in that he excused himself from the group of well-wishers that had surrounded him.

"Good evening, Dunbarton," Alexander greeted him easily. They had never exchanged much more than pleasantries over cards and there was absolutely no reason to believe the man would want him dead. Donbarton was a Whig, but when the earl had vehemently opposed the marquess on the American war, Alexander had accused him of Toryism. It seemed ridiculous to ascribe that as a reason to kill him. These days, Donbarton spent more time with his horses, cards, and mistress than he did with politics. Still, the possibility that Donbarton was part of some larger plot could not be discounted. Perhaps he and the duke of Mallentrye were in league, though it seemed unlikely. Ludicrous as the idea was, Alexander had found Donbarton's snuffbox at Hartforde Hall, and he intended to find out how it had got there.

"Well, Hartforde!" Donbarton smiled and saluted him heartily. "I understand congratulations are in order. A lovely young bride and two strapping sons all in short order!" He clapped him on the back. "'Fore George, Lady Donbarton is green with envy. The old

warhorse had her nose put out of joint when she found
she was damned near the last one to know!"

Alexander relaxed a little. He did not believe Donbarton could be so casual around a man he had tried to
have assassinated. "I believe I have something belong-
ing to you." He took out the snuffbox and held it in
the palm of his hand. His fingers closed around it
when Donbarton recognized it.

"Damme, if you don't! I've been bloody well down
about it since I lost the thing. Belonged to my father,
you know. He was going to give it to the duke when
he got back from France, but he liked the deuced thing
so well he kept it himself. How did you come by it?"
Donbarton looked wistfully at the box. It was his favorite and it had been a bitter disappointment to lose
it.

"I found it in Hartfordeshire."

Donbarton looked at Alexander with amazement.
"Hartfordeshire? 'Pon my honor, Hartforde, that's
bloody peculiar! I expected you to tell me you got it
from William Fordham—you know, that little fellow
the duke of Mallentrye took such a liking to."

"What's he to do with it?"

"I lost it to him at hazard!"

"When was that?"

"I really haven't any idea. A month or two, maybe.
Why does it matter?"

"Because some weeks ago an attempt was made on
my life, and on that day I found this"—he lifted the
snuffbox in his hand—"in my drive."

"Gadzooks!"

Chapter 36

I

"Well, you're the last person I expected to call on me so early in the morning!" Fordham smiled nervously at Alexander when he stepped into the carriage waiting for him. He would have backed down, but, unluckily, the footman had stood in such a way as to make the maneuver impossible. The door clanked shut after him.

"I've discovered we have some business to take care of." Hartforde thumped on the roof with the carved head of his walking stick, signaling the driver to move on.

"Really?"

"Yes. First, of course, there's this letter." He pulled it out for Fordham's inspection. "You recognize it, do you?" A smile curled on his lips. "Then, there's the additional matter of your attempt on my life." His voice was smooth. "As you can see, the attempt was bungled. However, my wife was very nearly killed. But perhaps you did not know I was married to Miss St. James some months ago."

"And you think I had something to do with it? That's insane!" Fordham stared nervously at Alexander. "I had nothing to do with any shooting."

"I don't recall mentioning a shooting." His green eyes narrowed dangerously.

"Of course you did!" Fordham's laugh sounded shrill when Alexander shook his head. "A lucky guess, I suppose."

"Then, Mr. Fordham, how do you explain my finding this lying in my drive in Hartfordeshire on the very day my wife was shot?" He pulled out the snuff-box and set it carefully on the seat next to him.

"I don't have the slightest idea." Fordham shrugged. "It isn't mine. I've never seen the damned thing before." His eyes darted to the doors.

"If you try to jump, I'll shoot you through," Alexander said calmly, taking a pistol from his coat pocket and leveling it at Fordham's heart with a sincere smile. "Lord Donbarton assures me he lost it to you at hazard." He gave a slight nod downward at the snuffbox.

"You can't prove anything!" Fordham snarled.

"'Tis only a matter of time 'til I find Wickenstand. But I can prove it without him. Do you know how I got this letter?" He waited a beat. "From Ian Boxham—who, I understand, knows a great deal of what went on between you and Mallentrye."

"What's the point of all this?"

Alexander crossed his legs, casually resting the pistol on the top of his knee. When Fordham laughed nervously, Hartforde smiled and softly said, "Ah, yes, you wanted to know the point. I am giving you a great honor. Normally I would simply kill vermin like you. I intend to give you a sporting chance. The choice of weapons is yours."

"You mean to duel?" He was horrified.

"I mean to kill you, but you may call it a duel if you choose."

"I haven't a second!"

"I've taken the liberty of seeing to that. We'll be picking up our seconds shortly."

A few minutes later, the carriage pulled to a stop. When the door opened, Lord Burke and another man climbed in. "Mr. Peters, here"—Alexander indicated the man who sat next to him—"has agreed to be your second. Mr. Peters is my valet, and I assure you, he is a good man, and better than you deserve. This is Charles, Lord Burke. He is my second. We should be arriving at any moment. What weapon do you choose?"

It was not yet six o'clock when the carriage drove up St. James's Street, slowed, then turned into the secluded little court on the east side of St. James's, where it pulled to a stop. Pickering Place was the spot preferred for the settling of affairs of honor because it offered a good deal more privacy than the parks. A few minutes later a second carriage arrived. A small man dressed in somber clothes alighted and, after conversing a few moments with Lord Hartforde, took up a spot on the street well away from the other men.

"Pistols," Fordham said.

"Very well," said Alexander.

II

Some quarter of an hour later, the small man was bending over a body, probing with practiced fingers. "Well, will he live?" Peters cried.

"No, I expect he will not." The doctor ignored the valet's outburst and peered into the dying man's face. "Ah, 'tis over, then." He sighed and, dropping the wrist he had been pressing to feel for a pulse, pulled the eyes shut with the fingers of one hand. Still bending over the corpse, he pulled out a handkerchief and wiped the blood from his fingers.

"Then, my man, you'd best be on your way," Alexander said calmly. When the physic had removed all traces of what had just transpired, the three remaining men got back into the carriage and waited.

At half past six, another carriage arrived at Pickering Place.

"Duke," Alexander said grimly to the last of the three men who alighted from the carriage. "My Lord Fistersham." He nodded to the duke's second, then briefly to the physic.

"Are you sure, Hartforde, you agree to pistols?" Mallentrye laughed.

"I assure you, Your Grace, my aim is excellent. I have every intention of killing you."

"You're a damned fool, Hartforde!"

"I should be a damned fool, Your Grace, if I let you destroy both my marriages. Are you ready?"

Mallentrye gave his strange barking laugh again. "Indeed, Hartforde, I am ready."

At a quarter to seven the physic bent over yet another body, and at five minutes to the hour, Pickering Place was deserted.

Chapter 37

I

"Ah, Lord Hartforde! I've been expecting you. Lady Hartforde intimated you might be round shortly." Mr. Avery, the solicitor, made a neat bow.

"You've seen her?" Alexander felt himself go limp with relief.

"Why, of course, milord! She was here, oh, one or two weeks ago—several days, at any rate. If you will forgive me, milord, she insisted you were seeking a divorce."

"I have no intention of divorcing my wife." Alexander sat down heavily.

"Then I must inform you that she intends to take you to law, my lord. Though 'tis my opinion if you oppose her in the matter, there's little chance she'll succeed. This puts me in mind of Lord Vane and his unfortunate wife"—he looked startled when he realized what he had said—"though there is absolutely no indication she is with someone else, nor, I am sure, my Lord Hartforde, have you mistreated your wife."

"Where is she?" He was close to throttling the man.

"Well, let me see if I can find the bill. . . ." Mr. Avery began rummaging through the voluminous amount of paper scattered over his desk. "I took the liberty of sending her to your banker . . . assured her any preliminary extraordinary bills would be paid . . . until I had further instructions from you, my lord. I hope it is not against your lordship's wishes in the matter." He peered up at Alexander. "The clerk must have the deuced thing. Mr. Watterby!" he shouted. "Divorces generally take some time." He continued looking through the papers. "I hope you understand that, in the meantime . . . obliged for her upkeep, milord. Though if you prefer to cut her off, 'twould be no great difficulty, either."

"Blast you, man! I've told you I have no intention of divorcing my wife. Just tell me where she is!"

"Glad to hear it, my lord. Ah! Here 'tis! Never mind, Mr. Watterby!" he shouted. "I've found it." He waved the clerk out of the room. "Jermyn Street, St. James's Hotel." He was about to drop the paper back onto his desk when Alexander leaned forward.

"Give me that!" He snatched the paper from his hand and was out the door before the surprised attorney could say another word.

II

For the second time that day, Alexander's carriage came down St. James's Street. This time, though, it turned onto Jermyn Street and pulled to a stop at the St. James's Hotel. He had to give the clerk a five pound note before he learned that Isobel's rooms were on the second floor, in the back. Impatiently, Alexander knocked loudly on the plain wooden door. Just as he was about to give up and rouse the proprietor for the key, the door swung open. "Lady Hartforde is not at home today," said the servant who pulled the door open. "Would you care to leave your card?"

"I assure you, madam, she will be at home to me." Alexander pushed past the surprised woman and strode into the room. He found Isobel in a sparsely furnished sitting room. She was holding one of the twins, and John Faircourt was holding the other. A young woman, obviously the nurse, stood a respectful distance from them. When Faircourt saw Alexander storm in, he handed the baby to the nurse, then jumped up.

"Will you please excuse us?" Alexander asked.

"My lord." Faircourt bowed and looked nervous. "I fear I cannot go"—he looked at Isobel—"unless her ladyship desires me to. She has told me—"

"Send him away, Isobel"—he half drew his sword—"or I shall run him through on the spot!"

"Perhaps you'd best go," Isobel said softly.

"If you insist, Lady Hartforde."

"I do."

"As you wish." He looked rather relieved as he bowed over her hand. "My lord." He inclined his head at Alexander.

"What are you doing here?" she demanded when Faircourt was gone.

"I came to take you back to Albemarle Street—where you belong."

She gave a short laugh. "Have you forgotten the duke? And, of course, now you've seen me with John Faircourt."

"It doesn't matter," he said, eyes locked with hers so she was unable to look away. "With any luck, the duke is dead by now, and if I thought it was necessary, I'd kill Faircourt, too." He reached to touch her cheek. "I love you, Isobel."

"Do you?" she whispered.

"I suppose I deserve that." He laughed and shook

his head. "I do love you, Isobel. I was a bloody fool to believe you would go to Mallentrye. I was an even greater fool not to admit to myself how I feel about you." Isobel tore her eyes away from him. The emotion in his voice was bringing an uncomfortable lump to her throat. She was startled when he crossed the room and went down on one knee before her. "All I know is that I'd follow you to Hades and back again." He lifted her hand to his lips. "I know I told you I'd divorce you, but I didn't mean it, not ever. I've been wanting to beg your forgiveness and tell you how much I love you. I listened to that damned physic when he said I should leave you alone until you were recovered. I was frantic when you left! I thought I would go out of my mind! I've been all over this bloody town looking for you, and now that I've found you, I want there to be no more misunderstandings. I love you, Isobel, as I've never loved anyone." When she said nothing, he whispered, "Did you save my life only to take it away from me now?"

Isobel listened to Alexander and wondered why she felt nothing. "You're saying what I've longed to hear, and I ought to be falling into your arms and telling you I love you, too, but—" She shook her head. "I look at you and still think you are the most beautiful man I have ever seen, but it's as though my heart is shut off from all feeling. I've wished for so long that I didn't love you . . . maybe I've got my wish," she said softly. "I don't know what to say, Alexander."

He kissed her hand again, and when he lifted his head she saw tears glistening in his eyes. "I'll make you love me," he said. He stood up and, taking the infant from her, cradled him in his arms. Tiny fingers gripped his, and as he smiled down at the child he saw his eyes were just beginning to turn green.

"That's Laurence Alexander, and this is Charles St. James," the nurse said in a choked voice when she saw Lady Hartforde would not, or perhaps could not, answer.

"Well, young man," he said to his son, "shall we go home?"

Chapter 38

I

"Milord, my lady's things have arrived. I've had them sent to her room," Mrs. Peaslea said after giving a quick curtsy.

"Very good, Mrs. Peaslea," he answered, without looking up from his desk.

"Milord?"

"Yes?" He looked up impatiently.

"This must have been mixed up with my lady's things." The woman held out a bulging leather case. "Though I don't know as why she'd have it."

"Put it here." He pointed to the corner of the desk. When she was gone, he picked up the case and looked at it. The housekeeper had not known it was Isobel's because the initials embossed on it were I.F.B. His curiosity got the better of him and he opened the case to pull out the sheaves of crisp paper that filled it nearly to bursting. It was music, page after page of it. He barely recognized the scrawled hand as his wife's. The manuscript of her first symphony was there, and as he sorted through the papers, he found there were three more symphonies, a violin concerto, and several shorter pieces for the fortepiano. From the dates he could find, she must have been writing almost constantly during the time she was at Hartforde Hall. He put the manuscripts carefully back in the case and ordered up the carriage.

II

Isobel sat at the fortepiano but, though her hands rested on the keys, she was not playing. It was as if the instrument were foreign to her. Her fingers could move over the keys in the correct sequence, but the notes sounded flat and uninspired. She had expected the music would come back to her, but it had not. There had never ever been a time when it was not there, crowding her mind until it finally demanded she write it down. Now there was nothing and she was deathly afraid it would never come back. It was a desolate, empty feeling.

The loss of her manuscripts had been a blow. The case had not been there among her things delivered from Jermyn Street, and though she had told Molly time after time to look again, it had vanished. Reconstructing all her compositions was a task for which she hadn't the energy. What would be the use? she asked herself. Music had made her who she was; without it, she was less than no one. Her mistake had been to fall in love with Alexander. Had she not, she would still be Ian. It seemed unfair that falling in love should have such disastrous consequences. But, then, one of the results of her falling in love had been the twins, and how could she wish her boys had not been born? Her passion for Alexander had been a heady thing, and she almost believed its course had been inevitable. He had so overwhelmed her that she would never have been able to refuse him. Every time she saw him, he still made her heart leap to her throat, but the price of her love had been steep. She got up from the fortepiano, wondering if she would ever play again.

Chapter 39

I

"Well, what do you think?" Alexander asked impatiently. "Will you do it?"

"Lord Hartforde, I should be honored to conduct Lady Hartforde's symphony." Faircourt bowed his acceptance of Lord Hartforde's generous offer. "It isn't often I am the first to perform the work of a genius, and if it will bring her back, I'm willing to try anything."

"Excellent! How soon will you be ready for a first performance?"

"I imagine in about a month's time. Will you attend the rehearsals?"

"With pleasure."

Faircourt bowed again as Lord Hartforde left, and when he was alone he began to leaf through the manuscripts.

II

"Hurry, Isobel, or we shall be late!" Alexander admonished her for ascending the stairs so slowly.

"I don't want to go!" She scowled at him. He was cruel to take her to the symphony, and if she'd known his intentions, she would have refused altogether to leave Albemarle Street. Music was no longer a part of her life and she wanted nothing to do with it.

"Nevertheless, we are going." They paused at the landing. "I have a new protégé I insist you must hear. I've spent a good deal of money to get this music performed, and I want to know if you think it's worth my spending more money on the fellow."

He took her hand and pulled her up the stairs after him. As it was, they barely had time to get to their box before the overture started. Isobel didn't know what to think when she realized what Alexander had done. He looked steadily at her. "Faircourt has told me more than once that the composer is a genius. Do you not agree?" He saw the uncertainty in her eyes and he took her hand. "Ian Boxham isn't dead, Isobel. I want you to make him live forever." His eyes shone with an intense light that made her tremble when they locked with hers. "I love you, Isobel, and that means I love Ian Boxham. Whatever you decide to do with your music, you have my full support. Ian deserves a patron, and I intend to be an unstinting one."

"How long have you been planning this?" she asked, trying to suppress the queer feeling constricting her chest. She looked at him and suddenly felt the wall she had constructed around her heart begin to crumble. He understood that without music she wasn't whole, just as she couldn't be whole without him. It was as though the world had suddenly opened up to her again, and there was Alexander and her music at the very center of it.

"Ever since Mrs. Peaslea mistakenly gave me your music," he was explaining. "I had it printed, and your manuscripts bound, as well. Then I hired the hall, the musicians, and, of course, John Faircourt." He was startled to see a tear trickle down her cheek. "Have I done the right thing?" he asked, a stricken look on the handsome face she loved so well.

"Oh, Alexander!" She threw her arms around him and began to cry. "You've done exactly the right thing!"